BLUE HAWAIIAN

BLACKWOOD CELLARS SERIES #1

CARLA LUNA

moonmanorpress.com

MOON MANOR PRESS

First paperback edition: June 2021

Cover Design: *Bailey McGinn*
Editing: *Free Bird Editing*
Proofreading: *One Love Editing*
ISBN 9781736866108 (paperback)
ISBN 9781736866115 (ebook)

Published by Moon Manor Press
carlalunabooks.com

❀ Created with Vellum

For Mike, and memories of Maui

CHAPTER 1

*B*y the time her plane touched down in Maui, Jessica Chavez swore she'd never fly again. Slightly problematic given that she was now on an island in the South Pacific. But after three flight delays, sickening turbulence, and a drunken seat partner, she was done.

As Jess turned her phone back on, the sheer number of text notifications made her cringe.

Nineteen messages.

All from her older sister, Gabriela, who was getting married in six days. Since Gabi had expected Jess to show up at noon, she'd planned for them to spend the rest of the day together, running errands and catching up on family gossip. Though Gabi didn't blame her for arriving eleven hours late, her texts displayed an escalating level of irritation. By the last one, she'd dispensed with the smiley faces and heart emojis.

Damn. Jess had been in Maui for all of ten minutes and she was already failing as Gabi's maid of honor. That couldn't happen. This wedding was her chance to prove she could handle responsibility without screwing up.

No easy feat, considering her life was a raging dumpster fire.

When the Fasten Seatbelt sign blinked off, Jess grabbed her faded Art Institute of Chicago tote bag and hustled off the plane. All she wanted to do was get to her hotel room, raid the minibar, and crash for the next eight hours.

Though it was almost midnight, the baggage claim was packed with brightly dressed tourists, all waiting on their luggage. An announcement came over the loudspeakers: "Passengers on Hawaiian Air Flight 262 from Los Angeles, your bags will be on Carousel 3. Passengers arriving from San Diego, your bags are on Carousel 4."

San Diego.

According to Gabi, Connor Blackwood was arriving tonight, on a flight inbound from San Diego. Jess had assumed she wouldn't run into him, because his plane was scheduled to land much later than hers. That was before she'd been delayed eleven hours.

Please don't let him be here. Not when I look like hell.

She'd have to face him at some point. Not only was he first cousins with Gabi's fiancé, Marc Blackwood, he was a groomsman in the wedding. But she wanted Connor to see her as a sexy, confident woman who no longer cared that he'd broken her heart five years ago. Instead, she was frazzled and exhausted.

Rather than risk running into Connor at the baggage claim, she took refuge in the ladies' room. The reflection that greeted her made her recoil. Under the harsh fluorescent lights, her skin looked completely washed-out. Her dark brown curls were tangled beyond redemption. And her eyes sported the raccoon effect caused by smeared mascara and eyeliner.

In other words, a hot mess.

After cleaning up as best she could, she left the restroom and planted herself on a bench by the exit. If she kept her head down, Connor might miss her on his way out. The wait gave her a chance to text Gabi and explain her late arrival.

By the time she headed over to Carousel 3, the area had cleared out, but her battered green suitcase was nowhere to be seen. Heart pounding, she searched everywhere. Nothing. Her bag must have been rerouted at some point between Chicago, L.A., and Maui.

Seriously, universe, could my life get any worse?

Not only was she attending Gabi's wedding without a date, but she was jobless and temporarily homeless. Next month, she'd have to leave Chicago for good and drive back home to Riverside, California, in utter defeat.

But first, she had to survive the wedding.

As she took her place in line at the lost luggage counter, her phone buzzed with a text from Gabi. *Sorry today was such a mess! Tomorrow will be better! I'd wait up for you but Marc's calling me to bed.*

Followed by a wink emoji.

She groaned. "TMI, Gabi. Rub it in, why don't you."

Oops. Had she said that out loud?

Apparently, she had, because the man in front of her turned around.

And after five years apart, she was face-to-face with *him*.

His eyes widened. "Jess. I thought it sounded like you."

It was official. Her life *could* get worse. "Hello, Connor."

He was hotter than she remembered, with his piercing blue eyes and his thick black hair that begged for the touch of her fingers. Though he needed a shave, the stubble added to his rugged look. Beneath his t-shirt and jeans, his body appeared as firm and well-muscled as it was five years ago. Why couldn't he have put on sixty pounds or grown a thick lumberjack beard? Although, on him, a beard would look sexy as hell.

For an awkward moment, neither of them spoke, and she was tempted to run in the other direction.

Until he frowned at her. "You're not supposed to be here."

Indignation flared up inside of her, bringing a warm flush to her cheeks. "I'm Gabi's maid of honor. Of course, I'm supposed to be here."

"I meant, your plane. Marc told me you were arriving at noon."

She winced as the implication hit her. Connor hadn't wanted to run into her. She shouldn't have been surprised. He'd been the one to block her after they broke up.

"You were hoping you'd miss me?" she said. "Fat chance, seeing as how I'll be in Maui all week."

He let out his breath. "Sorry. It's been a long day."

His weak-ass apology didn't cut it. "You want to talk long days? I've been up since 3:00 a.m., Chicago time."

"It's not a competition."

"Who says? You had one crappy flight, while I've *literally* been to hell and back."

His shoulders slumped in defeat. "Jess…"

"What?"

"I'm probably the last person you want to see right now. But I'm exhausted, and I'm sure you are, too. For tonight, can we try to be civil?"

He had no business telling her how to behave. But after the day she'd had, arguing with him would only worsen her mood.

Since they were stuck in line together, she had two options: ignore him completely or strike a temporary truce. The second option was more appealing. Even though she hadn't forgiven him for ghosting her after their breakup, she and Connor had a long history together. They'd once been good friends, bonded by all the summers their families had spent vacationing up at Big Bear Lake.

She blew out a resigned breath. "Okay. That works for me." She waited to see if he'd turn away, but his eyes were still fixed on her. "What? I know I look like shit."

"It's just…" A wry smile played across his lips. "What's the deal with your shirt?"

Damn, if his smile didn't pierce her defensive armor. Because the shirt in question was beyond tacky—a tight pink, scoop-neck tee, emblazoned with "I Heart L.A." in glittery purple letters. It wasn't the shirt she'd been wearing when she left Chicago, but a *lot* had happened in the past twenty hours.

She placed her hands on her hips, striking a cocky pose. If she kept things light between them, she might not feel as vulnerable. "Not everyone can pull off this look, you know. It takes a certain level of audacity."

"That it does." His eyes gleamed with amusement. "But I'm not sure Gabi would approve."

"True. It's hardly in keeping with her wedding aesthetic. Which means I won't be posting it on Instagram anytime soon. I'm already in enough trouble, seeing as how I'm arriving criminally late and don't have my luggage."

"Even your dress for the big day?"

Jess shivered, not wanting to imagine how her sister would react if one of those custom-made dresses went missing. "Gabi brought them with her. The garment bag probably flew first class."

"I would have thought you'd get VIP treatment. Didn't you say you're the maid of honor?"

She snorted. "I'm the *second-string* maid of honor." Though she could joke about it, the title stung. She had assumed she'd be Gabi's first choice, but her sister hadn't thought Jess could handle all the responsibility.

Connor regarded her with a sly expression. "What happened to Gabi's first-round draft pick? Did she flee the country?"

"You're not wrong." She shouldn't be making light of the situation, but she couldn't resist. As kids, she and Connor had often joked about Gabi's demanding personality.

"Wait. Seriously?" He started laughing. "I realize Gabi's high-maintenance, but that seems like an extreme reaction."

"Just stop." A hint of a grin crossed her face. "It wasn't because of Gabi. Her friend Carly took a job working for Doctors Without Borders two months ago. She's stationed in a remote village in Nepal."

Fortunately for Jess, Carly had done most of the groundwork as maid of honor. But Gabi had still been reluctant to hand over the position to Jess. Which made her feel even guiltier about missing her first official day of duty.

The clerk called the next person in line, and Jess and Connor inched forward. "I take it the airline lost your luggage, too?" she asked.

"Only the garment bag with my tux. The rest is in my carry-on." He pointed to a rolling black suitcase beside him.

"Sorry your tux went missing. But I lost everything. No dresses, no swimsuits, no cute outfits for all our activities." She grimaced as she imagined her sister's reaction if she were to show up at every event wearing the hideous pink t-shirt. "I'm not even worthy to be the second-string maid of honor."

He placed his hand on her arm. "You're here, aren't you? That's what counts. It's not your fault the airline lost your suitcase."

Goose bumps prickled her skin. Even after all this time, his touch still had a powerful effect on her. "True, but Gabi suggested I squeeze everything into a carry-on. I ignored her, and look what happened."

Not that her sister had followed her own advice. But Gabi didn't suffer from the bad-luck gene like Jess. Both of Gabi's suitcases had arrived when she did.

Connor gave her a sympathetic shrug. "Don't sweat it. There's no way you could have known."

She regarded him with uncertainty. Bantering with her was one thing. But he was treating her decently. Like he *cared* about her.

What was his game? Was he trying to bridge the gap he'd created between them?

Or did he have a different agenda?

Connor turned his attention to the counter clerk, who had called him to the front. As he approached the shapely blond woman behind the desk, he said something that made her lean forward and laugh appreciatively.

Jess clenched her jaw. How could she have forgotten what a player Connor was? Around women, he wielded his charm like a weapon. She should have been immune to it, but she'd allowed him to slip past her defenses. And she'd been joking with him as if they were friends.

But their friendship had ended five years ago, after she'd made the mistake of sleeping with him and thinking it *meant* something.

At the time, she was eighteen and he was twenty-two. She'd been house-sitting for her mom's boss at his cabin on Big Bear Lake when Connor showed up at his family's lodge next door. Though they'd known each other for ten years, they'd never been alone like this. Just the two of them, both adults, without their families around to pass judgment.

Within a day, they gave in to temptation and ended up in bed. Over the next two weeks, her childhood crush on Connor grew into a deep, passionate love. Like a fool, she professed her feelings the morning he was scheduled to leave. But her confession only drove him further away.

After he left, she texted him in desperation, begging him to reconsider. But he cut her off completely, rupturing their long-standing friendship.

She hadn't heard from him since.

Get over it. You're here for Gabi.

Gabi had asked Jess to stand in as maid of honor only after she promised to be on her best behavior. No emotional breakdowns, no sudden crises, and no romantic catastrophes. She intended to keep her word. Better than that—she intended to show everyone she wasn't the same disaster-prone drama queen she'd always been. She was twenty-three, which meant it was time she started acting like an adult.

That was the plan, anyway.

But when had her life ever gone according to plan?

She seethed as Connor took his time with the clerk, laying it on extra thick. When she came up to the counter, the woman told her, without a shred of compassion, that her suitcase might not arrive for another two days.

Connor leaned against the wall, waiting for her to finish. Jess made no attempt to hide her annoyance. "So, did you slip her your number?"

"What are you talking about?" he asked.

Who was he trying to fool? "The clerk. I saw the way you chatted her up."

"I didn't hit on her. I was trying to lighten things up because she said she'd had a rough day. How'd you like to be stuck listening to everyone whine about their luggage?"

She flinched as the guilt hit her in full force. Her last temp job had been in customer service, and the experience had been humbling. "Sorry. I'm not at my best. But I've been traveling for twenty hours straight." And she still had another forty minutes to go, assuming she could get a ride-share at this hour.

"No problem. Do you want a ride to the resort? I'm getting a rental car."

"You're renting a car? Why? Gabi told me she hired a shuttle van for our excursions." Panic surged through her, sending her pulse racing. Should she have rented a car? Gabi had sent so many texts over the last week she might have missed a few.

"Relax," he said. "This is for me. I wanted to have a little freedom."

Freedom to do what? Hit the club scene and pick up women? Her earlier irritation rose back to the surface. "I'll take a Lyft," she said.

"Come on, Jess. It's after midnight. At this hour, it'll probably cost you fifty bucks."

She didn't have fifty bucks to spare. "Fine. I'll ride with you."

She could endure a forty-minute drive with Connor.

But if he thought she'd forgiven him, he was sadly mistaken.

CHAPTER 2

Connor wanted to kick himself for the surly way he'd greeted Jess. But the long, stifling flight from San Diego had left him with a headache. He hadn't expected to run into anyone until the following morning, at the "mandatory" beach outing Marc and Gabi had scheduled for the entire wedding party. By then, he hoped to be well rested and in full vacation mode.

To make up for his rudeness, the least he could do was offer Jess a ride.

If he was being honest, he owed her a hell of a lot more.

He pointed to the doors leading outside. "Let's go. We'll have to take a shuttle to the rental car place."

Jess hiked her tote bag over her shoulder and followed him. "Sounds good. I'm wiped."

"Want me to take your bag?" he asked. "It looks like it weighs a ton."

"Only because I'm carrying the world's largest binder." She set down the tote and pulled out a thick white binder labeled *Gabi & Marc Wedding*. "Have a look."

He flipped through the gigantic tome and reeled at the sheer mass of information and instructions, subdivided into specific categories. Interspersed among the pages were swatches of fabric, printed menus, and photos of elaborate place settings.

He passed it back to her. "You're in charge of all this? No wonder Gabi's friend bailed."

"No. Gabi put this together. This isn't even the original binder. She keeps that one with her at all times. This is the *backup* binder. She insisted I carry it on my person in case my luggage got lost." She pushed it back into her tote bag. "Smart move on her part, but it's a pain to lug around."

Who creates two wedding binders? He'd always considered Gabi a control freak, but this was extreme. He held out his hand. "Let me take it. I don't mind."

"Thanks. Just don't let it out of your sight."

The bag was even heavier than it looked. He felt a pang of sympathy for Jess, who'd been forced to carry it all day.

Outside the terminal, the night air was balmy and fragrant. After hours inside a plane with the air-conditioning cranked to the max, Connor appreciated the warm, tropical breeze. The palm trees across the road brought LAX to mind, but without the smog and traffic.

As they waited at the curb, he stole another glance at Jess. Her pink t-shirt was one of the ugliest things he'd ever seen. Not that it detracted from her appearance. If anything, the low-cut neck put her generous cleavage on full display. He couldn't fault the yoga pants either, since the thin black fabric molded nicely to the curve of her butt. Her dark brown curls were wildly out of control, but he liked them that way. He had a sudden flash of memory as he recalled tangling his fingers in her thick, unruly hair when they were in bed together.

Damn, but those nights had been incredible.

Don't even think about it. Jess looks as if she wants to kill someone. Possibly you.

She glared at him. "Are you checking me out?"

Busted. He held up his hands. "No. But I'm curious about your shirt. Are the bridesmaids doing a photo shoot wearing trashy t-shirts?"

She granted him the faintest of smiles. "Do you honestly think Gabi would *ever* go for something so basic? I got drenched with coffee halfway between Chicago and L.A., so I had to find a new top at LAX. I wanted to spend as little as possible, since I purchased a bunch of clothes for this trip. Now they're missing, and I have nothing to wear." She sighed. "I should have seen it coming. I'm cursed when it comes to planes."

Even as a kid, Jess tended to exaggerate. "You had one bad day. It happens."

"If you're me, it happens all the time. When I went home for Thanksgiving last year, a blizzard shut down O'Hare Airport. Home for Christmas? Mechanical issues. And on the return? A series of ice storms in the south that delayed air travel all over the U.S."

"What about today?" he asked. "It's July, so the weather couldn't have been an issue."

"You'd think so, wouldn't you? But summer in Chicago means big thunderstorms. The storm system grounded the planes at O'Hare for *five hours.*" She gave him a cheeky grin. "All because I chose to fly."

"That's kind of scary. Remind me never to fly with you."

"Gabi calls me a bad-luck magnet. Not that I blame her. Bad luck seems to follow me wherever I go."

Bad luck or bad choices? Like him, Jess tended to act before thinking. When they'd hooked up at Big Bear, they leapt into bed without setting any ground rules. At the time, he couldn't imagine wanting more than a fling. He assumed Jess felt the same way, since their lives were going in different directions. While she was about to start college, he'd recently graduated. The visit to Big Bear was a way for him to kill time and avoid his father before heading off to Spain on a monthlong assignment for his family's wine empire.

In hindsight, he should have made his expectations clear, right from the start. No strings and no promises. When Jess confessed her love for him, he was blindsided.

To say he hadn't handled it well was an understatement.

He didn't know if he'd ever earn her friendship back. But he'd missed her and the bond they shared after countless summers at Big Bear. Especially the nights when they'd stayed up late, sitting out by the firepit and talking.

More than once, he'd considered calling her to apologize. But for years he'd been mired in a cycle of shitty, self-destructive behavior. He'd hit rock bottom seven months ago after a bad breakup. That was when he finally put a stop to the drunken bar crawls and mindless hookups. And he tried to live by the words his younger sister, Victoria, had drummed into him: "If you can't treat a woman with respect, asshole, then you don't deserve her."

After what he'd done to Jess, he definitely didn't deserve her, even if the thought of exploring those sexy curves sent his fantasies into overdrive.

Nope. Not going there.

If he wanted to regain her friendship, he needed to stop thinking about her that way.

Time to focus on something else.

He brought out his phone and scrolled through his messages. Nothing from his dad yet. But his older brother had sent him a text. *Don't think you can escape Dad's wrath because you're in Maui. He's going to give you hell as soon as he arrives.*

Connor's gut tightened. His decision to leave the family company hadn't come easily. But if his plan succeeded, he'd be free to chart his own course.

With a light touch on his arm, Jess brought him back into the present. Her voice bore none of the irritation she'd shown earlier. "Hey. You okay?"

He exhaled. "Just…family stuff."

"That's the problem with a family wedding. Too much family." She stepped to the side as a parking shuttle stopped in front of them and an elderly couple got on board. "Don't get me wrong— I'm excited to visit Maui. But…"

"But it might be more relaxing on our own?"

"Exactly."

He gave her a sly grin. "I saw a flight on the departures board, leaving for Honolulu at one thirty. There's still time to make our escape."

She laughed. "As if. We'd be in so much trouble."

The Avis shuttle pulled up to the curb, and they climbed on board. At the rental car agency, Connor filled out the paperwork and declined the expensive add-ons. Once he and Jess located the car, he entered the resort's address into his phone. But before he could engage her in conversation, she closed her eyes and conked out immediately.

Lost in thought, he barely noticed the view outside his window until he reached the west side of the island, just past Maalaea. On his left, the Pacific Ocean stretched out endlessly, the inky waves shimmering in the moonlight. He eased his grip on the steering wheel and allowed himself to relax. When he glanced over at Jess, she looked as beautiful as she'd been at eighteen. Though he didn't regret a minute of the time they'd spent together, he wished he could take back those years they'd lost.

❧

CONNOR DROVE through the gates of the Grand Ka'anapali Resort and continued along the winding road leading toward the beach. Palm trees illuminated with strings of white lights guided the way. He nudged Jess's shoulder. "Wake up, Sleeping Beauty. We're here."

She blinked and rubbed her eyes. "Holy shit. This place is *huge.*"

"It's a five-star resort. You knew that, right?"

"Yeah, but the last hotel I stayed at was a Super 8 with a broken TV." She lowered the window. "Ahhh. It even smells like paradise."

He chuckled. "Isn't that a bit much?"

"Are you mocking me? If your family weren't paying for my room, I'd be stuck at a cheap motel. I'm not filthy rich like you are."

Her words rankled him. "I'm not that rich."

"But you will be, eventually."

In theory. Thanks to the Blackwoods' wine empire, his family was loaded. Blackwood Cellars had started with a modest winery in the Temecula Valley, northeast of San Diego, and had eventually grown to include wineries in Napa, Oregon, and Spain. Most of his family worked in Temecula, except for his cousin Marc, who helped run the Napa office.

At the moment, Connor had no desire to dwell on Blackwood Cellars. Not when he was on the verge of turning his back on it and starting his own venture.

He drove past a cluster of private bungalows, then passed two enormous swimming pools and a set of tennis courts. After parking the car, he walked with Jess toward the Dolphin Tower, the high-rise where the wedding party was staying. The lobby was a bright, open space, with high ceilings and a wall of windows looking onto the Pacific Ocean. A giant, tiled fountain stood off to one side, strewn with pink and orange flowers.

Jess was right. The place did smell like paradise. Assuming paradise smelled like a mix of chlorine, coconut sunscreen, and cloying tropical blooms.

At check-in, the young clerk appeared unusually perky, despite the late hour. "Welcome to the Grand Ka'anapali!" he said. "Checking in together?"

Jess spoke up quickly. "Nope. Different rooms." She brought out her driver's license. "Jessica Chavez. My room should be in the Chavez-Blackwood wedding block."

"Found it," the clerk said. "And—you're in luck—it's one of the only rooms left in that block with an ocean view."

She sighed. "Perfect. Thank you so much."

An ocean view sounded ideal. "Do you have any more rooms facing the beach?" Connor asked, bringing out his ID. "I'm also in the wedding block."

"Indeed, I do. One left, and it's right next door." The clerk beamed. "Isn't that fantastic?"

Jess groaned. "You can't be serious."

Connor couldn't resist flashing her a cocky grin. "Don't worry. I'll behave. But can you make the same promise?"

"Don't flatter yourself," she said.

After the clerk ran Connor's credit card, he handed him a gift bag. "This was left for you by Marc Blackwood."

He took the bag and peeked inside. A large bottle of Valois Brandy, one of Blackwood Cellars' premier products. Trust his cousin to know *exactly* what he needed.

"Here are your key cards. I gave you both an extra one—*just in case*," the clerk said.

As they headed toward the elevator, Jess let out her breath in a huff. "What did he mean—*just in case*? What did that twerp think's going to happen?"

"It's not hard to make the leap, seeing as how we checked in together, and it's after midnight." Connor nudged her playfully, trying to defuse her anger. "If you want my extra key card, say the word. Then you can visit me whenever you feel like it."

She smacked him in the arm. "Not a chance. Just because you're in the room next to me doesn't mean you can take advantage."

"Wouldn't dream of it."

A total and utter lie. After the day he'd had, he could use a little release. But if he wanted to mend things with Jess, he had no business making a play for her.

Their rooms were on the ninth floor, next to the ice machine. Connor hadn't intended to start in on the brandy this soon, but a drink might take the edge off the day. "You up for a nightcap?" he asked. "Marc gave me a bottle of brandy, and I'd be glad to share."

She scowled at him as she opened her door. "No, thank you. Unlike you, I'm not exactly equipped for relaxing. I have no luggage. That means no toiletries and nothing to change into."

He leaned against the doorframe. "You can always sleep in the buff. Isn't that what—"

"Good night, Connor." She entered her room and let the door slam shut behind her.

Maybe he was pushing her more than he should have.

But he was every bit as attracted to her as he had been five years ago.

Maybe even more.

CHAPTER 3

Jess leaned against the door, her head swimming with frustration. Connor hadn't reached out to her in *five years*. And from the way he'd greeted her at the airport, he hadn't been thrilled to see her. Completely understandable since she hadn't wanted to run into him either.

Yet, instead of freezing him out, she'd let him breach her defenses. She even bantered with him, as if they were still friends.

Damn, but she was an idiot.

Clearly, she wasn't over him yet. But she needed to keep her guard up. He'd hurt her before, and he could do it again. And she was more vulnerable now, given the toxic way her last ex had treated her. Simon the Terrible, who'd lured her to Chicago last fall, then slowly turned on her. When she suspected him of cheating, he spent weeks gaslighting her. Learning the truth almost came as a relief.

She tossed her tote bag on the bed. It had been a *day*, all right. At least her room was a sweet slice of heaven. Decorated in bright, tropical prints, it included a king-sized bed, a couch, a large work desk, a small bar with a full coffee station, and a balcony facing the ocean.

The room would have been more perfect if she had someone to share the bed with. Or the shower. A memory came to her, unbidden, of showering with Connor in his family's lodge. They'd gotten so carried away they'd used up all the hot water.

Just stop.

She found a basket of complimentary toiletries in the bathroom and freshened up as best she could. She was giving the sleeping-naked option consideration when a knock came at the door. A glance through the peephole revealed Connor. What kind of game was he playing? Did he think she was so desperate for great sex that she'd invite him into bed?

The truth was, she couldn't remember the last time she'd had great sex. Simon hadn't exactly been a generous lover. Long before he dumped her, he was indifferent in bed. Though she didn't miss him anymore, the memory of his betrayal still stung. She'd come home from work, on a rainy night in March, only to find him entwined on the couch with a woman from his MFA program. Rather than make excuses, he broke up with Jess and kicked her out of the apartment.

It had been painful as hell, but a few nights of wild, uninhibited sex might ease that pain. And what better place to have a scorching hot affair than a tropical wedding?

But not with Connor. She wouldn't make that mistake again.

She was tempted to leave him hanging, but she wanted to shoot him down to his face. She flung open the door. "What is it?"

He held out a gray t-shirt embellished with the L.A. Dodgers logo. "I thought you might want something comfortable to sleep in. Unless you *like* that pink thing."

She accepted the shirt. "Umm…thanks."

"No problem. Need anything else?"

Did he have an agenda? Or was he just being considerate?

She inched back a few paces. "I'm okay for now."

"All right. 'Night, Jess." With a little wave, he turned and left.

That was it. No hint he'd like to come into her room. No lewd remarks. Not the slightest flicker of interest. It was kind of insulting, to be honest.

She brought the shirt to her nose and inhaled. The aroma was distinctly Connor—pinewoods and all male. Great. Now she'd have a harder time getting him off her mind.

Maybe that was his intention. *Devious bastard.*

Whatever the case, she couldn't stand the obnoxious pink shirt another minute. She ditched it, along with her bra, and put on Connor's shirt. Even if it was far too long, years of wear had made it soft and worn. Like the shirt she'd borrowed from him after their first night together. Was that why he lent it to her? Was he hoping to trigger old memories?

Stop it. You're overthinking everything.

Needing to cool down, she opened the sliding glass door that led to her balcony. As she stepped outside, she gasped in awe at the sight of the Pacific Ocean, gleaming under the light of a near-full moon. The sound of the waves, crashing against the shore in a steady rhythm, soothed her frazzled nerves.

For the first time since leaving Chicago, her mood lifted. Even if her life was a disaster, even if her ex was sleeping *right next door*, she might seize a little joy during this vacation. And she'd start by indulging in a late-night cocktail.

She went back into her room and checked out the minibar. Since she wasn't on the hook for the hotel bill, she could treat herself. She pulled out a small bottle of orange juice and a mini bottle of vodka, intending to make a screwdriver. Now all she needed was ice.

She cracked open her door and peered into the hallway. With no one around, she could venture out, as is. Who would be roaming the hotel at one thirty in the morning, anyway? She reached for the envelope containing her key cards, took one out, and headed into the hall to fill her ice bucket.

But when she tried to get back into her room, the card didn't work.

She waited another minute, took a deep breath, and tried again. The light beside the door handle flashed red. She flipped it over and tried once more. Still red.

Shit.

The clerk must have activated only one of her cards. And she'd picked the wrong one. Now she was locked out, wearing nothing but an oversize t-shirt and a lacy pink thong. The only way to resolve this crisis would be to go down to the lobby and ask the overly enthusiastic hotel clerk to fix her card, subjecting herself to complete humiliation.

Or...

Gritting her teeth, she knocked on Connor's door.

No answer. Was it possible he'd fallen asleep already? Her pulse raced as she tried again, rapping with a little more force.

He opened the door and gave her a wicked smile. "I'm glad you changed your mind about a nightcap. And you brought your own ice. Very thoughtful." He took her elbow and ushered her in.

For a moment, she could barely move, aware he was looking her over, taking in her nighttime ensemble. His gaze lingered on her bare legs and stopped at her chest, where her nipples were visible through the thin cotton shirt. Her face flamed, but she didn't allow herself to look away. Bad idea, since he was wearing nothing but pajama bottoms, putting his bare chest on display. She recalled lying in bed with him, placing soft kisses on his chest, as her mouth moved lower and lower down his body...

Get a grip, Jess.

She walked over to the couch and plopped down on it. With a flush of embarrassment, she crossed her arms, trying to hide her traitorous nipples, which had tightened at the thought of his touch. "I came because I got locked out."

"Already? We've only been here fifteen minutes."

"My key card isn't working."

"You used it earlier."

She groaned in frustration. "The clerk gave us *two* cards,

remember? *Just in case*? This one's a dud. Now I can't get into my room. I need you to go to the lobby and ask the clerk to fix my card."

He raised his eyebrows. "Kind of bossy, aren't we?"

Bastard. He was enjoying this far too much. "Please? I can't go down there like this." She tugged on the L.A. Dodgers shirt, wishing it covered more of her. "Will you *please* help me out?"

His smug expression was almost unbearable. "Maybe. What do I get in return?"

She swallowed, aware of his nearness and her growing desire. But she was stressed and exhausted. Hardly the best time to be making decisions of a sexual nature. "Depends on what you're asking."

"Share a drink with me." He gestured to a bottle of brandy, sitting on top of the room's mini fridge. "Valois Brandy, courtesy of Blackwood Cellars."

His offer sounded more enjoyable than drinking by herself. But she needed to be cautious. She'd made too many stupid mistakes while under the influence. "I don't know if that's such a good idea."

"Come on. One drink. I need to unwind, and I'd rather not do it alone."

Back when they were waiting for the shuttle, he'd looked unsettled. Maybe he just wanted to talk.

She handed him the bucket. He filled two hotel glasses with ice, uncapped the brandy, and poured it into the glasses. She took one and tried a sip. The taste reminded her of whiskey, only sweeter, and filled her with a delicious, soothing warmth.

"Thanks. I needed that," she said.

"You and me both."

There it was again—the slight edge to his voice. "Aren't you happy to be here? I thought you and Marc were close."

He set the bottle on an end table and grabbed a shirt from the bed. After putting it on, he joined her on the couch. "I'd do anything for my cousin. But I can't say the same for the rest of my family. The less time spent with my dad, the better. Yesterday afternoon, I left a business proposal on his desk. He'll probably tear me a new one when he gets here."

At Big Bear, Connor's dad had always come across as a hardass. Whenever Connor had gotten into trouble—and he'd gotten into *plenty* of trouble—Brian Blackwood had punished him harshly. More than once, Jess was there to offer sympathy when Connor complained about his dad's unfair treatment.

"Things aren't going well at Blackwood Cellars?" she asked.

"For everyone else, maybe. Not for me."

"Darren still the same as ever?" If there was one Blackwood she didn't miss, it was Connor's older brother, Darren, who always treated Jess and Gabi like they didn't belong up at the lake.

"He's gotten worse. He lives for the chance to humiliate me in front of his underlings, since I can't do a damn thing about it." Connor let out his breath. "Forget it. How's the writing gig going?"

"How'd you know I was writing?"

"Marc showed me a couple of articles you wrote for *Chicago Live*. It's great you found work as a writer. How do you like Chicago?"

She cringed, remembering her initial enthusiasm. After graduation, she'd taken a bold risk, following Simon to a new city, miles away from Southern California. She'd even secured a decent job as a full-time writer for a website called *Chicago Live* that catered to locals and tourists looking for fun and excitement in the Windy City. But that was before winter set in. Before March, when everything went to hell.

In the space of two weeks, she lost her boyfriend, her apartment, and her job. Now, after four months of slogging through temp work and burning through her savings, she had to move back home to Riverside. But she hadn't told anyone yet. If she let the news slip while she was in Maui, her mom and her sister would see her as they always had—the same old Jess, prone to bad judgment and epic screwups. Rather than admit her failure right away, she planned to wait until after the wedding to drop the bomb.

The touch of Connor's hand, resting on her bare knee, brought her back to the present. She shivered. "What?"

"Are you okay?" he said. "I lost you there for a moment."

"Sorry. I was thinking about Chicago. What did you ask me?"

He gave her a quizzical look. "If you liked it there."

She shrugged. "It's okay."

"Just okay?"

She couldn't tell him the truth. Not when it would reveal how much she'd failed. But her breakup wasn't something she had to hide. "I don't know if Marc told you, but I moved there with my boyfriend, Simon. Or rather, my *ex*-boyfriend."

"Your ex, huh? What happened?"

She looked away, her gaze falling on the sliding door leading to the balcony. Like her, Connor had left the door open, allowing the roar of the waves to filter in. She inhaled deeply, trying to cast off any lingering sorrow over the breakup. Simon hadn't just replaced her with someone else; he'd delivered the news in the cruelest way possible. He told Jess he'd fallen for a *real* writer. Not someone who churned out tourist propaganda.

When she was able to face Connor again, she had her emotions under control. "Simon dumped me in March and gave me two days to move out of the apartment. His new girlfriend didn't exactly want me around." At Connor's shocked look, she added, "I'm camping out on a friend's couch. But it's only temporary."

Until I move back home in a month, like the loser I am.

Connor scowled. "Sounds like a jerk."

"He didn't start out that way. When I met him, I was blown away by his writing. He's incredibly talented. But..." She paused, aware she was sharing more than she had intended.

Connor rested his hand on her knee again. "But what?"

She was tempted to push it away, but it had been too long since anyone had touched her with affection. "The longer we were together, the less he respected me, because I was writing lifestyle articles for a tourism website while he was pursuing his MFA in Creative Writing."

"You've done more than write articles. What about your fantasy epic?"

Heat rose in her cheeks. The shame left a sour taste in her mouth.

"Jess. What did he think of it?"

She kept her voice even, not wanting to reveal how hurt she'd been. "He said it sounded like something a teenager would write. Which is partially true. I never let him read the manuscript because I was afraid he'd laugh at me."

Connor's lip curled in disgust. "What an ass. He didn't deserve you. And he didn't deserve to read *Queen of the Forgotten Lands* either."

She laughed. "I can't believe you remember the title."

"Did you ever finish it?"

"No, I set it aside." She held up her hand to stop him from protesting. "It was eight hundred pages, and I'd been working on it for seven years. I was never going to finish. But I did start something new after the breakup."

"Another fantasy novel?"

"Nope. It's a mystery. All twisty and everything, with lots of red herrings."

Her new project was the one silver lining in her whole miserable spring. When she'd been at her lowest, she channeled her emotions into her writing, creating a story unlike anything she'd ever written. A mystery complete with messy family dynamics and a dual timeline. She was still in the early stages, but the story held a lot of promise.

"Sounds great." Connor raised his glass. "Here's to new beginnings."

She clinked glasses with him, then downed the rest of her drink. Heartbreak aside, she'd forgotten how much she liked being with Connor.

He poured another splash of brandy into her glass. "Good stuff, isn't it?"

"Yeah. These Blackwoods know a thing or two about booze." She swallowed the brandy in a quick gulp, sighing as the warmth flooded her body.

"Easy there, tiger. You're probably dehydrated from the flight." He stood up. "I'm going to get you another key card. Sit tight."

While he was gone, she poured herself more brandy but sipped it slowly. As good as it would feel to get tipsy and put the awful day behind her, she had to watch herself around Connor. Even if he was behaving himself, he wasn't someone she could trust. From what she'd heard via Marc and Gabi, he still had a reputation for wild nights and casual hookups.

When Connor returned, he handed her the card and the ice bucket. "Here you go."

She stood to face him and contemplated closing the distance between them. He wanted her, she was sure of it. And she couldn't deny her attraction to him.

Why not? They were alone, they were adults, and they both knew how good it could be.

No way. Because it won't mean anything to him except sex. You'll wake up tomorrow and hate yourself.

She wished him good night and went back to her room.

Alone.

CHAPTER 4

$\mathcal{C}$onnor woke to the buzzing of his phone. Pulling himself out of a deep sleep, he sat up and rubbed his eyes. He couldn't remember the last time he'd slept that soundly. It must have been the brandy. Or the satisfaction he'd gotten from connecting with Jess. He hadn't expected her to warm up to him so quickly. Though he suspected she still hadn't forgiven him, he liked the way she let down her guard.

His phone buzzed again, and he picked it up from the nightstand.

Missed call from Marc Blackwood.

He sent his cousin a text. *What's up?*

Marc replied immediately. *You up for a run on the beach?*

Though Connor wasn't fully awake yet, the fresh air might jump-start his day. He grabbed his running gear from his suitcase and returned Marc's text. *Be there in 15.*

On leaving his room, he passed by Jess's door, which now sported a "Do Not Disturb" sign. Not surprising, considering she'd left his room at one thirty in the morning. Though he'd respected her boundaries, he'd definitely been tempted. How could he be anything but tempted when she came to him wearing a thin cotton t-shirt that barely covered her ass? But he'd behaved admirably, treating her like a friend rather than a potential conquest.

At times, the tug of attraction between them was hard to resist. The old Connor might have pulled out all the stops, trying to sweet-talk her into bed. But he wasn't going to backslide. Not if he wanted Jess to trust him.

Damn, but it was hard being responsible.

He rode the elevator to the lobby, then went to the side of the resort facing the ocean. Coming from Southern California, he was used to palm trees and warm weather, but Maui had a completely different vibe. Maybe it was the tropical breeze. Or the pounding surf. Either way, he was grateful to be miles away from his office at Blackwood Cellars.

Marc jogged over to meet him, wearing a t-shirt bearing a logo for the Napa Valley 10K. "About time you dragged your lazy ass out of bed."

"Lazy? I got in after midnight. And it's not like I went to sleep right away."

His cousin grinned. "You had company already? You don't miss a trick. Someone you met on the plane? Or here at the resort?"

Enough. I'm not that guy anymore.

"Just a drink, to unwind after a long day," he said. "Thanks for the brandy."

"Glad you liked it. You ready for a run on the beach? It's a tougher workout."

Typical Marc. He wasn't happy unless he was pushing himself at the gym or training for a triathlon. Naturally, he had no problem running on sand, while the resistance slowed Connor down. At least the view was spectacular. They ran in silence, breathing in the salt air, until they reached a comfortable pace.

"How's it going?" he asked Marc. "All set for Saturday?"

"Yeah, it's great."

Marc's words sounded so flat Connor resisted the urge to bust his balls. If something was off about the wedding, the least he could do was listen. "You don't sound too excited."

"It's all good. I guess."

"You guess?"

"Gabi's so stressed out. I thought she'd chill once she got here, but…"

But Gabi didn't know the meaning of the word "chill." When they'd played together as kids, she was the one who followed *all* the rules. A total buzzkill. Unlike Connor and Jess, she thrived on schedules and organization.

"Don't you have a coordinator to handle all the little shit?" Connor asked.

"Sure, but you know Gabi. She has to micromanage everything." Marc let out a long breath. "The first night was perfect. We stayed up late and closed down the bar. But yesterday morning, she had a flower crisis."

"A flower crisis? What does that mean?"

"The type of plumeria she wanted wasn't available, and now her color scheme is messed up. And then she freaked out because her sister's arrival kept getting delayed. She wanted Jess to help her out with a bunch of errands yesterday, but she didn't get into Maui until midnight."

"I know. She and I arrived at the same time." As they passed a couple of female joggers, the prettier of the two gave Connor a sexy smile. He smiled in return, but his mind was still on Jess. "She wasn't in a great mood, given that her plane was ten hours late."

Marc laughed. "Dude, even if she had a perfect travel day, she wouldn't have been happy to see you. She hates you."

He stopped short, his feet skidding on the sand. "No, she doesn't."

"Come on. You broke her heart."

"I didn't mean to." He hadn't wanted to hurt her. But when

she'd professed her love, he was so overwhelmed he had to put some distance between them.

"She was *eighteen*. You should have known better." Marc cleared his throat. "Speaking of which, Gabi wanted me to ask you something. It's none of my business, but…"

From the awkward look on Marc's face, Connor could guess what he was asking. Or rather, what *Gabi* was asking. "Is this about Jess?"

"Yeah. Gabi doesn't want you getting involved with her. She's worried Jess's breakup with Simon left her extra vulnerable."

A lump of irritation lodged in Connor's throat. Even if Gabi was just trying to protect her sister, he didn't appreciate her setting constraints on his love life.

Then again, this was *her* week.

"Don't worry about it," he said. "I have no interest in hooking up with Jess."

"Good. Besides, Gabi convinced me to set her up with Lance. He'll keep her busy."

Why did Gabi need to set Jess up with *anyone*?

Connor strained to keep his voice level. "Who's Lance?"

"You met him before. My old roommate from UC Davis. He was at my housewarming party two years ago."

As they resumed running, Connor tried to recall Lance. He didn't like what he remembered. At the party, the guy had bragged about his sexual exploits to anyone who would listen. "Isn't he kind of a player?"

"In college, yeah, but he's settled down since then. Gabi thought he might help Jess snap out of her funk. Simon really dicked her over."

And you think a douchey frat boy's going to give her the respect she deserves?

But he didn't say it. After the way he'd treated Jess, he had no right to interfere.

They ran for a few minutes in silence until Connor got his

annoyance under control. "About the wedding—anything you need?"

"Just show up for some of the activities. Mostly the big events, like the sunset cruise and the luau. And...I know you're on the outs with your dad, but..."

"But what? Don't stir up any shit?" Connor couldn't help the edge that slipped into his voice. He was starting to wish he hadn't joined Marc on his morning run.

"Sorry. I sounded like a dick, didn't I?"

Connor immediately regretted his tone. Marc had enough on his plate, what with Gabi being so high-maintenance. "I get it. This is supposed to be a nice family get-together. The last thing you need is me getting into a shouting match with Dad. Or telling Darren what I think of him. Don't worry. I'll be on my best behavior."

"Thanks. Gabi already took a lot of heat from her family for having her wedding here. Some of the Blackwoods weren't too happy about it either."

"We're in Maui. What's not to like?" Considering how wealthy his family was, they could all afford the flight and the hotel costs.

"There's Great-Aunt Nina, who refuses to fly. And the Sacramento cousins, who didn't want to travel thousands of miles to attend a destination wedding. I got an earful from them."

Connor could only imagine. The Sacramento bunch were entitled as hell. "Then it's a good thing my sister's having her giant wedding extravaganza at the Blackwood Estate in five months. That way the entire family can participate."

"Speaking of which—we had lunch with Victoria yesterday. All she could do was brag about her Christmas wedding, as if ours pales in comparison."

As much as Connor loved his little sister, she was so obsessed with her upcoming wedding to a senator's son she was veering close to Bridezilla territory. "The way she tells it, everything on the planet will pale in comparison."

They ran past an older couple, out for a morning walk along the beach. The woman cradled a small, yappy dog that barked at them maniacally. Connor nearly stumbled as he attempted to give them a wide berth.

"After Victoria's wedding, I'm guessing Brody will be next," Marc said. "That leaves only you."

"Don't hold your breath. Once I turn my back on Blackwood Cellars, I won't be such a prize." Connor tried to keep the bitterness out of his voice, but he was still stung by the way his ex had left him, back in December.

Up until he'd shared his plans for the future with her, his girlfriend Natasha had been all in. But after he confessed he wanted to leave the family business and start his own winery? She was done. Without his money and his connections, he wasn't worth her time.

"Screw Natasha," Marc said. "All she cared about was your money."

He'd heard as much from everyone in his family. But their words hadn't lessened the blow. If anything, they made him feel like an idiot for trusting Natasha. "Victoria pegged her as a gold-digger. Then again, she thinks everyone's after our money."

"No kidding," Marc said. "She even made a few digs about Gabi until I told her to shut up."

Connor stopped short again. "Has she forgotten you've been in love with Gabi since you were ten?"

Marc skidded to a stop beside him. "Let's head back. I told Gabi I wouldn't be gone long. And for the record, I wasn't *ten*."

"Bull. She beat you in that swimming race, and from then on, you were whipped." The memory still made Connor smile.

"I let her beat me. I felt sorry for her."

"She kicked your ass, fair and square. It was hilarious."

Every summer, as far back as Connor could remember, his family and Marc's had spent two weeks at Blackwood Lodge, located on Big Bear Lake. Connor always relished the time with

Marc and Brody—his two closest cousins—but the year he turned twelve, the Chavez girls showed up and changed everything.

The three boys had gone down to their private dock to swim, only to see two girls playing on the Blackwoods' Aqua Trampoline. When Marc ordered them to leave, Jessica Chavez—a spunky, pigtailed eight-year-old—stood up to him and issued a challenge. If her big sister, Gabi, could beat him in a swimming race, then they could stay. If not, they'd leave. Marc took the bet, and Gabi trounced him. After that first day, they became fast friends and spent the next two weeks together running wild.

From then on, the girls showed up every summer. Like the Blackwoods, they always came right around Independence Day and stayed for two weeks. Some of Connor's best memories were made during those summers. But the last time he and Jess were there together, he'd made a terrible judgment call.

Somehow, he suspected he wasn't done paying for it yet.

CHAPTER 5

The sound of someone pounding on the door roused
Jess from her slumber. She stretched out her arms,
slowly coming into full consciousness. For the first time in
months, she'd slept a full eight hours without waking. A welcome
change from the restless nights she'd spent on her friend's lumpy
couch in Chicago. She got up, shambled over to the door, and
checked the peephole. Gabi.

As she opened the door, she braced herself, unsure as to
whether she'd be facing accusatory Gabi or welcoming Gabi. Her
sister stood in the hallway, dressed in khaki shorts and a purple
Hawaiian shirt. Her sleek black hair was cut in a stylish, short do
that accentuated her cheekbones. In her hand was a large
shopping bag and a sheaf of papers.

Gabi strode forward and embraced her. "You're here! After
yesterday, I was worried your plane was going to end up at the
bottom of the Pacific Ocean."

Jess couldn't help but laugh. Now that she'd had a decent
night's sleep, the hell of yesterday's travel ordeal had diminished
slightly. She shut the door behind Gabi. "Knowing my luck, it's
entirely possible. Sorry I wasn't around to help you out."

Gabi shrugged. "Luisa pitched in. That sucks about your luggage, though. I'm so relieved I brought all the bridesmaids' dresses with me. I can't imagine replacing your dress on such short notice."

Jess raised her eyebrows, as if to remind her a lost dress was hardly comparable to losing one's entire travel wardrobe.

Gabi cringed visibly. "Sorry. But the dresses were custom-made and…"

And my clothes are cheap and easily replaceable? But she didn't say it. Gabi had spent hours poring over options for the bridesmaids' dresses, sending her countless photos before settling on a style they both liked.

"It's fine." Jess retreated until she was sitting on the bed, since she felt underdressed clad in nothing except Connor's shirt. "What can I do to help out? Any errands we need to run? I'll be good to go once I get some coffee into my system."

Though she would have preferred a relaxed morning, she didn't want to let Gabi down.

"I did most of the big errands yesterday with Luisa. But now that you're here, you can get up to speed on all our activities." Gabi took her phone out of her purse. "Did you get the link I sent you for the calendar app? It lists our full itinerary for the next six days."

There had been *so* many messages and group texts from Gabi that Jess had scanned them quickly. Maybe *too* quickly. "Sorry. I haven't installed it yet."

Gabi's mouth quirked up in a smile. "I figured as much." She handed Jess a piece of paper. "Download the app when you get a chance. In the meantime, here's a copy of the itinerary. This will give you the most up-to-date version of all the events."

Jess gave the paper a once-over and reeled at the list of activities. Given a choice, she would have been happy to spend the next five days lying on the beach and drinking fruity cocktails. "Wow. This is extensive."

"Too much?"

She pinched her thumb and finger together. "Maybe a little?"

Like always, her job was to rein in Gabi's obsessive desire for perfection. In turn, Gabi tried to help her out with impulse control. Their success rate hovered around fifty percent.

"Some of the events are optional," Gabi said. "But Marc and I are the only ones who've been here before, so I wanted to make sure everyone got a chance to experience the best parts of the island. I also included a list of all the bars, restaurants, and coffeehouses in the area, along with my recommendations for other points of interest." Gabi passed over a second sheet of paper. "Here's an updated list of the wedding party, including their arrival and departure times."

Jess reviewed the list. "Who all from the group is here?"

"You and Connor arrived last night. Victoria, Luisa, and Lance got here yesterday morning. Most of the other Blackwoods will be arriving later tonight. Mama's coming tomorrow afternoon, but we don't have to worry about picking her up, because she's on the same flight as Brody. He's renting a car, so he offered to drive her here."

"Brody's flying in tomorrow? I'm excited to see him again."

Few people were as laid-back and understanding as Marc's younger brother, Brody. Jess had spent more time with him at Big Bear than with anyone else in the Blackwood family. But she'd never developed romantic feelings for him, probably because she'd been carrying a torch for Connor since she was twelve. If anything, she regarded Brody more like a fun older brother.

Gabi clasped her hands together. "Remember how Mama always wanted you and Brody to get together? Any chance that might finally happen? It would be perfect symmetry."

"Or maybe a little weird. Two sisters marrying two brothers? Sounds like a Hallmark movie."

Her sister giggled. "Except if it were a Hallmark movie, we'd be twins, and they'd get us mixed up."

"And they'd be twins as well. They'd call it *Doule Trouble* or something." Jess tried to recall if she and Gabi had watched a movie with that premise. Over the years, they'd seen so many cheesy holiday movies the plots had blended together.

"Actually, I think he might be dating someone. But you don't need him. Not when you'll have fun with Lance."

Lance. Jess looked down, toying with the hem of Connor's shirt. She poked at a tiny hole in the fabric. "I'm good. You don't need to set me up."

"You sure? When I told you about him last month, you said he sounded like fun. Remember?"

Sure, she'd said it. But she hadn't *meant* it. She'd wanted to placate Gabi, who was worried she'd feel awkward without a plus-one. "I'll be fine on my own. I'm completely over Simon."

Gabi strode over to the window and pulled up the blinds. Bright sunlight streamed in. She turned and scowled at Jess. "Simon's not the issue. I set you up with Lance so you wouldn't obsess over Connor."

Jess recoiled at the sudden brightness, like a vampire caught off guard. "What are you talking about? Connor's in the past."

"Then why'd you ask me when his plane was arriving? Or whether he was involved with anyone? You're still into him." Gabi's jaw tightened. "The last thing I want is for you two to get back together."

The hostility in her sister's voice took Jess by surprise. "Why do you care?"

"Why?" Gabi clenched her fists. "Because he shattered your heart into a thousand pieces. And I was the one who helped you recover. If he wasn't Marc's cousin, I wouldn't want him anywhere near our wedding. When it comes to women, Connor's a total dick."

A week ago, Jess would have agreed. But Connor hadn't been

a dick last night. He'd loaned her his shirt and fetched her a new key card without asking for anything in return. Except one drink. Even then, he'd behaved. "Maybe he's changed."

Gabi rubbed her forehead. "I know you were in love with him, but *please* don't delude yourself."

"But—"

"Stop. I'm going to make an executive decision. I don't want any Connor-drama at this wedding. Got it?"

Though Jess chafed at her sister's tone, she reminded herself that Gabi was looking after her. Her older sister had been the one to prop up her battered ego after Connor left. Still, this trip was also her vacation. Her *only* vacation until she replenished her meager savings account.

"What makes you think there would be any drama?" she asked.

"You're the biggest drama queen I know." Gabi's voice rose. "Every time you have a personal crisis, you suck up all the attention in the room. You *ruined* my graduation weekend."

"I didn't mean to."

"Then why'd you go to Vic Sandovsky's house party the night before my graduation? You knew what those parties were like. When the cops showed up, you were drunk and half-naked. Mama *loved* getting that call."

"I'll admit that was big mistake on my part." She hadn't even liked Vic very much. But after a few rum and Cokes, she'd let things get pretty far—at least until the cops arrived and broke up the party. Spending a few hours at the police station was nothing compared to the tongue-lashing she'd endured from her mom. Even now, the memory of that weekend made her face prickle with heat.

Gabi continued. "And what about my seventeenth birthday, when you had to be rushed to the emergency room?"

Another painful, stomach-churning memory. "I got food poisoning, remember?"

"Because you were the only one at the restaurant who tried to eat the Flaming Wings of Death. Once again, you had to steal the spotlight. I realize you like being 'impulsive,' but this is my wedding week. I don't have the bandwidth to deal with your drama." She clasped her hands together. "Please?"

The "please" did it. Besides, Gabi was right. Jess needed to grow up. She stood and faced her sister. "There will be zero drama at this wedding. I'm way more responsible now."

More than ever, she was glad she hadn't told Gabi she'd been laid off. Or that she was out of money and planned to move back home in a month. If she wanted to prove she was worthy of being her sister's maid of honor, she needed to act like her life was under control. No big reveals. No tearful confessions. No meltdowns.

Above all, she couldn't let her mom know or she'd fuss over Jess instead of Gabi. Once the wedding was over, she could tell everyone the truth. She'd handle the pity and the questions then. But not until Gabi received her long-awaited moment in the sun.

Gabi let out a long breath. "I trust you, so let's move on. Okay?" When Jess nodded, Gabi handed her the shopping bag. "Here. Hopefully, your suitcase will arrive soon. If not, these clothes will get you through today."

Jess sat back on the bed, setting the bag beside her. She pulled out a ruby-red bikini, a tropical-print cover-up, a bright fuchsia Hawaiian shirt, a minidress, and a pair of strappy sandals with precariously high heels. Her earlier frustration ebbed away.

"These are great. Thank you."

Gabi beamed. "You're welcome. I already had your measurements from ordering your dress, and the shoes are a loan from Victoria because you wear the same size. I thought the dress would look cute on you, but it's a little short."

Jess held the dress up against herself. Though it wasn't much longer than Connor's shirt, the jade-colored fabric shimmered beautifully under the light. Without looking at the price tag, she could tell it was a cut above her usual wardrobe choices, most of which came from Old Navy or H&M. Included in the shopping bag was a small cosmetics case, stuffed with basic makeup—mascara, eyeliner, foundation, blush, and lipstick. She tested the lipstick against her wrist, pleased at the bright coral color. Perfect for a tropical look.

"Thanks for everything," she said.

"No problem. Glad I could help."

Jess stared at Gabi. Her flat tone didn't inspire confidence. "Are you okay?"

Gabi sat beside her on the bed. "This is a big undertaking. Six days of events, including the rehearsal dinner and the wedding. I want everything to be perfect."

Jess placed her hand over her sister's and gave it a squeeze. "You don't have to try so hard. We're in Maui. You could tell everyone to go fuck off and they'd still enjoy themselves."

Gabi frowned. "I could never do that. The Blackwoods are expecting me to play hostess. I have to live up to their expectations."

"Why? It's not like you're trying to impress a group of strangers. We've known them since we were kids. After all those summers at Big Bear, we're practically family." They'd eaten so many "second breakfasts" at the Blackwood Lodge that Jess could recall every detail of the kitchen, right down to the big Garfield mug she'd used to hold her daily cocoa.

"Seriously?" Gabi's voice tightened. "We were *never* in the same league."

The inklings of a caffeine-withdrawal headache needled Jess's brain. She got up, ambled over to the coffee station, and turned on the mini Keurig. "Do you want any coffee?"

Gabi shook her head. "I had three cups already."

Maybe that's the problem, right there.

She selected an Italian roast coffee pod and inserted it into the machine. "Back to what you were saying—even if we weren't as rich as the Blackwoods, they didn't care. We stayed at the cabin right next door."

"Only because Mama's boss let us stay there. We both know why."

Not this again. "What's the big deal? He wanted to help us out."

"He felt *sorry* for us. Like we were some kind of charity case."

What did it matter if Zach Horton took pity on them? For years, their mom had busted her ass working as Zach's administrative assistant, putting in long hours, even weekends. Given that he was a wealthy real estate developer with multiple homes, he could afford to give his assistant two weeks paid vacation at his family's cabin in the mountains. For Jess, those Big Bear vacations were the highlight of her summer, regardless of whether they were offered out of pity or generosity.

"Don't fool yourself," Gabi said. "We're nothing like the Blackwoods. They're worth millions and we're—"

"We're what? *Not* rich? Most people aren't rich. That's why they call them the one percent. At least Mama has a decent job. You should be proud of her." Jess took a sip of coffee, wincing at the bitterness. She usually took it with cream, but she hated the powdered stuff.

Gabi crossed her arms. "What about Dad? Should we be proud of him?"

"Forget that asshole. We haven't seen him in twenty years. We don't even share his last name." Jess had always been proud to call herself a Chavez girl rather than Teddy Carter's daughter.

"We're still related. Last I heard he was back in jail."

Jess let out her breath in frustration. To her, being poor and biracial was nothing to feel ashamed of. If anything, she was proud as hell to be half Latina. But even though she and Gabi were light enough to pass as white, her sister had always been more conscious of differences in race and class. Especially since she was marrying a white guy from an extremely wealthy family.

"It doesn't matter where we came from. Marc loves you." Jess gestured to the sliding door leading to the balcony. "Look outside. We are *literally* in a tropical paradise. You need to chill."

"Only if you promise you won't screw up. No getting drunk. No food poisoning. No hooking up with Connor. I'm counting on you."

Jess swallowed, the bitter coffee unsettling her stomach. A twinge of disappointment ate at her, but she pushed it aside. "I'll behave. I promise. What's on the agenda today?"

"Since we have the sunset cruise tonight, we're doing a low-key beach day, with a little swimming and snorkeling. We'll meet in the lobby at ten thirty and head out to Ka'anapali Beach."

Jess held up the bikini, which was a lot more revealing than the black tankini she'd packed in her luggage. "Perfect. Thanks for getting me something to wear."

Once Gabi had left, Jess felt her muscles slowly loosen. Being around her older sister was exhausting. Gabi had always striven for perfection, but now she was going off the deep end. Jess was caught in the middle, trying to be the perfect sister, the perfect maid of honor, the perfect everything, when she'd never been perfect at anything in her life.

But she wouldn't forgive herself if she screwed up Gabi's wedding. Which was why she needed to be on her best behavior.

She gave her newly acquired bikini another glance. The skimpy material would barely cover her curves. But if she wanted to spend time on the beach, she'd have to put it on.

Maybe Lance would be impressed.

Maybe Connor, too.

Not that she cared what *he* thought.

CHAPTER 6

The stretch of beach bordering their resort lived up to all of Jess's tropical fantasies. Golden-white sand, turquoise water, palm trees, and a perfect temperature of 80 degrees. Gabi and Marc brought a picnic basket filled with muffins, dried pineapple slices, and macadamia nuts, as well as a cooler stocked with water and passion-orange-guava juice. Marc even rented snorkel gear from the hotel. Jess laid her towel next to the spot Gabi had staked out, beside their cousin Luisa.

Since Luisa was Gabi's age, they'd been tight as kids and had often shut Jess out at family get-togethers. But even if Luisa wasn't Jess's favorite cousin, she was still family. And she was the *only* cousin attending the wedding. It didn't seem right that Luisa's parents or her siblings hadn't come to Maui with her. But none of the extended Chavez family had been able to afford the costs of the airfare and the hotel.

As always, Luisa looked completely put together, dressed in a skimpy black bikini that put her toned figure on display. Her thick black hair fell to her shoulders in loose waves, with none of the humidity-induced frizz that plagued Jess.

"Great to see you," she said. "We were wondering whether

your plane would arrive in Maui or end up somewhere random, like Tahiti."

By tomorrow, Jess hoped everyone would be done mentioning her travel mishaps. She plastered a bright smile on her face. "I arrived in one piece. Thanks for helping out with Gabi's wedding errands."

"No problem. I'm glad my boss gave me the week off. Though I expect he'll be checking in constantly. I'm pretty much indispensable."

Jess bit back a laugh as she caught Gabi's eye. The two of them had spent numerous holidays listening to Luisa extol her position as a powerful player in a cutthroat marketing firm. "Are you planning on doing any work while you're here?" Jess asked her.

"Planning? No. But I'm sure I'll be asked to put out a few fires." Luisa peered at the water, where Connor and Marc were tossing a Frisbee back and forth. "In the meantime, I can have fun. Marc's cousin looks very promising."

Don't even think about it.

Not that Jess had any claim over Connor. But she didn't want Luisa fawning over him either.

Gabi spoke up quickly. "Don't waste your time. The guy will break your heart."

"Speaking from experience?" Luisa asked.

Jess's chest tightened as she waited for Gabi to mention Big Bear. But her sister shrugged off the question. "That's just what I've heard from Marc."

"I'm not looking for anything long-term," Luisa said. "My job's *much* too demanding. But I wouldn't say no to a little vacation romp." She stood up. "Let's go in the water."

As Gabi got to her feet, she shot Jess a sympathetic look. "You want to join us?"

Jess fought the urge to retreat to her room. This was her vacation, and she wasn't about to let Connor or Luisa ruin it. She flashed her sister an ultra-fake smile, as if to signal she was one hundred percent okay. "Sure, but I should put on some sunblock first. Did you bring any?"

Gabi handed her a bottle of Banana Boat sunscreen. "Here. You're going to need it, otherwise you'll fry. The sun's stronger than you're used to."

After Gabi and Luisa left, Jess began the slow process of applying sunscreen to her body—pretty much her *entire* body, since her new bikini was so damn tiny. Marc waded out of the water and approached her.

"You coming in?" he asked.

"In a few minutes." She waited, curious as to why he'd sought her out privately.

He rubbed the back of his neck. "Hey, listen. I got a text from Lance. He was planning to join us, but he's got a wicked hangover. Apparently, he was at the bar until two last night."

She kept her smile in place, despite the unease coursing through her. "No problem."

"I'm sure he'll be up for tonight's cruise. He loves sailing."

"Great." She tried to muster up an appropriate level of enthusiasm. "I can't wait to meet him."

Marc ran into the water and splashed the girls. Despite her best intentions, Jess let her gaze drift over to Connor, who was horsing around with Luisa. In swim trunks, he was a sight to behold, with his muscular legs, broad shoulders, and tight abs on display.

A snarky voice broke into her daydreams. "Please tell me you're not pining over my obnoxious man-whore of a brother?"

Coming from anyone else, the comment would have made her flush with shame. But not when the speaker was Connor's younger sister, Victoria, who delighted at shooting barbs at everyone in the family.

Jess laughed. "I was just objectifying him a little. I didn't realize it was that obvious."

"You were all but drooling. Believe me, he's not worth it." Victoria set down her towel. "By now, you must be over him."

"Of course. He's old news." Jess cringed at how false she sounded. She passed Victoria the bottle of sunscreen. "Do you want some?"

"You think I'm putting a ten-dollar bottle of grease on this skin?" Victoria opened her rattan bag and brought out a tube of La Mer SPF50. "This is the only brand I'll use."

Knowing Victoria, the brand was probably endorsed by Gwyneth Paltrow or some other lifestyle guru. "You haven't changed one bit."

"And I don't intend to." Victoria gathered her curtain of raven-black hair into a topknot, then rubbed sunscreen over her long, slender arms.

When Jess first met Victoria, she had pegged her as a spoiled princess and a daddy's girl—both of which had proved to be true. But underneath the hauteur and the bragging, Victoria was a lot of fun. At times, Jess found her a welcome relief from Gabi, who rarely allowed her petty side to show.

Victoria narrowed her eyes at Luisa, who was in the water up to her waist. "Who's the chick flirting with Connor?"

"She's not flirting. I mean…she's just having fun with him, that's all. She's my cousin Luisa." Even if Jess occasionally resented Luisa, she felt the need to defend her. "She's one of the few people here repping the Chavez clan."

"What's up with that? Did your family have a falling-out?" Victoria took out a pair of oversize sunglasses and put them on.

"Not really." Jess looked away, unsure of how much to reveal. "But this trip was beyond everyone's budget. I'm only here because Marc paid my way." Rather than deal with Victoria's pity, she scrambled to explain further. "Gabi's having a big party when we get back. That way the rest of the family can celebrate together."

When Gabi initially announced her wedding plans, she caused

a huge eruption. The fallout included numerous group texts, a lot of shade, and a few heated arguments. But Gabi held her ground and insisted on having the tropical wedding of her dreams. Jess firmly backed her up, even if she secretly thought her sister's decision was a little selfish.

"I didn't mean to pry," Victoria said.

Jess didn't want to belabor the subject. Victoria had lived in a rich-girl bubble for so long she probably couldn't grasp the concept of a budget.

"How's your wedding planning going?" she asked. "It's coming up soon, right?"

Victoria gave a heavy sigh. "Too soon. It's going to be a Christmas-wedding extravaganza at the Blackwood Cellars Estate, the likes of which the Temecula Valley has never seen. Two hundred guests, including two state senators. Daddy's thrilled."

Victoria, however, sounded less than thrilled. Why was everyone acting like weddings were such a huge chore? Shouldn't they be less about expectations and more about joy?

"You don't sound too excited," Jess said.

"I should be." Victoria's shoulders sagged. "But Ben hasn't been the ideal fiancé. Don't spread it around, but I caught him cheating last month."

Jess winced as Victoria's words triggered a painful flashback. Two bodies on the couch. Shared laughter. And the horrible sensation of walking into a bad dream. "I'm sorry. I went through that in March with my ex. It sucks."

"The worst part was the humiliation. You know?"

"I do. But...you're still going ahead with the wedding?"

"Afraid so. Daddy wouldn't have it any other way. Ben is Senator Macalister's son, which makes him an ideal catch. And I can't afford to make waves right now." Victoria's phone trilled, and she blanched at the picture on the screen. "Speak of the devil.

I should probably take this so Ben doesn't think I'm *deliberately* ignoring him."

Jess left Victoria to her conversation. She wished she could offer a little advice, but given how oblivious she'd been to Simon's cheating, she was hardly an expert in relationships. She stood and made her way down to the ocean. Unlike the beaches in Los Angeles, where the waves were bracing at first contact, the water was warm.

She let out a groan of pleasure. "This feels amazing."

"It's the perfect temperature," Marc said. "I could stay in all day."

While they took turns tossing the Frisbee, Jess continued sneaking glances at Connor to see how much attention he was paying to Luisa. Was he going to make a play for her? She hated how much the idea bothered her.

Maybe her sister had been right to set her up with Lance. If she had fun with him, she might stop obsessing over Connor.

After an hour, Marc suggested snorkeling. He gave the group a brief rundown on technique, and everyone grabbed a mask, snorkel, and fins. Once Jess caught on, she swam off from the group. The view took her breath away. Coral in shades of brown, purple, and orange. Yellow-and-black striped fish. A long, tubelike creature with a needle-nose. And an orange fish that reminded her of *Finding Nemo*. As she floated atop the sea, bobbing amid the gentle waves, the tension eased from her body.

She had no idea how long she was immersed in her own undersea paradise, but when she stood up to take a break, Connor was standing next to her. His nearness made her self-conscious, especially since she was wearing the world's smallest bikini.

"What are you doing here?" she asked.

"Just wanted a little quiet. Did you get your luggage yet?"

"Hardly. I'll be lucky if it arrives before the wedding."

His gaze was bold, traveling over every inch of her body. "Then where'd you get the bikini?"

Pushing past the urge to duck back into the water, she placed her hands on her hips, putting her barely covered curves on full display. If Connor wanted an eyeful, she'd give him one. "It was a gift from Gabi. Do you like it?"

His approval shouldn't matter. But she was gratified when he gave her a wicked smile that made her toes curl. "Definitely. Gabi has excellent taste." He took a few steps closer. "Just a warning. You might want to keep an eye out for sharks. Maui's known for them."

Ice water shot through her veins. "Sharks? Gabi didn't mention sharks." She scanned the horizon. "Shouldn't there be signs up?" She was about to wade back to the beach, but Connor caught her arm. The sensation sent tingles through her.

"Kidding. I wanted to see if you were still scared of them."

She smacked him in the chest. "You bastard. If I'm afraid of sharks, it's because you forced me to watch *Jaws*." She lifted her hand to smack him again, but he grabbed her wrist and held it tight. She stumbled, and he steadied her with his other hand. They were inches apart, and she was more aware of his physical presence than ever. She swallowed, torn between enjoying his touch and putting some distance between them.

"*Jaws* is a classic," he said. "Every movie buff needs to watch it at least once."

"But you told me sharks had been sighted at Big Bear Lake. It was beyond cruel."

He chuckled. "It was a freshwater lake in the mountains. Zero chance of a shark attack."

She'd forgotten how much she loved his laugh. Or how much she enjoyed teasing him. "At least I didn't freak out and claim a rogue grizzly was rooting through our garbage like you did that summer."

"Hey, it was pitch-dark outside. And it sounded like a bear."

She gave him a huge eye roll. "It was a raccoon, you big dork. You had bears on the brain after we watched *The Revenant*. Worst movie choice ever."

"I had to put it on my bucket list. Leo won an Oscar for that movie."

The sparks between them made Jess's pulse race. She licked her lips, tasting salt water, only to find Connor staring at her unashamedly, as if he wanted to claim those lips for himself. She forced herself to pull away and take a few steps back before she did something stupid, like kiss him.

"I...I watched some of the movies on the list you gave me."

He placed his hand over his heart. "My cinematic bucket list. And?"

"Some of them were great. *Snowpiercer* was brilliant, but so dark. *The Blair Witch Project* gave me chills. But *2001: A Space Odyssey* was a total snoozefest."

"Remember how we wanted to do a *Jurassic Park* marathon and watch all the movies back-to-back?" he said.

She laughed. "Until your mom reminded us the purpose of being up in the mountains was to get outside and enjoy the fresh air."

As much as she'd loved being outdoors with the whole gang, she'd treasured the times she and Connor had spent watching movies, hidden away in his family's cushy media room at the lodge.

He pointed to her arm. "You're looking a little pink. You might need more sunscreen."

She pressed her fingers against her skin, which had grown sensitive to the touch. Even though she'd practically bathed in Coppertone, she was on the verge of a sunburn. "Thanks. You should do the same." She took off her fins and tucked them under one arm.

As they waded back toward the others, Luisa approached them and flashed Connor a sweet smile. She placed her hand on his arm. "I need a break from the sun, so I'm heading inside. But I'll see you tonight. Should I come to your room, or should we meet at the shuttle?"

Connor had the courtesy to look uneasy. "Ah...how about the shuttle?"

"Perfect." She gave his arm a squeeze. "I'm glad I won't be flying solo on the cruise."

Jess wanted to keep silent. She *needed* to keep silent. But as soon as Luisa walked back to shore, she turned on Connor, her voice dripping with venom. "Nice work. You're here less than twenty-four hours and you're already hitting on my cousin?"

"I wasn't hitting on her."

"The hell you weren't." Here she was, falling prey to his charm, even *flirting* with him, and he was up to his old tricks.

"For your information, Luisa approached *me*. Everyone else on the cruise is part of a couple, and she didn't want to feel left out. We're going as friends."

"Is she aware of that? Because she seemed into you." Jess knew she was crossing a line, but she didn't care.

"Who are you to judge, seeing as how you're spending the evening with *Lance*?"

The disdain in his voice told her exactly how he regarded the arrangement. "What's wrong with that? It's *my* vacation. I could use a little fun."

He crossed his arms. "I get it. But you might want to tone down the judgment. And stop assuming the worst of me. We haven't talked for five years. Maybe I've changed."

"I wouldn't know, since you blocked me from your life. Which was a dick move, by the way. That's not how friends treat each other."

He gave an exasperated sigh. "Because you didn't want to be friends then. You wanted a relationship. And that wasn't going to happen. I did it for your own good."

Nothing worse than a man telling you he'd done something

for your own good. "You did it because you couldn't be bothered with me. You got what you wanted and decided to bail."

"Jess, you were eighteen. And you were leaving for college in three weeks. It wouldn't have worked out."

"You could have told me that up front. If I'd known all you wanted was sex, I never would have jumped into bed with you."

"Liar. You wanted it every bit as much as I did."

She stared at him in rage, itching to smack the knowing smile right off his face. Not because his words stung. Because they were true.

Gabi appeared beside her. "Everything okay here? Jess, you should get out of the sun for a while. You look flushed."

"It has nothing to do with the sun," Jess said. But she was glad for a reason to end the conversation. She turned and waded back to the shore with Gabi.

"I thought you guys were getting along," Gabi said. "You seemed fine at first."

"Until I remembered what a jerk he was." Now she regretted the way she'd confided in him over brandy.

"Just forget about him, okay? You and Lance will have a great time tonight."

She intended to. More than anything, she wanted to make Connor jealous. She wanted him to realize what he'd given up and make him regret it.

CHAPTER 7

*A*s Connor headed back to his room, he cursed himself for fighting with Jess.

Last night, he'd taken the first step in reaching out to her after five years apart.

But now he'd fucked things up again.

The beach outing had offered him the perfect opportunity to apologize to her. Instead, he'd argued with her about Luisa. Which was ridiculous. Even if he found Luisa attractive, he didn't plan to take things any further. Not when he was trying to clean up his reputation.

Besides, if he wanted anyone, it was Jess.

Damn it.

He could blame his attraction on the sight of her in that minuscule bikini. But it wasn't only the physical contact he craved. He missed the connection they'd shared. Not just their love of movies, but the way they'd commiserated with each other as kids, both living in the shadows of their perfect siblings. They were the troublemakers, the screwups, the ones least likely to succeed.

And for years, he'd been the only one who knew about her writing.

When he first found out about it, he was sixteen. After a night of partying on Big Bear Lake, he returned to Blackwood Lodge at 2:00 a.m., only to discover he was locked out. He wandered over to the cabin where the Chavez girls were staying. Seeing Jess's light on, he threw rocks at her window until she came down and let him in. She confessed she'd been up late, writing a fantasy novel in secret, because she didn't want her family to know about it.

He'd never told anyone. But every year, when their families were at Big Bear, he asked her for updates. In turn, she filled him in on the latest plot developments, excited to be sharing her story with someone.

You have to try harder to fix things with her. And apologize properly, for fuck's sake.

But not tonight. Because *Lance* would be in the picture.

AFTER SHOWERING off the sand and saltwater, Connor spent a few hours on a shaded chaise at one of the resort's pools, engrossed in a gripping mystery novel. He'd considered driving into Lahaina, but he was still wiped from yesterday's travel. After a late-afternoon nap, he arose in time to dress for the sunset cruise.

If it were up to him, he would have skipped the outing completely. He'd just as soon take his car and drive to a secluded beach to watch the sunset. But after promising Marc he'd participate in some of the planned activities, he didn't want to let his cousin down.

As he left his hotel room, Jess emerged at the same time. At first, he was too stunned to speak. During their summers at Big Bear, she'd always worn shorts and t-shirts and barely any makeup. This Jess was someone he didn't recognize. Her dark curls were artfully tamed, and her body was poured into a tight, jade-green dress that bared her shoulders and scarcely covered her butt. High-heeled sandals accentuated her shapely legs.

Ignoring him, she turned and walked toward the elevator.

"Jess. Wait up."

She continued to walk, giving him a delightful view of her tight, round backside. Damn, but that dress was tempting. Lance didn't deserve her.

When she stopped at the elevator, he caught up with her. "You look great."

She arched her eyebrows at him. "Not so much a kid anymore, right?"

"Definitely not." If anything, she looked too sexy. Lance would consider it an open invitation. Connor cleared his throat, knowing he was venturing into dangerous territory. "It's none of my business, but—"

"But what?"

"I met Lance two years ago. The guy goes through women like Kleenex."

"Didn't you just agree I was no longer a kid? What's with the older-brother advice?"

"Because I don't want you to go into tonight thinking it might *mean* something, when all he's after is a little tail." He sounded patronizing as hell, but his concern was valid. She'd been through enough grief in Chicago with Simon. She didn't need another guy jerking her around.

"Maybe I'm the same way. I want the fun without any strings. Great, mind-blowing sex with no commitment. Is that too hard to imagine?"

He smirked. "It is when it's coming from you. I know you, Jess."

"No, you don't. Like you said, we haven't seen each other in five years. A lot has changed."

"Has it? Have you been with anyone since you broke up with

Simon? Any one-night stands? Any flings?" When she didn't respond, he felt vindicated. "I thought so. You haven't changed that much."

The elevator opened and they got in. Jess pressed the button for the lobby, then turned on him with a scowl. "Why do you care if Lance fucks me tonight and walks away tomorrow? Isn't that exactly what you did to me?"

He clenched his fists. It wasn't the same at all. They'd spent *two weeks* together. And their attraction had stemmed from a ten-year friendship. What they'd shared had gone far beyond anything he'd ever experienced with any of his casual hookups.

"Well?" she said.

God, he was fucking this up *again*. "Look, Jess, I—"

The elevator stopped and the door opened, ending the conversation. He caught a whiff of gardenia-scented perfume as Luisa entered the tiny space. Like Jess, she was clad in a sleek minidress and high heels. The silver bracelets around her wrist shone under the harsh fluorescent lights.

"Good timing." Luisa beamed at him. "We must be on the same wavelength."

He forced a smile. "Apparently so."

Why had he agreed to this? The night had disaster written all over it.

Luisa turned to Jess. "Looking forward to tonight's cruise?"

"I can't wait. Gabi set me up with one of Marc's college buddies."

"Ooh. Is he cute? Or are you meeting him sight unseen?"

"I haven't met him yet. But I've seen a few photos. He's smoking hot. Apparently, he has this incredible workout regimen."

"Mmm. I love a man with a good body."

Connor could barely contain his revulsion. The elevator ride couldn't end soon enough.

Marc was waiting in the lobby, and he directed them outside

to a shuttle van emblazoned with the words "Island Excursions" in bright pink letters. Gabi stood next to the shuttle, handing out leis. Beside her was the infamous Lance. The guy was trying way too hard, rocking the full nautical look—navy blazer, blue button-down, white shorts, topsiders. Did he think he was going to sail the boat himself? *Idiot.*

But Jess bestowed him with a full-wattage smile. "Lance, I presume?"

"In the flesh." He placed a lei around her neck. "You look even more gorgeous in person. Let's hope this isn't the only time you get lei'd tonight."

Lei jokes? Really? What was this guy—thirteen? Connor tried to hide his disgust. What rankled him the most was the way Jess was staring at Lance, all starry-eyed, like he was the embodiment of her bedroom fantasies.

For a brief moment, Connor contemplated bailing on the cruise, using seasickness as an excuse. But his family would never buy it, given how much time he'd spent on the water at Big Bear Lake. Besides, he'd be letting Luisa down. He'd have to suck it up and be a good sport.

The shuttle took them to Lahaina Harbor. Marc led the group down the dock, past charter boats and smaller craft, until they reached Pier 11, where their boat *The Wind Rider* was waiting. Connor had expected a big party ship, with lots of guests and a live band, but this was a more intimate, private charter. In addition to the wedding party, a few other couples were present —all friends of Gabi and Marc's who had come to Maui a few days early. All of them were paired off. No wonder Luisa hadn't wanted to show up without a date.

Once everyone settled onto padded benches around the railing, the captain reviewed the boat's safety features and pointed out the bar at the front of the ship. As the boat left the harbor, the knots eased from Connor's shoulders. Even if he had to watch Jess swoon over someone else, he was out on the water, at sunset, on a perfect summer evening. It was a good place to be.

He turned to Luisa, who was seated beside him. Though the bar wasn't more than a hundred feet away, her gravity-defying heels weren't conducive to navigating a moving boat. "Would you like a drink?"

"Thanks. I'll take a mai tai."

"You got it."

As he stood up, he made a mental note to limit himself to two drinks, max. Under no circumstances could he get wasted and lose control. He moved to the front of the boat, where Lance waited in line to place his order with the bartender.

"How's it going?" Connor asked.

Lance let out a sigh of contentment. "Fantastic. I love weddings."

"You do?" Connor did a double take. "Didn't peg you as the romantic type."

"Hardly. But I've never found anywhere better for picking up hot, desperate women."

The guy had seen *The Wedding Crashers* one too many times. "That's your big move?"

"Hell, yeah. Take your average single woman. It doesn't matter how much of a ballbuster she is in the boardroom. When she watches one of her friends get married, she starts feeling desperate, and the last thing she wants to do is go to bed alone. That's where I come in."

Connor was by no means a romantic, but he wasn't a calculating douchebag like Lance either. "I wouldn't call Jess desperate. She's only twenty-three."

"Right, but Marc told me she's coming off a bad breakup. She's vulnerable. So..." He grinned, showing perfect white teeth. "Shouldn't be too much of a challenge."

"It might not be that easy."

Lance laughed. "Not for you, maybe. But I've got this move down."

The urge to punch him in the mouth was so strong Connor had to take a few calming breaths. He didn't have any right to Jess. And he couldn't stop her if she wanted Lance.

But he damn well wanted to try.

CHAPTER 8

$\mathcal{B}$y the end of the sunset cruise, Jess had learned more than she ever needed to know about Lance Wilmington. At first, she'd been flattered by his attention, until she realized all he wanted to talk about was himself.

She'd heard not one, not two, but *four* stories of his legendary escapades at the frat house. Then he regaled her with tales of his gap year in Europe, followed by a lengthy description of his triathlete training. But she smiled and laughed in all the right places, mostly because Connor was sitting on a bench across from them, with Luisa at his side. Though Jess had no idea if Connor was truly interested in her cousin, she retaliated by leaning closer to Lance, as though hanging on his every word.

Admittedly, her attempts to make Connor jealous were immature as hell. But she was still annoyed at the way he'd talked down to her earlier.

As they sailed back to the harbor, a bearded guitar player serenaded them with songs from the Jimmy Buffett canon. While Jess wasn't a big fan of "Cheeseburger in Paradise," anything was preferable to more Lance stories. With the sun setting, the air had grown cooler. She shivered, wishing she'd borrowed a wrap from Gabi.

Lance put his arm around her bare shoulder. "Aww, you're cold." His breath tickled her ear. "Don't worry. We can warm up once we're back in your room."

She tried not to flinch at his touch. They'd been together for two hours, but she hadn't felt a single flicker of attraction. "Slow your roll, sailor. We're still at sea."

"We'll be back soon. Then the real fun begins." He nuzzled her neck. "I can't wait."

She stiffened. "But…but it's not even nine."

"Gives us more time, am I right?" He nibbled on her earlobe.

She downed the last of her drink. With two mai tais under her belt, she was tipsy but not wasted enough to contemplate sex with Lance. Not that drunken hookups had ever been her thing.

Maybe it's time you switched things up.

All through college, she'd plunged headfirst into angst-filled relationships, only to end up getting dumped. Why couldn't she treat sex the way guys did, like a mindless diversion? She might have more fun if she let go of her inhibitions and succumbed to a night of no-strings sex.

But she wasn't quite there yet. She'd gotten more aroused flirting with Connor on the beach than she'd been at any time during the cruise.

"I'm not sure if we're heading back to the hotel yet. Gabi might have more stuff planned." She whipped out her phone, grateful she'd installed her sister's calendar app. "Yep, after the cruise ends, we're going to a bar in Lahaina called the Blue Lagoon."

Lance leaned in again to whisper in her ear. "Wouldn't you rather go back to your room and get the party started?"

She fumbled for a response. "I…I'd love to, but I'm the maid of honor. I'm not supposed to skip any of my sister's activities."

"All right. Later, then."

She exhaled in relief. Maybe after another drink, Lance would seem like a palatable companion for the night. He was easy on the eyes, and anyone who boasted a workout regimen like his must have a good body.

Why, then, was she so reluctant to seize the moment? And why did she keep checking out Connor?

She *had* to get over him.

At the Blue Lagoon, their group commandeered a large table at the back. The place had a funky vibe, decked out with brightly colored surf boards, hanging nets with blue glass floats, and a bamboo dance floor.

Jess pulled up a chair and grabbed one of the laminated menus, which felt sticky to the touch. The vibrantly colored pictures highlighted tropical drinks with names like Blue Hawaiian, Planter's Punch, and Samoan Typhoon. All of them looked like a one-way ticket to Drunk Town, so she played it safe and ordered a mojito.

She took a few sips and willed herself to relax. As the tension eased from her shoulders, she favored Lance with a flirty smile. Only to have him reciprocate by sliding his hand under her dress to caress her bare thigh. His bold gesture should have excited her; instead, it made her shudder with revulsion. She wanted to squirm away, but not with Connor watching. Catching his eye, she held up her glass in a salute and slammed half her cocktail in one gulp. The rum hit her like a freight train, but she kept going until she'd finished the entire drink.

"Can I have another?" she asked.

Lance laughed but extricated his hand from beneath her dress. He got up and headed toward the bar.

She licked her lips, tasting mint and lime. It might be her imagination, but the room was swaying, ever so slightly.

A catchy dance tune came on, and Gabi leapt up from her seat. She tugged on Marc's arm, roused the other couples from the table, and led them onto the dance floor.

Luisa grabbed Connor's arm. "Let's go dance."

"In a sec," he said. "You start without me."

Luisa frowned but got up to join the others. As Lance was returning from the bar, she snagged him. "Come dance with us."

Lance set Jess's drink in front of her. "You up for it?"

She waved him away. "I'm good. I'll watch." Considering she could barely walk in Victoria's heels, dancing was out of the question. She took a sip of her mojito. *Mmm.* It went down just as easy as the first one.

Connor leaned across the table. "Slow down. That's your fourth drink."

"You're counting?"

"I'm watching out for you. Ease up, okay? Do you really want Lance taking advantage of you when you're drunk?"

"I want *someone* taking advantage of me. Why is that so hard for you to understand?"

He grabbed her wrist. "Because Lance is just trying to get laid. He doesn't give a shit about you."

"And you do? Don't be such a fucking hypocrite." She wrenched her wrist out of his grasp and lurched away from him. But when she stood, her head spun. She braced herself on the table until the dizziness faded.

"Are you okay?" he asked.

"I'm fine. I need to use the bathroom."

She tottered toward the ladies' room, occasionally stopping to brace herself against the wall. Once inside the restroom, she splashed cold water on her face.

Get it together. You're going to have a great night with Lance. Wild, passionate sex, just like you wanted.

Leaning on the sink, she tried to picture Lance's face. His body. But all she could conjure up was Connor's face. The image of his chiseled, naked body, illuminated by the firelight, when they'd made love in front of the fireplace at Big Bear. No matter how hard she'd tried to forget that night, it was seared onto her brain.

If she wasn't careful, all the memories would come flooding back. During the two weeks she'd been with Connor, they hadn't been able to keep their hands off each other. Nothing she'd experienced since then had ever come close.

"Jess? Are you all right?" Luisa stood beside her, applying a fresh coat of lipstick.

"I think...I...might have had too much to drink." Jess looked away in shame.

"Why don't you call a ride-share and go back to the hotel? I can go with you."

Her cousin's compassion made Jess even more aware of her pathetic state. "What about you and Connor?"

"Honestly?" Luisa laughed and tossed her hair. "He's hot, but he's been staring at you all night. I can't compete."

Hearing that news played havoc with Jess's shaky equilibrium. She didn't want Connor. She *couldn't* want him. What she wanted was to have great sex with Lance so she'd get Connor out of her mind. "*Oh*. We...um...had a thing a long time ago. But it's over. Way over. And I promised Gabi I'd spend the evening with Lance."

"But not if you're this wasted." Luisa gave her a hard stare. "You realize you don't owe him anything, right?"

She nodded, feeling chastised.

"Let me know if you want to go back, okay? I don't mind cutting out early." Luisa gave her hair an extra fluff, then strolled out of the ladies' room.

Even if her cousin's advice had been well-meaning, Jess chose to ignore it. If she turned Lance down tonight, he'd find someone else tomorrow. And, once again, she'd be tempted to chase after Connor. But if she gave in to him, she'd get her heart broken all over again.

She *needed* this distraction.

She took a few deep breaths and headed toward the bar. A shot of something potent might get her back in the game. She caught the bartender's attention. "Hey there, handsome. Can I get a Fireball Shooter?"

One of her favorites when she needed a second wind, back when she and her friends used to close down the bar in college.

"You sure?" he asked. "You look like you've had a lot already."

Was it that obvious? She batted her lashes at him. "I'm *fine*. And I'm not driving anywhere. Hit me."

As she downed the potent combination of rum, cinnamon schnapps, and Tabasco, her eyes watered. She gave a full-body shudder, blinked a few times, and set the shot glass back on the bar. "Thanks. I needed that."

She turned to leave, only to plow into Gabi. "Oops. Sorry. Didn't see you there."

Gabi grabbed her arm and pulled her aside. "What the hell are you doing?"

"Um...drinking? It's a *bar*, Gabi."

Her sister's voice was terse. "You're drunk. I can smell it on your breath. It's time for you to call it a night. The party's over."

Jess grinned at Gabi, hoping she'd lighten up. "Nope. The party's just getting started.'"

Gabi let out her breath. "Enough. You need to act like an adult."

"And you need to get that stick out of your ass." Giving her sister a little salute, Jess tugged her arm out of her grasp. If she spent any more time with Gabi, she'd ruin her buzz.

She wove back to her table, only to find everyone had vanished except Lance. "Where'd the party go?"

"The dance floor, baby. Which means we *finally* get a little alone time."

The minute she sat down, he pulled her toward him, capturing her lips in a demanding kiss. He tasted of rum and lime juice, and he clearly knew what he was doing. As he threaded his hands through her hair, she twined her tongue with his, hoping to feel a rush of desire.

But even if his technique was masterful, it left her cold.

No tingle of lust. No rush of anticipation. No throbbing ache that cried out for attention.

After another kiss, she was convinced. Lance might be a world-class stud, but he wasn't doing it for her. The smart move would be to bow out now. But then what? Go back to her hotel room and pine over Connor?

No. She'd stick it out with Lance.

After another hour at the Blue Lagoon, she was so drunk she could barely see straight, let alone walk. Lance led her into the shuttle and stayed by her side as they entered the lobby of the hotel. With his arm around her shoulders, he guided her to the bank of elevators.

Damn, but she was smashed.

Just how much had she imbibed, anyway?

Two mai tais. Two mojitos. That idiotic Fireball. And half a rum and Coke. Three and a half drinks too many.

She tripped as she exited the elevator. Stupid heels. She couldn't wait to get them off. Same with the too-tight dress. At this point, sex was out of the question. She was so dizzy all she wanted to do was face-plant on her bed, crash into oblivion, and forget the whole night.

"Which room number?" Lance asked.

"Umm...954. No, wait. 945." She struggled against the fog overtaking her brain. "It's close to the ice machine."

Lance stopped in front of 945. As Jess stumbled on her heels —again—she was hit with a massive head rush. She had crossed the line from happily tipsy to what-the-hell-was-I-thinking. The next stop on the drunk train would be the Vomit Station, and she did *not* want to go there.

"You okay?" Lance asked.

"Not really." Her stomach lurched. *Vomit Station, dead ahead.* "I think I'm done."

"Done?" His voice hardened. "As in done drinking or done for the night?"

"For the night." She squinted at him, aware he was scowling. "Are you mad? Don't be mad."

He stepped closer, his eyes clouding over with fury. "This is bullshit. You've been teasing me all night."

"Back off. I can say no if I want."

When he refused to move, she pushed him away. He retreated, making her lose her balance. She teetered, then fell, her knees hitting the carpeted hallway. The clasp of her purse popped open, and the contents spilled out. She clutched her stomach and groaned as another wave of nausea rolled over her.

She no longer cared about Lance *or* Connor. She just wanted this miserable night to be over.

CHAPTER 9

Connor rode the elevator up to his room alone. Though he'd enjoyed Luisa's company, he had no urge to take things any further. If she was disappointed, she gave no indication. Instead, she wished him good night and went off to bed.

Not that anyone was around to hand him a trophy, but for him, this was a huge victory. It wasn't as substantial as saving Jess from that arrogant frat boy, but better than seeking out a mindless hookup in retaliation and hurting someone in the process.

As he got off the elevator, a sharp moan drew his attention. Jess was on her hands and knees outside the door to her room, with the contents of her purse littering the hallway. Lance stood over her, a scowl etched on his face. Connor fisted his hands and strode toward them. If that bastard had hurt Jess in any way, he'd make him pay.

"What's going on?" he growled.

Lance held up his hands. "Chill, bro. It's nothing. Jess had too much to drink."

"And you were planning to take advantage of her?" Connor asked. "Not cool, asshole."

Jess pushed her curls out of her face and glared up at him. "Mind your own business. I'm not some freaking damsel in distress."

"No, but you're drunk and about to do something stupid," Connor said. Never mind that he'd enjoyed his share of equally stupid hookups in the past. He didn't want Jess to make the same mistake. Especially since she was in no position to actively consent to *anything*.

Lance gave a snort of disgust. "She's shit-faced. If you want her, she's all yours."

Connor moved in closer. Even if he'd promised Marc to keep things under control, he was itching to put this douchebag in his place. He kept his voice low, tamping down the rage building up inside him. "Get the fuck out of here. *Now*."

Muttering curses under his breath, Lance stomped off toward the elevator.

Connor bent down next to Jess. "Come on. Let's get you back to your room."

She pulled away from him. "I don't need your help."

This was the thanks he got for sticking his neck out? He wanted to scold her for acting like an idiot, but at this point, she was too drunk to care. He knelt and swept up all the crap from her purse. Once he was done, he pulled her up and set her back on her feet. She swayed precariously but managed to stay upright.

"What are you doing?" she demanded.

"Getting you into your room so you can sleep there instead of out in the hallway." He held out his hand. "Key card?"

"In my purse."

He rifled through the contents, smirking as he pulled out a couple of condoms. "I see you came prepared for your date with Lance. Too bad you won't get to use them."

"Shut up. Just find my damn key card."

He looked through her purse twice. "It isn't in there. Are you sure you took it with you?"

"I think so?" She closed her eyes and leaned against him. "I just wanna go to bed and make the spinning stop."

He set her against the door while he scoured the hallway again. No sign of it. Either she'd forgotten it completely or it had slid under someone's door. Either way, he didn't want to waste any more time.

"Let's go in my room. You can wait there while I get you another card from the front desk."

"Not a chance. You just want to have your way with me."

He sucked in his breath. "Believe it or not, I find you remarkably easy to resist."

She could have stripped naked and he still would have turned her down. Only a player like Lance would take advantage of a woman when she was this far gone.

He led her into his room and turned on the light. A wave of fatigue crested over him, making him long for the comfort of his bed, but he needed to take care of Jess first. He went into the bathroom to fetch her two ibuprofen, then grabbed a bottle of water from the mini fridge. He handed them to her.

"Here. Take these. And drink all the water."

She plopped onto his bed and kicked off her heels but made no move to drink the water until he pushed it at her again. "Fine," she said. "You're so damn bossy."

He dragged a wastebasket beside the bed. "Stay here while I get you another key card. Don't lie down, okay? I don't want you passing out on my bed. And don't throw up. But if you feel the urge to vomit, use the trash can, not the bed."

"You use that line on all your dates? You're a real ladies' man, aren't you?" She snorted with laughter.

Once she'd drained half the water bottle, he left the room. He took the elevator to the lobby, grumbling the whole way. Why was he helping her? She certainly didn't appreciate it. If anything, she resented him more for interfering.

Maybe it was his way of making up for what he'd done to her five years ago. For leaving her so abruptly and cutting her out of his life. But if he hadn't severed their ties, he might have sought her out after he returned from Spain. Which would have been a huge mistake. Because once he started working under his brother, Darren, he'd been miserable. And he hadn't handled it well. Instead of channeling his frustrations into running or joining a boxing gym, he'd spent too many nights at the bar, getting drunk and picking up women. Jess had been better off without him.

But he hadn't explained his actions. Or apologized. Instead, he made her feel like their two weeks together had been easily forgettable. That she was just another fling, rather than a woman who'd affected him deeply.

When he returned with a new key card, she was sprawled across his bed, sleeping soundly. He nudged her shoulder. "Jess? *Jess*. Get up."

Nothing.

He closed his eyes and let out a weary sigh. She was hogging half the bed. If he tried to move her, he might wake her. In her state, she was better off sleeping. The bed was big enough for three or four people, but if she woke and found him lying next to her, she'd probably smack him in the face with a pillow.

He grabbed a couple of pillows and opted for the couch.

Given his height, it was hardly the most comfortable option. But one thought gave him consolation—Jess had ended up in *his* bed and not Lance's.

CHAPTER 10

Jess woke to bright sunlight streaming into the room. Her head throbbed like it had been slammed by Thor's hammer. Her mouth was so dry she could barely swallow. And her stomach roiled with discomfort.

What the hell had she done?

She propped herself up on her elbow and forced her eyes fully open.

Oh God.

She was still wearing last night's dress. And she was in *Connor's* room. She'd spent the night in his bed, but if the pillows on the couch were any indication, he hadn't joined her.

She sat up slowly. The previous night's antics came back in shameful waves. How could she have been so irresponsible? Four and a half cocktails. A Fireball. And no water in between to lessen the effects of the booze. She shuddered as she recalled Lance's furious reaction after she turned him down.

That's one bullet you've dodged.

But the bullet she hadn't dodged? Connor. After spending all night fighting her attraction to him, she'd ended up in his bed. Her bossy white knight, who'd watched out for her but hadn't laid a finger on her. Because if she and Connor had done *anything*, she would have remembered it, no matter how plastered she was.

"Connor?" She rubbed her eyes. On the nightstand, a bottle of red Gatorade rested atop a sheet of paper, with the words "Drink Me" scrawled in Connor's messy handwriting. Feeling like Alice in Wonderland, she uncapped the beverage and took a few grateful sips. In college, she and her roommates had kept a supply of Gatorade on hand to lessen their post-party hangovers.

After downing the rest of the bottle, she stood on unsteady legs. No sign of Connor anywhere. She checked the desk for a note. Nothing. After retrieving her purse from the bed, she fished out her phone, hoping he'd sent a text, but the battery had died.

Time to go back to her room and salvage the day. The first order of business was a searing-hot shower, followed by a vat of coffee.

Until she remembered another detail. No key card. She must have passed out while waiting for Connor to return with it. Rather than wake her, he'd let her sleep. She scanned the room for her card but didn't spot it. She could look for it later, after she'd done some damage control.

She stumbled to the bathroom, splashed cold water on her face, and took stock. *Hideous.* Under no circumstances could she face Connor this way. She went back into his room and found one of the resort's leopard-print bathrobes hanging in the closet. She grabbed it and returned to the bathroom. The shower had open glass panels rather than a curtain, which meant she'd be partially exposed.

To hell with it. She needed a shower.

She moaned in pleasure as the scalding hot spray coursed down her back. Thanks to the body wash and shampoo provided by the hotel—a Hawaiian brand that smelled like coconuts—she no longer reeked of booze. After giving herself a final rinse, she turned off the water. Only to freeze in shock when the bathroom door opened wide.

Shit. In her haste, she'd forgotten to lock it.

"Jess? You in there?" Connor stepped inside the bathroom.

Despite the cloud of steam she'd worked up, she was still visible. She scooted back toward the wall. "Go away!"

He stopped but didn't turn away. In his eyes, she saw raw desire. The same powerful attraction they'd shared on the beach. She swallowed. If he took off his clothes and jumped in with her, all her willpower would vanish.

Shaking his head, he took a few steps back. "Sorry. I'll wait for you in the room." He walked out, shutting the door behind him.

She cursed her body's traitorous reaction. Even now, she was fighting off fantasies of him stripping down to nothing, coming into the shower, and pressing his hard, naked body against hers. She dried herself off, then put on the plush bathrobe, belted it tightly, and left the bathroom.

Connor sat on his bed, scrolling through his phone. He pointed to the chair beside the desk. "Have a seat. We need to talk."

Her hackles rose. "If you're going to lecture me—"

"I am. What were you thinking last night? You were drunk off your ass."

"So what? I wanted to get drunk. How else..." She broke off, not wanting to admit the truth.

His smile was far too knowing. "How else were you going to stomach sleeping with Lance? Is that what you were going to say?"

"No!"

He leaned back and crossed his arms. "You're lying."

"Am not."

"Are too. Admit it—you didn't want him. You were trying to make me jealous."

Even if he was right, his smug expression infuriated her. "Not everything is about you!"

"Last night was."

Indignation rose inside her. "What about you and Luisa? Were you into her or were you deliberately trying to piss me off?"

He shrugged. "Like I said, she wanted someone to hang out with on the cruise. But that's it. I didn't hit on her. If I wanted her, do you think I would have spent the night on the couch?"

Jess sat down at the desk, taken aback by his honesty. "Still... you didn't need to come to my aid. I was handling things fine on my own."

Even as she said it, her face heated up with shame. She hadn't been fine. She'd come perilously close to face-planting in the hallway.

"Sorry if I was out of line," he said. "But I still care about you. No one should be left alone when they're that drunk."

He was apologizing? Once again, she wondered if he had an agenda, but he looked genuinely contrite. "Thanks. I...kind of lost control."

Her skin crawled when she thought of how far she'd let things go, with a man she didn't like. And she'd done it to make Connor jealous.

Gabi was right. Even after five years, she was still obsessed with him.

She looked away, not wanting to meet his gaze. She didn't want him to know how conflicted her feelings were or that she'd spent the last twenty-four hours wavering between resentment and longing.

On his desk was a cardboard to-go cup and a pecan bun on a paper plate. She inhaled the tantalizing aroma of French roast. "Is that coffee for me?"

"Yep. Same with the sticky bun. I consider coffee and carbs to be the perfect post-hangover breakfast. Provided you drank the Gatorade I left you?"

She gave him a wry smile. "We share the same remedy. Thanks. Did you manage to snag me another key card?"

"It's on the desk. Don't lose it this time."

"Where? I didn't see it."

"Hang on." He pushed aside a pile of clutter—brochures, a Maui guidebook, and a printed map of the resort—until he located the card and gave it to her.

She tucked it in the pocket of the robe and took a sip of coffee. Heavenly. He'd flavored it the way she liked it—with a light splash of cream, no sugar.

"You missed your other surprise." He pointed to a green suitcase, now propped against the couch.

Ignoring her throbbing head, she jumped up in excitement. "Oh my God! When did it get here?"

"Last night, maybe? The front desk texted me this morning about my garment bag. On the chance your suitcase arrived, I asked if they'd let me pick it up. I needed ID, so I grabbed your driver's license from your purse." He took it from his pocket and handed it to her. "I figured you'd rather have me get it than go down to the lobby wearing last night's clothes."

Connor had given her his bed, bought her breakfast, *and* retrieved her suitcase. All of which struck her as incredibly considerate gestures. Maybe it was time she put the past aside.

"Thanks. Sorry you had to sleep on the couch."

"No harm done."

They sat in silence, sipping their coffee, but Jess had a hard time reining in her fantasies. Now that her irritation at Connor had faded, her attraction had ramped up, once again. She was alone with him. Wearing nothing but a bathrobe. What would happen if she flung it off and tackled him on the bed? Would he still want her? Or was he totally turned off since he'd seen her at her worst last night?

Just stop. You're here for Gabi's wedding. Everything else comes second.

"What's on tap for today?" she asked. "My phone's dead, so I can't pull up the itinerary."

"Let me see." Connor checked his phone. "The rest of the Blackwood clan—except Brody—arrived late last night, so this morning there's a family brunch at the Banyan Tree restaurant, at 10:00 a.m. sharp. Blackwoods only."

"No loss there." In her present state, a formal brunch with the Blackwoods sounded excruciating.

"Then at one, tee time at the Ka'anapali Golf Course, followed by cocktails."

She grimaced. The few times she'd tried golf, she played terribly. Gabi had only taken up the sport after Marc had given her a full set of clubs for her birthday.

"Are you going?" she asked.

"No. I'm not ready to face my dad yet, so I made other plans. I'm doing the Road to Hana."

She'd read about the Road to Hana on Gabi's list of recommendations. It covered fifty miles of the island's eastern coast, on a winding route that included six hundred curves and crossed fifty-nine bridges. Along the way were black-sand beaches, bamboo forests, and waterfalls. The only reason Gabi hadn't included it in her itinerary was because the full trip—there and back—took seven hours minimum.

"I hate to kick you out of here, but I need to take off soon," Connor said. "I want to be on the road by nine, plus I need to pick up lunch."

"You're going by yourself?" That seemed like a lonely undertaking during a family vacation. Then again, he probably wanted to avoid his father for as long as possible.

"No one else was into it. Unless you want to come?"

"Are you sure?"

He wanted to spend the day with her? After the way she'd treated him? Maybe he truly wanted to be friends again. The idea appealed to her. If she joined him on this expedition, they'd have a chance to reconnect, without their families interfering.

"Absolutely," he said. "As long as you're up for some hiking and maybe a dip under a waterfall. But we won't be back until dinner."

"Sounds like fun. But I don't think Gabi would appreciate it if I took the day off. She's probably still pissed about last night." Hadn't Gabi asked her not to get drunk? In typical fashion, she'd already broken one of her promises.

"She might not have noticed. Most of the group was hammered by the time we got back."

"But not you?"

"Not anymore. I've made too many dumb-ass mistakes when I've been drunk. Besides…I was sort of…"

"What?" The words came out with more force than she intended. "Watching out for me?"

He gave her an apologetic grin. "Not my business, but…"

His protective streak should have annoyed her. Instead, she found it endearing he cared. "It's fine. I'm glad I didn't do something I'd regret."

Like sleep with Lance.

"So—Hana? You in?" he asked.

She considered her responsibilities. Though her mom was flying in at four, she was planning to catch a ride with Brody. But even if Jess was off the hook for airport pickup duty, Gabi might have other expectations for her.

"If Gabi isn't going to the Blackwood brunch, I should see if she has something else planned. Or if she wants me to run errands. I don't want to let her down."

Connor perused his phone again. "You're not on the morning's itinerary. The only thing I see is *Gabi and Luisa: 10 a.m. kitesurfing lessons.*"

She was a little hurt at being excluded even if kitesurfing sounded like a wreck waiting to happen. "I'm free all day?"

"Sadly, no. You're listed on the golf outing. I didn't realize you played golf."

"I don't. Not even a little."

"Come with me instead. Wouldn't you like to see more of Maui?"

Exploring the island with Connor was bound to be more fun than flailing around on a golf course. But wasn't this scenario *exactly* what Gabi wanted her to avoid? She was about to turn him down, but she couldn't do it. This might be her one chance to rebuild their friendship, in a setting where no one else was around to pass judgment.

"Why don't you text Gabi and see if she'll let you have a free day?" Connor asked. His smile was so encouraging, her heart swelled. Damn if she wasn't reverting to her eighteen-year-old self already.

"Okay. Maybe she won't care if I miss golf."

"I'll stop by your room to check in fifteen minutes," he said. "You'll need sunscreen, a water bottle, shoes for hiking, a towel, and…" He grinned. "Bring your bikini. The one you wore to the beach yesterday."

How could she resist an invitation like that?

CHAPTER 11

*J*ess went back to her room and plugged in her phone.
Before she lost her nerve, she called her sister. A text
would have been easier, but she wanted to face the
issue head-on. If Gabi showed any sign of irritation, then she'd
suck it up and act like she wanted to spend three painful hours
on a golf course.

When Gabi's phone went to voicemail, Jess was so surprised
she hung up. After taking a moment to compose the proper
excuse, she tried again, this time leaving a long message.

"Hi, Gabi. It's Jess. Last night was so fun! Sorry if I had a little
too much to drink. Anyway, I saw you're busy with kitesurfing
this morning, so I'm going to explore Lahaina. And I'm gonna
pass on golf because I'd just slow the group down. So...I guess I'll
see you at dinner tonight. Have a great day!"

On the chance Gabi didn't need her, she prepared for her
outing with Connor. Opening her suitcase, she squealed in
delight at all her clothing options. Though she'd packed two
swimsuits, she chose the ruby-red bikini because Connor had
admired it. Over it, she put on a tank top and shorts. As she
prepared her backpack, she found herself humming.

Get a hold of yourself.

Whatever happened today, even if she and Connor rekindled their friendship, she could *not* let him charm her into bed. Other than their fling at Big Bear, they'd grown up as friends. Not lovers, but actual friends who'd shared jokes and confided in each other for years.

That was what she should be focusing on. Not sex.

A sharp rap on the door made her heart leap in response. She fumbled as she unplugged her phone, only to drop it on the floor. With trembling hands, she stuffed it and the charger in her backpack.

Chill out. If you don't calm down, you'll scare Connor away.

He stood waiting at the door, dressed in a t-shirt, shorts, and hiking boots. On his back was an olive-gray knapsack. "Did you get the all clear?"

She tried not to stare at his muscular legs. Or his broad chest, which filled out his shirt nicely. She was going on this excursion as his travel buddy. Nothing else. "Gabi didn't answer, but I think it'll be okay. As long as I don't miss the big family dinner."

"You won't, I promise. I need to be there, too."

"Okay, then. Let's go."

Alone with Connor in the elevator, she was drawn in by his physical presence. A glimpse of his scruffy stubble made her wonder what it might feel like, grazing the inside of her thighs. She took a deep breath to center herself, only to catch a whiff of his delicious pinewoods scent. The same scent as the shirt he'd loaned her. A shirt she *never* intended to return.

She tensed when they walked through the hotel lobby, afraid they might run into someone from the wedding party. She didn't want Gabi to find out, secondhand, that her little sister had blatantly disobeyed her orders. As they pulled away from the resort in Connor's rental car, a frisson of excitement passed through her. She was going on an all-day expedition with Connor. Anything could happen.

Not that anything *would* happen. She'd make sure of it.

~

THE ROAD to Hana started from the town of Paia, an hour's drive from the hotel. After picking up box lunches from a local deli, they set out, with Jess on map duty. On either side of them, the dense, tropical vegetation made her feel like they were driving through a leafy green tunnel. At first, the twisty curves unsettled her stomach. But Connor had come prepared with a bag of candied ginger in his pack. Though Jess was skeptical at first, a few handfuls of the crystallized candy eased her discomfort. After her nausea had passed, she looked up at the road ahead and stared in disbelief.

"Connor. *Connor.* Do you see that bridge?"

"What about it?"

"It's *one* lane. How's that supposed to work?"

He shrugged. "The bigger car gets the right-of-way?"

"We're in a compact. You couldn't have upgraded to an SUV?" As they approached the narrow bridge, she clenched her fists, worried another vehicle would speed around the blind corner and smack into them, but they passed over it without incident.

"Relax," he said. "This time of day, everyone's going *to* Hana. No one's going in the other direction."

"If you say so." She unfolded the oversize map and tried to pinpoint their location based on the road markers. "I can't believe you're making me use a map. Like an old-time explorer."

"The cell reception's spotty here. Besides, I like maps."

"Okay, *Grandpa.*"

"I'm not the one who had a map of *Middle Earth* hanging up in my bedroom."

An embarrassing memory, to be sure. But it was touching he remembered. "True, but when we did that *Lord of the Rings* marathon up at Big Bear, you made us watch the *extended* versions. The last one was, like, five hours long."

He gave her a scornful look. "It was four. And totally worth it. It won the Oscar for Best Picture that year."

She poked his shoulder. "See, you're just as big a geek as I am."

"Nope. Not possible." He pointed to the map. "Get to work, missy."

She flattened the map over her thigh. "What am I supposed to be looking for?"

"Upper Waikani Falls. Find the mile marker. We can't park for long, but we can stop to take pictures."

"Found it. Mile Marker 19. It's coming up soon." She set the map at her feet and took a drink from her water bottle. By now, the last remnants of her headache had faded away, turning the previous evening's debacle into little more than a hazy memory.

She took out her phone to take a few photos, racking her brain for clever, waterfall-themed captions, like "go with the flow," or "chasing waterfalls, baby." But she caught herself in time. If she posted anything on Instagram, Gabi might see it. Then she'd know her naughty little sister hadn't spent the day in Lahaina.

Spotting a line of cars parked along the narrow road, she pointed ahead. "Up there. See? Where that red car's pulling out. But it's not a big space."

"I can make it work. And to think—you wanted me to rent an SUV."

For that, he got another shoulder poke. "Fine. Enjoy your tiny car."

"You know what they say—small car, big..." He grinned at her.

Warmth flooded her cheeks. *Nope. Not going down that road.*

Not when they were crammed together in a small vehicle. As he pulled into the spot, she rolled down her window and inhaled the humid, tropical air. Upper Waikani Falls wasn't just one waterfall, but three tall streams running side by side, cascading over rocky cliffs. Bright sunlight shimmered off the mist, creating a faint rainbow. Even from a distance, the roar of rushing water was audible. After she took few photos, she motioned to Connor.

"Pass me your phone. I have a better angle than you do."

As his hand brushed hers, the contact made her tingle. Though they'd been driving together for over an hour, she was suddenly aware of how close he was sitting. It would be far too easy to lean over and rest her hand on his muscular thigh. Or sneak in a quick kiss.

"Jess? We should get going. I think that convertible wants our spot."

She shook off her wicked thoughts and focused on the waterfalls, taking a slew of pictures for Connor before returning his phone.

As he eased back onto the road, she wiped her forehead, feeling uncomfortably warm. Being alone in a cramped car with Connor was more tempting than she'd imagined.

Forget an SUV. She would have been safer if he'd rented a minivan.

CHAPTER 12

When they reached the Pua'a Ka'a State Wayside Park at Mile 22, Connor pulled into a paved parking area. He'd chosen this spot as their first real stop since it contained shaded picnic tables and restrooms, with a waterfall and a swimming hole only a short hike away. At the sight of an empty table, Jess let out a cry of triumph and raced over to claim it. Once they were seated, he unpacked the box lunches and set out the food—sandwiches, chips, bottled juices, pineapple spears, and two huge brownies dusted with powdered sugar.

Jess grabbed one of the brownies and bit into it. She gave a blissful sigh. "Mmmm. Perfect."

"You're supposed to eat the dessert last," he said.

"Not me. Why save the good stuff for the end?" She took another bite and licked powdered sugar from her lips.

Her lips looked so soft and inviting he had to resist the urge to lean across the picnic table and lick the sugar off them. "Enjoying the drive so far?"

"Yeah. Thanks for inviting me. Thanks for everything, actually. You've been nice to me ever since we got to Maui, and I've been kind of a bitch. Sorry."

His resolve weakened even further. It didn't help that her low-cut tank top revealed a tantalizing hint of her cleavage. Or that he couldn't stop picturing her naked, in his shower. He'd wanted to strip down, kiss every inch of her delectable body, and take her up against the tiled wall.

Enough. You're acting like a sex-starved teenager.

"You don't have to apologize," he said.

"Sure, I do. I shouldn't have snapped at you when we were at the beach. But it still hurts, you know?" She uncapped one of the juice bottles and took a swig. "I realize it was partly my fault you cut me off after Big Bear. You were totally blindsided when I told you I loved you."

He recalled the gut-wrenching dread he'd felt during their last morning together, when she confessed her feelings. It was then he realized what a mistake he'd made, assuming she could keep things casual after sleeping with him for two weeks.

"I should have seen it coming," he said. "But I didn't, and I handled it badly. I'm sorry."

Her voice hardened. "I know I came on too strong. But you dismissed everything we shared with that last text. Do you remember what it said?" She blinked back tears.

He'd never forgotten. *It's over. You need to move on.* His callous words had done exactly what he hoped. She hadn't texted him again. At the time, he knew he was acting like a selfish jerk. If nothing else, he should have called her to talk things over one last time.

A family of picnickers passed them, laden with two coolers and a couple of folding chairs. Jess waited until they left before she spoke up again. "You have no idea how much you hurt me. I was devastated."

"I'm sorry. I was chickenshit, and I hated myself for it. But you telling me you loved me? That you'd wait for me to come back from Spain? I couldn't deal with that kind of pressure. Even though we had a great time together, there was no way I could handle a relationship. Not with you or anyone else."

She nodded, letting him talk.

"Getting away from California—from the whole family—was the break I needed. After I visited a bunch of vineyards in Spain, I spent a week in the mountains and cleared my head. That's when I realized how badly I'd fucked up. I should have told you how much those two weeks meant to me."

She sniffed and wiped her eyes. "You should have. Then I wouldn't have felt like another one of your disposable women."

The pain sliced into him, sharp as a knife. She'd spent five years feeling that way. Because of him. "I wanted to tell you once I got home."

"Then why didn't you?" Her grip tightened on her juice bottle. "You never reached out. And it wasn't hard to find me. I was at UC Irvine for four years."

If they were going to rehash the past, he needed to be completely honest. "I thought about visiting you. But I knew if I went to see you, I'd fall back into temptation. You didn't need that."

He'd never admitted it. Not to anyone. Instead, he'd acted like their fling hadn't affected him, like she'd been another of his conquests. But, in truth, those two weeks had been the best part of his summer. He spent hours during his hikes in the Pyrenees thinking of her and remembering the passion they'd shared.

Jess's eyes widened. "You...still wanted me?"

"I did. But you were away at college, meeting new people. And I couldn't give you what you wanted. I wasn't ready to commit to anyone. I figured if I cut you off, you'd be able to move on."

She stared at him, as though taking it in. "That helps a little. But moving on took me a long time. I'd been in love with you since I was twelve. And even if I *had* gotten over you, I still deserved an apology."

"I'm really sorry," he said. "Not just for what I did, but for assuming I knew what was best for you. I don't blame you for hating me."

She wiped her eyes again. "The thing is—I don't want to hate you. Not anymore." She let out her breath. "I'd like to be friends. But...I just don't know if I can trust you. Not entirely."

I wish you would.

But he understood her reluctance. For now, he was grateful she'd let him back into her life.

~

AFTER LUNCH, they hiked along the short, paved trail toward the lower falls. Compared to the waterfalls they'd seen on the drive, this one was on the small side—a five-foot torrent cascading into a swimming hole, amid dense tropical foliage. Still, the water looked cool and inviting. And it was blissfully free of other tourists.

"I can't believe we're the only ones here," Jess said. "Want to take a swim break?"

"Just to warn you—the water might be colder than you're expecting."

For that, he got a snort of derision. "When did you turn into such a wuss?"

She peeled off her tank top and shorts, revealing the sexy red bikini he'd ogled at the beach. Only two tiny pieces of fabric covered her luscious curves. This was more temptation than any man should have to withstand.

"Well?" She put her hands on her hips. "Are you coming in or not?"

If he stared at her a second longer, he wouldn't be able to control his hard-on, and it would be tricky to hide it in swim trunks.

Think unsexy thoughts. Like Great-Aunt Nina in a bikini.

That did the trick. He stripped down to his trunks, set his

clothes next to hers, then held out his hand. "We'll jump in together. All right?"

She took his hand and gripped it tight. "Just like at Big Bear. We were always the first ones in the lake, remember?"

"I remember. Count of three. One. Two. Three!" He jumped, pulling Jess in with him.

On first impact, the water was so cold it took his breath away, but Jess popped up and let out a whoop of joy. Before he could catch her, she dove under the water. He searched for her, startling when she tugged on his shorts and grabbed his butt. She surfaced again and splashed his face. He chased after her, but she managed to evade him.

As they swam and dove beneath the water, he let her think she'd won. But the minute she relaxed her guard, he pinned her against a rock. "Caught you."

She met his gaze with boldness. "The question is—what do you plan to do with me?"

With every inch of his being, he wanted to press his body against hers, devour her lips, and take her right there. As he smoothed the wet curls back from her face, he was struck by the desire in her eyes. When she parted her lips, he was ready to dive in.

The sound of voices shattered his fantasy. A group of elderly men and women tromped over to the swimming hole and began taking photos. Talk about a mood-killer.

He helped Jess out of the water, and they found a flat rock where they could sit and dry off. He noticed her staring at him under her lashes. "What's on your mind?"

She smiled. "I'm glad I don't have to hate you anymore."

"Did you really spend the past five years hating me?"

"Not exactly. But it hurt to think I'd gone from being a friend to another of your flings."

"You weren't, I promise." He rubbed his towel over his hair.

"Does that still happen a lot? Gabi made it sound like that's all you do—find girls in bars, hook up with them, and 'lose their number' the next day."

Trust Gabi to make him look like an asshole. "Not anymore. But for a while, that was my default."

And one of the main reasons he'd wanted to stay away from Jess. She didn't deserve that kind of treatment. No one did.

She pulled her tank top back on. "Why? Sure, you were kind of wild when we were kids—hell, we both were. But you never acted like a total dick. What changed?"

He raked his hand through his damp hair. "After I got back from Spain, Dad stuck me in the corporate side of Blackwood Cellars, working under Darren. He figured my dickhead older brother would whip me into shape. But it made us hate each other even more."

She let out her breath in disgust. "That guy has been an arrogant prick from day one."

"It was hell. I'd get off work, and all I wanted to do was get drunk, get laid, and forget I was stuck in a job I hated. Until last year, when I met someone and fell hard. Then I stopped fooling around."

Jess paled. "Gabi never mentioned you had a girlfriend."

Was she jealous? She didn't need to be. He never wanted to see Natasha again.

"It's over. It ended seven months ago." He stood up. "Want to head back?"

She nodded but didn't press him any further. Once they were walking, she spoke up again. "What happened? You don't have to tell me if you don't want, but I'm happy to listen."

He hadn't planned to bare his soul, but he'd always been able to open up around her.

"Not much to tell. Natasha and I only dated for about eight months, but things got intense quickly. We went out on New Year's Eve for a big romantic dinner, and I was going to ask her to move in with me. But I wanted to be honest with her, so I told her I was thinking of leaving Blackwood Cellars and going into business for myself. I was still in the planning stages, but my goal was to invest in a small winery and start my own label. No mass production, just handcrafted estate wine."

"Really? I love that idea."

He stopped short, surprised at her enthusiasm. Then again, she was the type who liked taking risks and trying new things.

"What did Natasha think?" she asked.

The pain had lessened now, but at the time, her rejection hit him like a blow. "At first, she laughed it off. Then she tried to talk me out of it. That's when she told me the truth—she was only with me because I was a Blackwood with a secure future. If I was planning on giving that up, then she was done."

"And you didn't back down?"

"I didn't. So, she left. I haven't heard from her since."

"I'm sorry."

There was no smugness in her voice that he'd been served a dose of his own medicine. Which made him feel marginally better.

"It was rough. After she left, I went on a couple of weekend benders. Lucky for me, some friends staged an intervention. And I realized what a dick I'd been. So, I've been trying to clean up my act. It hasn't been easy, but at least I don't wake up every morning hating myself."

"Has there been anyone since then?"

He wasn't going to lie to her. "A few women, here and there. But now I'm honest, right from the start. If they want to spend the night, I warn them they shouldn't expect anything long-term. The last thing I need—or want—is a serious relationship."

"Not ever?" The catch in her voice took him by surprise.

"Maybe someday. But right now, I need to stay focused. This new winery venture is stressful enough without getting in deep with someone again."

By now, they'd reached the car. Jess remained silent, no doubt processing everything he'd told her. A pang of regret sliced through him. He wished things had gone differently between them. He wished he'd sought her out and talked to her sooner.

Too late for that now.

But they could still be friends. And he could make sure they didn't lose touch once they left Maui.

They continued cruising along the Hana highway, occasionally stopping at some of the places on the map. At Wai'anapanapa State Park, a black-sand beach made from volcanic rock, they dodged the waves and checked out tide pools and lava tubes. They spent another hour along the Pipiwai Trail, hiking through a bamboo forest filled with stunning waterfalls.

On the drive back to Ka'anapali, Jess cued up her phone and cranked the volume, blasting him with a retro playlist that included tunes by the Beach Boys and Elvis Presley. Even if the music wasn't to his taste, he couldn't resist singing along with her. This was the Jess he'd grown up with, unafraid to champion the things she loved.

They'd been driving for another hour when she pointed to a sign.

"We need to stop. *Now*. Quick, there's a parking space." She flashed him a naughty grin. "It's just your size. Nice and small."

He put on his blinker and pulled over at a colorful sign advertising a small convenience store called Halfway to Hana. "What's so urgent?"

"This place. I read about it on Gabi's list of Maui must-sees. It's famous for banana bread. And shave ice. *And* coconut candy."

Her eagerness made him laugh. But now that she mentioned it, he could use a snack.

She got out of the car and posed for a selfie beside the Halfway to Hana sign. "Too bad I can't post this. Maybe after the wedding. Like, when Gabi and Marc are on their honeymoon and too busy banging to obsess over my personal life."

"Hang on," he said. "I want a picture of you." When she

frowned, he shook his head. "Not to post online. Just for me. To remember this day."

He wasn't likely to ever forget it, but he wanted a lasting reminder. Something he could look at, long after the trip was over. She cocked her hip, giving him a pose that was pure Jess.

At the stand, she bought two loaves of banana bread and a bag of coconut candy. He was tempted to get a cone of shave ice, but it looked too messy. He settled for a smoothie made with pineapple, banana, and coconut. When he gave her a sip, she let out an orgasmic groan, which made his dick spring to attention.

Down, boy. That groan wasn't about you.

"Oh my God, that's so good," she said. "I'm going to get one."

He loved that she had no qualms about eating or drinking whatever she pleased. Unlike Natasha, who'd avoided carbs at all costs.

Once they were back on the road, Jess unwrapped a loaf of banana bread and broke off a couple of pieces. She passed him one. "You have to try this. Best banana bread ever."

He took a bite, relishing the moist flavor, which tasted slightly of coconut. "You're right. It's delicious."

After wiping her hands on her shorts, she took out her phone. "Time to catch up on Gabi's Instagram. What has our favorite bride-to-be been up to? First up is kitesurfing, which looks low-key terrifying."

"Really? You were always the daredevil, not Gabi."

"True. But it's like a combination of surfing and flying a kite, and those waves look fierce. Knowing my luck, I'd lose control of the kite, plummet into the ocean, and get pulled under. Then someone would catch the whole thing on their phone, and the video would go viral." She snickered. "Do you remember the summer we tried to create those viral videos?"

"How could I forget? We wasted an entire day."

They'd spent hours setting up stunts on the Aqua Trampoline, only to fail, over and over again. After a while, Marc, Gabi, and

Victoria had walked away in frustration. But he and Jess kept at it, until they created a hilarious video worthy of YouTube.

"Do you still have any of the videos?" he asked. "We could show a few at the rehearsal dinner."

She snorted. "I'm sure Gabi would love that. But I don't think I have them anymore. When my last laptop died, I lost a bunch of files."

"Hopefully not your copy of *Queen of the Forgotten Lands*?"

She gave him a playful shove. "Will you stop? You're never going to read the final version. Especially since..."

He glanced over at her, curious at the flush on her cheeks. "What?"

"Let's just say...I may have based the roguish Prince Alaric on a certain someone."

"Me? You based your hero on me?"

She whapped him with the edge of the map. "Stop. You know I had a big crush on you."

"But still. To make me the hero of your book? That's next-level." He didn't know why the news filled him with such a swell of happiness. He'd never considered himself anyone's hero. "Now you have to finish it."

"Not an option unless I could get it down to a manageable length. Anywayyyy." She dragged out the word. "Next up is Victoria's feed. Apparently, she hit a hole in one. There's, like, four braggy posts about it."

More than ever, Connor was grateful he'd abandoned the family's golf outing. Tonight, he could play the part of the respectable son. He'd need to if he wanted to get his father on board with his winery plan. But enduring a golf game with the old man would have been hell.

Jess passed the banana bread his way. "Want another piece?"

"I'm good, thanks. Do you want to stop anywhere else?" If it hadn't been for the family dinner, he would have suggested they keep driving. Where they'd end up, he couldn't say. But they'd have fun.

"I'd love to, but I'd like to get back before the others return from golf."

They didn't reach the resort until ten minutes to five. Jess made a face when she saw her reflection in the rearview mirror, but Connor liked her curls wild and untamed. Though she'd looked gorgeous on the cruise, he'd take the natural Jess any day. Any place. A swimming hole. A hotel room. A rental car. *This* rental car, as a matter of fact.

Not that he'd act on his cravings. Once he was back in his hotel room, he could take a long, cold shower.

They headed toward the hotel lobby. "I have some serious work to do if I'm going to make myself presentable for dinner," Jess said.

"You look cute. The natural look suits you."

"It won't fly with Gabi. Or my mom." She groaned. "Everyone's going to be there."

"Don't worry," he said. "They won't see you until—"

The words died on his lips. As they entered the spacious lobby, they came face-to-face with the golf party. Not just Connor's family, but Marc and Gabi, as well as Marc's parents. And all of them stared at Jess and Connor like they couldn't believe their eyes.

CHAPTER 13

J ess was hit with a rush of guilt. Her hair was a
disaster, she'd lost all traces of makeup, and her
clothes were still damp. Worse yet, she couldn't
pretend she'd spent the day in Lahaina. Though she hadn't
broken her promise to Gabi, she'd flat-out lied about her plans.

Connor's father, Brian Blackwood, nailed his son with a
poisonous scowl. "Where were you? I expected to see you at golf."

"I told Marc I had other plans," Connor said. "You know I'm
not much of a golfer."

Victoria offered her brother a sly smile. "Agreed. The way you
play, you would have slowed us down considerably."

"That's still no excuse for putting your own needs in front of
the family's." Mr. Blackwood shook his head. "You're as selfish as
ever."

The disdain on the older man's face made Jess want to curl up
in a little ball, and she wasn't the one under fire. No wonder
Connor had dreaded facing him.

Ginny Blackwood placed a hand on her husband's arm. "Let's
not forget this is a vacation, dear. Connor's entitled to a little free
time."

Mr. Blackwood gave her a withering look. "Don't defend him. He knows what's expected. He just doesn't care enough to make the effort."

In response, Mrs. Blackwood lowered her head and nodded, like a child being chastised. Jess wanted to side with her, but she knew better than to cross Connor's dad.

"So," Victoria said brightly. "What were you two crazy kids up to?"

Jess tucked a damp strand of hair behind her ears. Caught in the spotlight, she fumbled for an answer that wouldn't upset Gabi. "Umm…Connor invited me to join him on the Road to Hana. We did some hiking and swimming and had a picnic lunch. And we stopped at Halfway to Hana for banana bread."

Gabi's uptight expression didn't change. "You do realize we have a family dinner at seven, right?"

Ease up, Gabi. That gives me two hours.

Unlike her sister, Jess didn't require hours of primping time. But she was grateful for a reason to beat a hasty exit.

"Then I'd better get going. See you all later." She wished she could squeeze Connor's hand or hug him—some gesture to show him how much she appreciated their day together—but the others might suspect something was up. She offered him a weak smile. "Thanks for taking me along. I had fun."

"Me too," he said. "See you at dinner."

Jess sensed Gabi wanted to grill her, but she couldn't handle a full-on interrogation in front of the Blackwoods. Later, she could take her sister aside and explain that she and Connor had spent the day together as friends. Nothing more.

Once she got to her room, she shucked off her damp clothes and took one of the leopard-print bathrobes from her closet. A shower and a full makeover were in order. Given that she hadn't seen her mother in six months, she wanted to make a good impression. Not that it would change her mom's viewpoint. She always compared Jess to her perfect big sister. Gabi, with the perfect grades, the perfect job, and the perfect, wealthy fiancé. Naturally, Jess fell short.

As she headed into the bathroom, her thoughts drifted back to Connor. Their day trip had gone better than she hoped. She'd had fun, and he'd behaved himself. By the end of the trip, she felt like they were friends again.

There was just one problem.

She couldn't stop thinking about him. Little details from their day kept flitting through her mind. Like their encounter at the swimming hole. When he'd caught her and pressed her up against a rock, she'd wanted him to take things further—to kiss her, peel off her bikini, and make love to her, right then and there. During the drive, she'd fantasized about pulling over at a wayside and stealing a quickie in his tiny rental car.

Oh, but she had it bad.

You idiot. You knew this was going to happen.

After spending the entire day with Connor, she couldn't deny the truth. She wanted him as much as she had five years ago.

Think about Gabi. She pleaded with you. You gave her your word.

But when would Jess get another chance for a passionate, no-strings affair? Certainly not over the next few months, when she'd be packing up her life in Chicago, driving across the country, and moving back home. Back to the same cramped, two-bedroom apartment she'd known since childhood, looking for work while her mom nagged her relentlessly.

You'll get your heart broken again.

No, I won't. Because this time, I won't let myself fall in love.

After four months of heartache, crappy temp jobs, and a steadily dwindling bank account, she needed a win. She needed joy, passion, and earth-shattering orgasms. Besides, if she played things carefully, she could balance her time with Connor *and* her role as Gabi's maid of honor.

What her sister didn't know wouldn't hurt her.

Before she lost her nerve, Jess slipped her key card into the pocket of her bathrobe, along with her phone and the condoms from her purse. She left her room and knocked on Connor's door.

He answered it, clad in nothing but his shorts. His hiking boots and shirt were on the floor, as though he'd been about to jump in the shower. Her breath caught as she stared at him, and she yearned to run her fingers over the smattering of dark hair that covered his broad, muscular chest.

"Lost your key card again?" he said. "Maybe you should wear it around your neck."

"Can I come in a second?"

He gestured for her to enter, then closed the door behind her. "What's up?"

"I wanted to say something. If I'm out of line, then I'll leave, I promise." She licked her lips, tasting brown sugar from the coconut candy she'd eaten on the drive back. "I know we aren't enemies anymore. But is there a chance we could be something else?"

He stepped closer and brushed his hand across her cheek. "Oh, Jess. This is such a bad idea."

That should have been her cue to leave. But his touch weakened her willpower. She stood frozen in place. "I know. Gabi made me promise I wouldn't hook up with you."

"Same with Marc."

"Are you kidding?" She could understand the request coming from Gabi, but not from Marc. "Why did he care?"

"Because of Gabi. He doesn't want her dealing with any drama—not from either of us. She's already under a lot of stress."

"Makes sense." She gnawed at her lip. She shouldn't give in to her impulsive side. Not with so much at stake. But she couldn't make herself turn and walk away. "The thing is—I still want you."

He smoothed the wayward curls from her face and kissed her forehead. "I want you, too. But I just got your friendship back. The last thing I want to do is hurt you again."

His reluctance gave her pause. But only for a second. This wasn't like last time. She didn't delude herself he'd ever fall in love with her. And she wasn't the same starry-eyed eighteen-year-old who still believed in soul mates and happy endings. This time, they'd set rules right from the start, knowing their fling had a definite end date.

"Right now, my life is as uncertain as yours," she said. "I don't want commitment."

"What do you want?" His fingers traced the curve of her lips, making her shiver.

"You. From now until we leave Maui, we make up for the five years we lost."

"And when we leave?"

"Then we say good-bye. No declarations of love. No tears. No frantic texts. Besides, I'm going back to Chicago, and you'll be in California. There wouldn't be any pressure."

The lie rolled off her tongue far too easily. But if she told him she was moving home in a month's time, she might scare him off. Since her mom's apartment was only an hour's drive from his condo, he might worry she'd be too close for comfort once she was back in Riverside. Back when she was eighteen, she'd brought up their proximity in a desperate attempt to sway him. It hadn't worked.

But now, if he assumed she was still living in Chicago, he'd have an easy out. And he wouldn't feel any guilt when they parted.

He kept his gaze fixed on her. "I can't promise you anything."

"I know. I don't want promises. No commitment and no regrets. Just great sex."

He cupped her face in his hands and kissed her. Gently at first, and then deeply. The sensation of his tongue against hers sent spirals of heat through her whole body. Her legs trembled, but not out of exhaustion from the day's hike. She ached to touch him, to reach into his shorts and stroke him until he was rock-hard, but that wouldn't be fair. He had to make the choice on his own, without any coercion.

"You're sure?" he whispered.

"I'm sure." Even as she said it, she knew she was crossing the point of no return. By becoming his lover again, she was setting herself up for another heartbreak.

It won't be like that. I know what I'm doing.

He undid the belt of her robe and eased it off her shoulders. She sucked in her breath as it fell to the floor, leaving her naked. Exposed like this, her insecurities eclipsed all rational thought.

When he frowned, she snatched up her robe and held it against her body. "If you're not sure, then I can go and—"

"No. Stay. *Please*. It's just…I didn't exactly plan for this."

"You don't have condoms? How is that possible?"

He chuckled. "I told you I was trying to clean up my act."

"Good thing one of us planned on getting laid." She fished the condoms out of the pocket of her robe and placed them on the nightstand. "Here. My emergency stash. Thanks to you, I didn't waste them on Lance."

From the gleam in his eye, she was certain he was gloating over her decision. "Excellent choice," he said. "Now for the important question—bed, couch, or shower? You pick."

Her heart raced in anticipation. Shower sex was high on her list of priorities, but not when the room held an enormous, king-size bed with 600-thread-count sheets waiting to be defiled. She pulled back the covers, eased herself onto the bed, and stretched out in what she hoped was a seductive pose.

He grinned. "Bed it is, then."

She gazed up at him, her pulse quickening, as he stripped off his shorts and boxers. The sight of him, naked and aroused, filled her with a throbbing ache. She wanted so badly to touch herself, to ease that ache just a little, but she held back. After months of self-medicating, it was time for someone else to make her happy.

He straddled her on the bed and gave her a long, appreciative look. "Do you have any idea how hard it was to restrain myself when you came into my room with that ice bucket?"

His confession filled her with a warm glow. "I felt the same way."

"Not possible. You were still mad at me."

"That doesn't mean I didn't want you." She traced one finger along his firm chest. "All you wanted was a measly drink."

"I was trying to behave myself. But not anymore."

He took one nipple between his fingers and tweaked it gently, making her gasp. First one, then the other, until she was desperate to feel his mouth on them. She moaned when he swirled his tongue around each nipple. As his rough stubble grazed against her bare skin, she wound her fingers through his hair and arched her back, her body ablaze with pent-up longing.

He drew himself up until he was facing her and held her in his gaze. "This is so much better than any of my fantasies."

"Same. And I had *so* many fantasies."

"Naughty girl." He ran his lips along the hollow of her throat. "Tell me about these fantasies."

"They were so delicious and wicked. Having sex on the fur rug in front of the fire. Up against the wall of the shower. In the hot tub." She'd had so many lonely nights where she'd consoled herself with memories, reliving each encounter they'd shared.

He murmured her name, then trailed soft kisses down her stomach, eliciting little cries from her. When he ran his tongue along the inside of her thighs, his stubble felt as arousing as she'd imagined. But better than anything she'd dreamed of, because it was real. Connor was here, with her, and he wanted this every bit as much as she did.

By the time he spread her legs and lowered his head, she was panting with need, her hands twisting the sheets. The things he was doing with his tongue were almost more than she could bear. She writhed under him, close to combustion.

Using his fingers and tongue to explore her slick folds, he

brought her so close to the edge she could hardly stand it. When he paused and looked up at her, she whimpered in protest. "Connor, please. You can't stop now."

His voice was warm and husky. "I want to hear you beg. Like you did at Big Bear."

"Bastard." But she was near to incinerating. "*Please*. Please don't stop."

He gripped her bottom tightly, holding her in place as he found her sweet spot. She moaned his name as the orgasm crashed over her. The sensations were so intense her whole body shuddered with the aftershock.

When he rose above her, with a satisfied grin on his lips, she couldn't help but laugh. "You don't have to look so fucking smug about it."

"I love it when you beg." He grabbed the condom from the nightstand. "Should we keep going?"

"Of course." She snatched the condom from him. "But you're not putting this on until I give you permission."

He raised his eyebrows. "Someone's getting saucy."

She pushed him back onto the bed and smoothed her hands over the ridges of the muscles in his chest. Lowering her head, she licked and sucked his nipples until she was rewarded with shameless groans of pleasure. His response fueled her lust even more. As her lips moved downward, she brushed her hair against his chest, stopping to take the hard length of him in her mouth. The taste of him excited her. She wanted to make him cry out in ecstasy, but he threaded his fingers through her hair and tugged her head back.

"Stop," he said. "I want to come inside of you."

She gave him a flirtatious smile but rolled over onto her back and handed him the condom. "Here. I yield."

His eyes skated across her body as he took it from her. "You are absolutely gorgeous. Even sexier than I remembered."

She flushed with happiness. "It's been a long time since anyone told me that."

"Then you've been with the wrong men. Because you're incredible. I've never stopped thinking about you."

He slipped on the condom and thrust himself deep inside her. She gasped at the feel of him and dug her fingers into his back. From the pocket of her robe, her phone began buzzing, but she ignored it. She was too far gone to care about anything except what was happening at this moment, in this bed, with this unbelievably sexy man.

He wasn't gentle, but she didn't want gentle. She wanted it hard and fast, with neither of them holding anything back. She rocked her hips, matching his rhythm, and held on tight. When he took one of her nipples between his teeth and tugged on it, the combination of pleasure and pain sent her careening over the edge. She came again in an intense orgasm that left her breathless and trembling. Connor gave a few more thrusts, then groaned in release seconds later.

Still atop her, he let out a soft chuckle. "That...might have gone a little quicker than I hoped."

"It was perfect. We can take it slow next time." She shivered as she imagined all the steamy encounters yet to come.

Whatever lay ahead of them, she had no regrets about her decision.

She just couldn't let anyone find out.

CHAPTER 14

Connor lay next to Jess feeling completely and utterly spent. A delicious exhaustion crept over him, the kind that made him want to fall asleep with her in his arms. He couldn't believe she'd willingly offered herself up after five years. And that they'd both enjoyed it so much. Now that he'd shown her how desirable she was, he wanted to do it again and again. Though, next time, he needed to pace himself better. He'd come faster than a horny teenager.

He ran his hand along her bare back, letting it rest on the curve of her ass. She gave a contented murmur and snuggled in closer.

As much as he wanted to spend the entire evening in bed with her, he couldn't consider it. He still had to face his dad. He disentangled himself and eased out of bed, disposing of the condom with a Kleenex. "Do you want a drink?"

Jess sat up and pushed her messy curls away from her face. "I'd love one."

She kept her eyes fixed on him as he retrieved the brandy from the top of the mini fridge. He poured them each a glass and set the bottle on the nightstand. As he passed her a glass, he raised his eyebrows. "Were you ogling me?"

"Of course. You have a damn fine ass. Plus, I'm making up for lost time."

He climbed back into bed beside her. "You go right ahead."

She took a sip of brandy and let out a long sigh. "This is heavenly. Why can't we just stay here and have sex, like three or four more times, then order room service?"

Three or four more times. He groaned. "You're killing me, you know."

"And we haven't had shower sex yet. Just imagine—you and me, all slick and soapy up against the wall."

Though the idea sounded tempting, he forced himself to rein in his lust. He'd made a choice when he left the business proposal for his father. For once in his life, he needed to act like an adult. He stared at the amber liquid in the glass, already anticipating the argument ahead.

Jess placed her hand on his shoulder. "Everything okay? You're not having second thoughts about us, are you?"

The vulnerability in her eyes pierced his heart. "Not a chance. I was thinking about tonight's dinner. I need to deal with my dad. The longer I keep him waiting, the worse it's going to be."

"What's going on? Does this have to do with starting your own winery?"

He nodded. "A couple of guys who used to work at Blackwood came to me late last year. Tom Bartolli's an expert winemaker, and Reb Larkins has years of experience as a vineyard manager. I worked under them before, during my summer jobs at Blackwood, but they left the company three years ago. They were thinking of starting their own winery, so I told them I was interested. A few months ago, they found a property, and now they want me to invest as a partner and help manage it."

"Is it in the Temecula Valley? On the same turf as Blackwood?"

"Yeah. Lucky for me, California doesn't have a noncompete clause. The property's on the east side of the valley. Sixty-five acres of prime vineyards, a winery, and a tasting room. The owners are ready to retire. The place has a ton of potential, but it needs a little TLC. Eventually, we want to add a farm-to-table restaurant."

He stopped, hoping Jess would respond as enthusiastically as she had during their hike.

She beamed. "That sounds ideal. You'd do so much better as your own boss. Why don't you ask your dad if he'll invest in it? Doesn't Blackwood Cellars own a bunch of different wineries?"

"Too many. Some of the wine is great, but a lot of it is mass-market crap, tailored to please as many middle-of-the-road consumers as possible. If my dad bought this winery, he'd bring it in line with Blackwood standards, and that's not what I want."

She traced her hand along his arm. "What do you want?"

"Ideally? If Dad would give me a loan, we'd have enough capital to do the renovations and work on the branding and marketing. But if he refuses to help me out, then I'll need to get a few more investors or a loan from the bank. It's a big risk."

A risk that could leave him broke and make him the laughingstock of the family. The thought of it twisted his insides in knots.

"But...you're a Blackwood. You must have cash lying around, right?"

He took a long swig of brandy. In hindsight, he should have started setting aside the seed money much sooner. "I've got enough to put a dent in the down payment. Trouble is, land in Temecula is unbelievably expensive. And our plans include a lot of renovations."

"Maybe your dad would want to sign on as an investor in return for a percentage of the profits?"

"I wish. But even if he wanted to make this kind of investment, he doesn't trust me. If I was still pulling the same old shit, I'd get it. But about a year ago—right after Natasha and I got serious—I started putting in the work. Long hours, weekends, whatever it took. Dad wanted to acquire a bunch of vineyards in the Willamette Valley, so I stepped up. I did all the legwork and the site visits, and it went great. But when it came time for the presentation to the board, Darren took all the credit. Of course, Dad believed him over me."

Jess scrunched up her brow. "What a shithead. I've never liked him. He always acted like Gabi and I weren't good enough for the Blackwoods."

He grimaced, remembering the handful of times Darren had muttered a few racial slurs about Mrs. Chavez. Only the threat of a beatdown had shut him up.

"There were other times, too, when I came up with ideas during our brainstorming sessions," he said. "My suggestions probably needed fine-tuning, but Darren always shot me down."

A few times Connor had sought out Darren alone, hoping he'd be more receptive if he wasn't surrounded by his underlings. But his older brother was so determined to maintain his alpha status that he never gave an inch.

"I can't believe your dad never called him on his behavior," Jess said.

"Dad's always favored him. Hell, if Darren wanted to open his own winery, Dad would be all in, but he's never had much faith in me." He finished his brandy and set down the glass.

"What about your mom? She always seemed more understanding. Could she help you out?"

"Dad would never let her. He likes controlling the family." For years, his father had belittled his mother, treating her as though her opinion meant nothing. "That's partly why I dread the thought of facing him. He hates it when anyone slips out from under his control."

"But you think he's going to want to talk about it *here*? At your cousin's wedding?"

"That's on me. Last Sunday, I left my business proposal on his desk, outlining my two-year plan. I told him I was doing it, with or without his help, but I'd appreciate his support."

"What did he say when he read it?"

"I…ah…timed it so he'd get the proposal *after* I left for Maui." Even as Connor said it, regret cut him to the core. He'd been such a fucking coward. "I know he got it because Darren texted me right after I arrived here. He said Dad read it, and he wasn't happy."

An understatement, if ever there was one.

"So, you're dealing with it now?" She gave him a playful shove. "Because everyone knows weddings are the most non-stress situations on the planet."

He placed his arm around her shoulder, pulling her closer. "Fair point, but I thought my dad might be less uptight if he was on vacation."

"I hope it goes okay. It's great you're going after your dream."

"Thanks." Having Jess at his side made the situation a little more bearable. "I've had days when I think it's never going to happen. But talking to you inspired me."

"*I* inspired you?"

"Yeah, because you're doing what you love. In college, you majored in journalism, even though your mom told you it wasn't practical. You proved you could make it work when you found a job as a writer. Not only that, but you had the guts to move to a brand-new city."

Jess traced her fingers around the rim of the glass. When she spoke, her voice was small. "Moving to Chicago wasn't that bold. I only went there because of Simon, and he turned out to be a big mistake."

Clearly, he'd hit a nerve. But he didn't want her to agonize over her shitty ex. "Don't be so hard on yourself. Even if Simon turned out to be a loser, you still took a huge risk, career-wise, and it paid off. Right?"

"I guess." But she still couldn't manage a smile.

He took the glass from her and set it beside his on the nightstand. The last thing either of them needed to do was dwell on their mistakes. Natasha and Simon were in the past.

He sought out her lips, capturing them in a sweet, tender kiss. Though his only goal was to console her, she responded with passion. She pulled him down until his body was flush against hers. The feel of her bare skin, so warm and soft, made him ache with desire.

She reached down and stroked him. "Do you think we could sneak in a quickie before dinner?"

"I'd love to." He kissed the soft curve of her neck, inhaling the scent of coconut sunscreen. "You brought two condoms, right?"

"Mmm-hmm." She wiggled beneath him, fumbling for the remaining condom on the nightstand, but stopped short when her phone buzzed from the pocket of her robe. "I should get that. It might be Gabi."

He released her, watching as she leapt out of bed and grabbed her robe from off the floor.

She pulled out her phone and answered it. "Gabi! What's up? No, I'm not ready yet. It's only—" As she looked over at the clock, her eyes grew wide. She pointed at it and mouthed the words, "It's six thirty."

Shit. He still had to shower and shave.

Jess was now in full apology mode. "I'm sorry. I lost track of time. But we still have half an hour. I'll be ready by then. Okay? I'll text you as soon as I'm good to go."

She ended the call, then let out her breath in a long exhale. "Damn it."

"What's wrong?" he asked.

"My mom wanted to meet with us before dinner. So, naturally Gabi's annoyed I'm not ready. Or maybe it's pre-wedding stress." She put her robe back on. "Speaking of stress, we should probably keep this a secret. I'm not ashamed to be with you or anything, but…"

But Gabi and Marc had asked them not to hook up. And he wanted his family to focus on his business plan, not his love life. "Works for me."

"Okay. Good. So…umm…will you be joining me after dinner?"

"Of course. Your room or mine?"

She grinned. "How about mine? Bring the brandy. I only brought a couple of condoms, so make sure you're adequately prepared."

He would be. Getting through tonight's dinner would be rough, but knowing he had a late-night rendezvous with Jess made it bearable.

CHAPTER 15

*J*ess dashed back into her room and took the world's fastest shower. She tackled her hair and makeup while waiting for the iron to heat up. Ironing was a task she avoided whenever possible, but her clothes were wrinkled from spending three days in a suitcase. As soon as her dress was presentable, she shimmied into it and smoothed the silken fabric over her hips. It was nothing fancy—just a little black dress—but she was impressed at her reflection in the room's full-length mirror. No doubt about it, she was rocking a definite glow. Maybe it was all those hours in the sun. Or the mind-blowing sex.

Oh, it was definitely the sex.

A quiver of excitement passed through her as she envisioned the next few days, sneaking off with Connor whenever possible. She'd forgotten what it felt like to be with a partner who cared about her pleasure. Who told her she looked gorgeous and treated her with kindness and affection. After this week, she'd have to remind herself never to settle for sub-par sex again.

At ten minutes to seven, a knock came at the door. Jess raced to open it. Naturally, her sister was early. Dressed in a dusky pink wrap dress and matching heels, Gabi radiated poise. Everything about her was perfectly understated, from the single strand of pearls around her neck to the light coat of polish adorning her nails.

Jess grabbed her jewelry pouch and sat on the bed. "Have a seat. I'll be ready as soon as I find two earrings that match."

Gabi did not sit. She strode over to the bed and stood above Jess, hands on her hips. "Did you have fun with Connor?"

If Jess reacted defensively, her sister would know something was up. She tried to sound humble. "Sorry you had to find out that way. I was going to tell you about it tonight. There's a good explanation."

"I hope so. You promised me you'd steer clear of Connor, and yet you spent the entire day with him. What happened?"

"I…ran into him in the lobby when I was getting coffee this morning. When I told him I was too tired for golf, he invited me to come to Hana. I thought it sounded like fun." With each lie she told, she expected her nose to start growing. But the truth would send Gabi off the deep end.

Gabi rubbed her forehead, as though Jess was giving her the world's biggest headache. "Fine. Just don't make the same mistakes you did last time."

Too late for that. "Of course."

"I can't handle one of your romantic crises. Dealing with the Blackwoods is stressful enough on its own."

"No crises, I promise. Connor and I are just friends." *With benefits.*

She found a pair of gold hoop earrings and put them on. "Besides, I had time to kill today. It's not like you invited me to go kitesurfing with you and Luisa."

"Sorry." Gabi sat on the bed next to her. "I should have included you, but we planned it on Sunday when your flights were delayed. I didn't think you'd be up for it."

Even if Gabi's outing with Luisa brought back bitter

memories of all the times they'd excluded Jess, she appreciated her sister's apology. Besides, if they'd invited her along, she would have missed her chance with Connor.

She tried to inject a little humor into her voice. "With my luck, I would have fallen and broken something. Not a great look, walking down the aisle in a cast."

"A fair point. But I promise not to leave you out again."

That was good enough for Jess. She stood up. "Should we go?"

"Not yet." Gabi rose beside her and let out a lengthy sigh. "Can you *please* promise me you'll keep things under control?"

Jess froze. Did Gabi know what she and Connor had been up to? "What do you mean?"

"Last night. What did I say about not getting drunk?"

Shit. Though her memories of the Blue Lagoon were something of a fog, she remembered arguing with Gabi. "I was rude, wasn't I?"

"You said I had a stick up my ass. Real classy."

"I'm sorry. That was out of line. I didn't mean it."

Gabi pursed her lips. "That's not the worst of it. Lance told Marc you almost passed out in the hallway after you got back to the hotel. Is that true?"

Jess hung her head as the shame gnawed away at her. "Yeah. Not my finest hour."

"This is my wedding week. Can you act like an adult for once?"

"I won't do it again, I promise. But…" She forced herself to face Gabi. At least in this instance, she could be truthful. "Lance was hot and all, but he wasn't doing it for me. I thought if I had enough to drink, he'd seem more appealing. And then we'd end up together, like you wanted."

Gabi groaned. "All I wanted was for you to have a date. A fun distraction. I never said anything about sex. Especially if you didn't want it."

"I thought I did at first. But I was wrong." Jess looked away, still ashamed she'd let the evening get so out of control.

"I know Simon messed with your self-esteem. And having Connor around can't be easy. But getting drunk and banging someone you don't like won't help you feel better. If anything, you'll end up feeling worse."

Jess couldn't repress her smile. "Did you actually use the word 'banging'? That's so unlike you."

Gabi laughed. "That's Marc's influence." She let out a breath, as if to remind herself she was still in big-sister mode. "For my sake, can you keep your shit together until after the wedding? I can't handle your drama right now."

Jess clenched her jaw to stop herself from snapping at her sister. True, she'd been rude to Gabi at the bar. And her fall in the hallway was embarrassing. But she hadn't made a public spectacle of herself at the Blue Lagoon. No drunken karaoke, loud sea shanties, or table dances.

All of which she'd done during her college years.

But she didn't want to fight with Gabi. "Got it. I'll be on my best behavior."

Besides, her sister had a point. Over the years, Jess had stirred up a lot of shit. When she was growing up, she'd gotten used to taking second place behind her perfect sister, who'd gotten straight As, been captain of the swim team, *and* landed a full ride to UC San Diego. The only way for Jess to stand out was to act on impulse and take risks, even if her behavior landed her in trouble. If anything, her ruse usually backfired, because afterward, her mom would throw up her hands in despair and beg her to be more like Gabriela.

Not that Gabi was to blame. She'd done her best to play the role of the caring big sister. Now Jess needed to show her the same level of support.

Gabi's phone rang, and she answered it in a clipped voice.

"Mama? Hi. Sorry to keep you waiting. Yes, we'll be right down." She ended the call and turned to Jess. "Let's go."

As they left her room, Jess tensed up, hoping Connor wouldn't emerge from his room at the same time. The last thing she needed was her sister questioning *why* he was staying right next door.

By the time they reached their mom's room on the sixth floor, Gloria Chavez had her door open in anticipation. Jess caught a whiff of her signature perfume, which smelled faintly of roses. Her mom had worn the same scent for years, no matter what the occasion.

As always, she looked put together, in a way Jess could never equal. Though they both shared the same dark curls, her mom's hair fell in stylish waves rather than obnoxious, brush-defying spirals. And she had a knack for scouring resale shops and finding fabulous outfits, most of which she altered on her trusty sewing machine. Like her dress tonight—a dark blue, tropical-print wrap dress that she'd accented with chunky gold bracelets and matching hoop earrings. Jess would have paid serious money for a dress that made her curves look that good.

Her mom gave both of them a hug, then stepped back to assess them. "You look radiant," she said to Gabi. "Your hair, your dress—everything. You'll be a perfect bride."

"Thanks, Mama." Gabi smoothed her hands over her dress. "You don't think this color is too pale?"

Jess refrained from rolling her eyes. Typical Gabi. Acting insecure when she knew damn well she looked fabulous.

Her mom beamed at Gabi. "Of course not. The pink goes so well with your tan." But when she appraised Jess, her brow creased in disapproval. "You're wearing black? Is this a Chicago thing?"

"You don't think it's appropriate?" Jess said.

"It's fine. A little tight, maybe. Have you put on weight?"

Jess flinched. Too many carb binges, too many nights of

Chinese takeout, and she was ten pounds heavier than when she'd left California. She forced a smile. "I was thinking of joining a gym, but my budget's stretched thin right now."

"Did you figure out your living situation in Chicago?" her mom asked. "You can't stay at your friend's apartment forever."

Jess did *not* want to be having this discussion. Not when she'd be spinning more lies. "Don't worry. I'll work something out."

Her mom shook her head sadly. "That Simon—I never liked him. He treated you so poorly."

"I'm okay. Gabi's probably sick of hearing about him by now."

"I wish you'd left him sooner," Gabi said. "Every week, it was something different—you were worried he was acting too distant, or losing interest, or cheating on you. You were right about the last one."

"Simon's over and done with," Jess said. "I've moved on. Besides, it's hard to be sad when you're in a tropical paradise. Right? Isn't this place fabulous?"

Her mom didn't smile. "It's a shame Carmen and Elena aren't here to enjoy it. Or the rest of your cousins. They're so disappointed they're missing out on your big day."

Now it was Gabi's turn to look uncomfortable. "I'm sorry. But this is my wedding. And I wanted it to be somewhere special and memorable, not boring old Riverside."

Ouch. Not an ideal choice of words, since the last few family weddings they'd attended had been in Riverside.

Rather than allow her sister to dig an even deeper hole, Jess stepped in. "But everyone's invited to your big celebration in August, right?"

Gabi flashed her a grateful smile. "Right. This way, no one will feel left out."

"And you're sure Marc's parents will pay for this celebration?" her mom asked.

"His parents will cover everything, just like they're paying for the wedding here. It's already decided."

When Gabi shot her a "save me" look, Jess responded quickly, grabbing her phone out of her purse. "Oh, wow. It's five after seven already. We should get going."

But their mom wasn't willing to let the subject drop. "It's good you're marrying someone who can take care of you, Gabriela. But make sure you keep up your career. You don't want to be stuck where I was, a single mother, working two jobs just to bring home enough food." She turned to Jess. "You need to be able to take care of yourself, too, no matter what a man does to you."

"Got it." More than ever, Jess dreaded telling her the truth. That she'd lost her job, run out of money, and was back to square one. That she'd be retreating home to Riverside in a month's time and moving back into her childhood bedroom.

For now, it was best not to think about the future.

Once the wedding was over, she could deliver the bad news.

CHAPTER 16

*B*lackwood family dinners usually required formality, but Connor had gotten a text from Victoria, reminding him the dress was "island casual." Perfect. He picked out a light blue Hawaiian shirt and a pair of khakis. Not his style but loads better than a business suit.

He headed down to the lobby, whistling. No matter what happened at dinner, he had a reward waiting for him at the end of the night.

Even in his wildest fantasies, he never would have imagined Jess coming to his room and asking for no-strings sex. In principle, he should have turned her down. Or tried harder to dissuade her. He didn't want her to get hurt. And, given that they were both trying to behave like mature adults, a secret fling seemed highly irresponsible.

But after spending the day with Jess, he'd been unable to resist her. Damn, if it hadn't been the hottest, most satisfying sex he'd had in months.

When he reached the Sunset Terrace, he took a deep breath to center himself. Two round tables, decorated with candles and colorful tropical flowers, were set up on an ocean-facing patio.

Overhead, crisscrossing strings of white lights and paper lanterns illuminated the area. The steady rumble of the surf, breaking onto the shore, created a soothing soundtrack.

It would have been the perfect setting for an intimate dinner with Jess. Too bad the rest of his family had to be there.

He strode toward the tables. And stopped short.

All the men present—his father, his uncle, his brother, and his cousins—were formally dressed. All the women wore dresses and heels. Victoria had set him up.

No surprise given their long history of pranking each other. But now he couldn't decide whether to keep walking or retreat to his room and change.

Victoria waved him over to her table. She pointed to an empty chair next to hers. "Don't you look cute? Only two days here and you're dressing like a local."

Rather than respond with irritation, he laughed. "You win this time. But payback's a bitch."

She tossed her hair. "As if you could ever fool me. I'm not as gullible as you are."

Though he'd never admit it to his devious younger sister, he'd rather spend the evening in a comfortable shirt than a confining button-down and a tie. Yet another reason he hated the office culture at Blackwood Cellars.

He sat in the spot Victoria had saved for him, pleased to see Jess seated in the chair to his right. In just half an hour, she'd cleaned up nicely, wearing a shimmery black dress that gave him a perfect view of her cleavage. He pressed his thigh against hers under the table and suppressed a grin of satisfaction when she shivered in response.

Bottles of Blackwood Reserve Cabernet and Chardonnay had already been set out for the guests. One of the waiters in attendance zipped over and filled Connor's glass. Though he hadn't planned on drinking, a little wine might help him relax.

As he glanced around the table, his mom's absence caught him off guard. Even if she usually lacked the courage to stand up for him, her presence sometimes served as a buffer between him and his domineering father. "Where's Mom?"

"Your mother decided to sit this one out," his father said. "She had a little too much sun today."

Connor's throat tightened. When he caught Victoria's eye, she gave a rueful shake of her head. Chances were good their mom had soothed her anxiety with too many post-golf cocktails and wasn't up to socializing.

The protracted silence was almost painful, until Victoria spoke up. She leaned over Connor to address Jess. "How's Chicago? Are you loving it there? Or are you homesick for Southern California?"

"A little of both," Jess said. "Chicago has great museums and shopping, but the weather takes some getting used to. I barely survived the winter."

"You think you'll stay out there?"

Jess hesitated, then took a long sip of wine. "Ah…no plans to leave just yet. But ask me again when the wind chill drops below zero."

Connor lifted his glass to salute her. "I think it's admirable you're trying life in a new city. Sometimes you have to take big risks, especially if you have big dreams."

There. He'd said it.

His father scowled at him. "Nothing wrong with a calculated risk, as long as it's well thought out. But people who chase their dreams without a backup plan? I'd call those people fools."

Did that mean his father placed him in the "fool" category? Wouldn't be the first time. Before Connor could respond, waiters came to their table and set down their salads—an unusual mix of field greens, toasted almonds, papaya, and mango. Baskets of bread appeared on the table, along with three different types of olive oil.

His father leaned forward. "Speaking of fools, I got your proposal, son."

Connor took a huge gulp of wine. Now he wished he had something stronger. "And?"

"Who do you think you are, turning your back on Blackwood Cellars? You're going to take everything you've learned—everything I've taught you—and compete against me?"

The words rankled him, considering how little his father had actually taught him. Everything Connor had learned about wine had come from his summer jobs at the Blackwood Cellars Estate, where he'd been lucky to work under people like the winemakers, vineyard foremen, and cellar supervisors, who were willing to answer his questions. He'd loved those jobs, and he'd been good at them. His career at Blackwood Cellars had only turned sour after he'd been stuck in the corporate office with Darren.

Jess stroked his leg. Was this her way of cautioning him against losing his cool? He appreciated the reminder. Yelling at his father wouldn't help his cause.

"I'd hardly call my venture competition," he said. "Blackwood holds ten percent of the global wine market. They're the fourth-largest producer in the U.S. Nothing I do will affect your sales."

His father reached across the table and took a piece of bread. "Every independent winery in the Temecula Valley affects our sales. We own half the vineyards and contract with dozens more. I don't need some upstart winery poaching from those vineyards and taking any of my market share."

"We won't be poaching. Our winery has its own vineyards. And the other vineyards we plan to work with are small players that don't have contracts with Blackwood."

"I still feel like this is the worst form of treachery. My own son—betraying me."

Why did his dad have to go all King Lear on him? In the scheme of things, this winery would be a drop in the barrel.

"Dad, Connor isn't trying to betray you," Victoria said. "He just has this idea he's following some noble pursuit."

Connor glared at her. "Will you stay out of it?"

"Why should I?" she said. "I actually like the concept. For years, I've listened to you bitch and moan about Blackwood Cellars—how you're sick of working for a big, corporate winery that churns out wine by the truckload. How you plan to be all artisanal and produce wine for people with a discriminating palate."

His father laughed. "Good luck with that. You know how many of those boutique wineries go under? Most of them end up selling their vineyards to me. Then they go back to San Diego or L.A. or wherever they came from before they decided they wanted to go 'back to the land' and live the simple, rural lifestyle. Simple, my ass. It's hard work."

Like I don't know that? During his summer jobs, Connor had done a lot of physical labor, everything from working in the fields to boxing and loading pallets on the bottling line.

He kept his voice even, not wanting to reveal the frustration building up inside of him. "I'm not doing this on my own. I'm going into partnership with Tom Bartolli and Reb Larkins."

"Both of whom used to work for me," his father said.

"Right. They know their stuff. And I do, too. I know you think I'm a slacker, but in the five years I worked under Darren, I learned a ton about distribution and marketing. I want to take my shot."

Connor flinched as someone clapped him on the shoulder. He turned to see Brody Blackwood, his youngest cousin, clad in a bright red Hawaiian shirt. Connor stood to give him a hug and slapped him on the back. "Hey, man. Great to see you."

"You too." Brody went to hug Jess, who was already on her feet.

She pointed to the empty chair on her other side. "Sit with us. Gabi and Marc's table is full."

Brody eased himself into the chair and glanced around the table. "Why isn't everyone wearing Hawaiian garb?"

Victoria trilled with laugher. "Only you and Connor fell for it."

"Nice one, cuz. Joke's on you because I love me some Hawaiian gear. I'm planning on buying a whole mess of shirts while I'm here."

Brody's timing was perfect. His nerdy humor was exactly what Connor needed to lighten up the conversation.

Brody held out his glass until a waiter came over and filled it. "What did I miss?"

"Connor's abandoning us and going rogue," Victoria said.

"You're going forward with it?" Brody took a sip of wine. "That's awesome. Let me know if you need any technical help—you'll want a kick-ass website."

His enthusiasm gave Connor's spirits a boost. "Thanks. Maybe in a month or so, once everything's finalized." He glanced over at his father to see if he'd make another cutting remark, but he'd turned his attention to Victoria's fiancé.

"Brody, where's Taylor?" Victoria asked. "I thought she'd be here with you."

Taylor was Brody's girlfriend of six months—an up-and-coming interior designer. Like so many of the women his geeky cousin had dated, she was flat-out gorgeous. Connor just hoped she treated Brody better than his previous girlfriends had. The poor guy always got his heart broken.

"She's in L.A., in the middle of a big project for one of her clients, but she'll be here by Friday." Brody took a piece of bread. "I can't wait for you to meet her."

"Think she's the one?" Jess asked.

"I sure hope so. She's an amazing woman."

Connor envied his cousin. He'd felt that way, once, but after Natasha left him, he couldn't imagine falling head over heels again. For now, he'd settle for great sex.

The servers whisked away their salads and brought out a series of family-style entrees: pork ribs, coconut shrimp, grilled vegetables, Hawaiian fried rice, and pineapple boats. Though his father didn't bring up the winery proposal again, Connor knew the discussion wasn't over. The old man always got the last word.

When dinner ended, Gabi stood at the other table and tapped on her wineglass. "Attention, everyone. Just a reminder the Mt. Haleakala tour will be leaving the hotel at 3:30 a.m. tomorrow. Be sure to pack warm clothes."

Victoria recoiled. "What? Why would we get up that early?"

Marc stood up beside Gabi. "We're going to catch the sunrise at Mt. Haleakala. It's a Maui tradition."

"Count me out," Victoria said. "I need my beauty sleep."

Ben, her uptight fiancé, nodded. "No sunrise is worth that much effort."

A few more people grumbled, and Gabi softened her tone. "Obviously, you can sleep in if you want. But we'll have blankets, and thermoses of coffee and cocoa, and Hawaiian banana bread. It'll be worth it, I promise."

"I can't wait," Jess said. "Sunrise on top of a volcano? It should be spectacular." She squeezed Connor's leg under the table again.

Getting up at three sounded like a miserable start to the day, but he wasn't about to disappoint Jess. "Sounds great. I'm in."

"Me too," Brody said.

Jess stood up. "If you'll all excuse me, I need to get ready for bed, since I'll be getting up in six hours. 'Night, everyone."

"Let's catch up tomorrow," Brody said. "I want to hear everything."

"How about on the ride up to the volcano?"

Brody laughed. "If you're awake enough to carry on a conversation. I don't remember you being a morning person."

She arched her eyebrows. "Maybe I've changed. Ever think of that?"

Connor watched as she walked away, savoring the sight of her rounded backside. Was she wearing black lingerie underneath that dress? He couldn't wait to find out. "I'd better get some sleep, too, if I'm planning to get up at three."

"Same." Brody stood up. "See you in the morning."

Before Connor could leave, his father's voice stopped him in place. "Not yet, son. We haven't finished our discussion."

CHAPTER 17

*C*onnor and his father ended up at the Coral Cove, an outdoor bar overlooking the resort's largest swimming pool. Victoria insisted on joining them, as did Darren. *Great.* Because what Connor wanted, more than anything, was to be lectured by his father and his know-it-all siblings.

By now, the pool was closed, but the bar was still open. Couples and small groups occupied the tables, taking advantage of the balmy temperature. Connor found an unoccupied table and his father bought a round of drinks. He let Victoria order a piña colada, but he ordered scotch for the rest of them. Connor slugged half his drink in one gulp, then braced himself for another tirade.

At first, his father kept the conversation light—talking about his golf game, the weather, and the upcoming wedding. He covered everything *except* Connor's proposal.

By the time they started their second round, Connor couldn't stand it any longer. "Well, Dad. Have at it. The rest of the wedding party isn't around, so you're free to put me in my place."

His father frowned. "Lose the attitude."

"Yeah, show some respect," Darren said.

Kiss-ass. "No one invited you to this discussion," Connor said.

"I *should* be here. After supervising you for five years, I'm aware of how much your work ethic sucks."

"Will you two stop?" Victoria said. "I can't stand this male-posturing bullshit."

His father took a sip of scotch. "Victoria's right. Let's cut to the chase. Darren, I know how you feel about Connor, because I've read your write-ups on his performance. And Connor, stop playing the martyr. You knew I'd be angry. Why else would you have left your proposal on my desk like a goddamn coward?"

As much as Connor hated to admit it, his father was right. "It was a bad move on my part. I apologize."

Darren opened his mouth—no doubt to gloat—but his father held up his hand. "Let me finish. It's one thing for you to turn your back on your family's legacy. It's another to think you can manage a winery on your own. In the five years you've worked for me, you've never shown initiative. You want to know the truth? If you weren't my son, I would have canned your ass three years ago."

Connor couldn't speak. Though he'd prepared himself for an angry confrontation, the words landed on him like a blow.

His father continued. "Whenever Darren or I gave you the slightest chance to make a decision, you botched things royally. Remember the Santo Domingo Winery in Spain? The one I bought, *on your recommendation*, only to see it wiped out by drought three years later?"

"I couldn't have seen that coming," Connor said. "The drought hit a lot of vineyards in the region. But what about those vineyards in the Willamette Valley? I'm the one who did the site visits and wrote up the proposal. Last year at the annual board meeting, you said they were one of the best acquisitions we'd ever made."

Darren scowled at him. "The Oregon acquisitions were *my*

proposal. All you did was travel on the company's dime and schmooze with the owners."

But that schmoozing had sealed the deal, especially when Connor had wielded his charm to convince the independent owners they belonged with Blackwood Cellars.

"I worked hard on that project," Connor said. "And I've come up with other ideas, too. But you always shoot them down."

"Anyone can come up with a great idea," Darren said. "You don't have the follow-through."

Their father gestured at Connor with his highball glass. "Work ethic aside, there's also the matter of your personal life. Think of all the weekends you've spent getting drunk and screwing every two-bit slut in the Temecula Valley, only to show up hungover on Monday morning. You're an embarrassment to the family."

The accusations hit their mark, making Connor recall the numerous times he'd been called into his father's office. Standing there, shamefaced, while enduring the old man's anger. But if he wanted to move past those memories, he needed to focus on the present.

"I know I was like that when I started. But I've changed. I haven't messed up once this year. I'm trying to be responsible."

"If you're so responsible, why'd you bail on us yesterday?" Darren asked. "You cut out on brunch and golf, all so you could dick around with your ex-girlfriend."

Connor wouldn't apologize for taking the day off. Not when his trip to Hana had given him the chance to reconnect with Jess. But he should have considered how his family would react.

"Seriously, Darren?" Victoria said. "This is our vacation. We're entitled to a little free time. Besides, you hate playing golf with Connor. You think he's too slow."

"At least he doesn't stop the game every five minutes to post on Instagram," Darren said. "Oh, *look at me*. I hit a hole in one."

"You're just jealous, asshole," she spat back.

Enough. If Darren and Victoria started arguing, Connor would never get in a free word. He addressed his father. "I didn't mean to let the family down. But right now, can we focus on my proposal? I'm serious about this winery business."

"Are you? Then why'd you limit yourself to a two-year plan? Because that's a guaranteed recipe for failure."

For the first time that night, Connor allowed himself a glimmer of hope. Even if he hadn't solidified his long-range plans, he'd discussed them with Tom and Reb. "I figured it was enough to give you an overview. But I can provide more information if you want. New projects, possible partnerships, plans for the restaurant, the whole deal. If I send you a five-year plan, would you consider it?"

His father said nothing, swirling the remaining scotch in his glass.

Darren spoke up, like the tool he was. "Don't fall for it. Connor's full of shit. If he's on his own, he'll tank within a year. Why should you have to pay for it?"

Connor hated how weak his voice sounded, but he had to make a final attempt. "Dad? Could you give me another chance?"

His father shook his head. "You've had plenty of chances, and you've blown them all."

Connor drained the rest of his scotch and stood up. "Then I guess we're done. 'Night, all." He kept his expression stone-faced, not wanting to reveal how deeply his father's words had cut into him. He strode away from the bar, eager to put some distance between them.

"Connor, wait."

Victoria stumbled as she attempted to catch up to him—no surprise, given her ridiculously high heels. He caught her arm. "Careful."

"I can ask Ben if he'd give you a loan. His dad's loaded."

"Don't bother. That's a hell of a thing to ask your fiancé."

"Then I'll ask around. I know a lot of people with money.

Sorority sisters from UCLA. Prep school friends. I've got connections. Maybe a few of them would be up for funding an artisanal winery, started by a hot, young maverick." She shuddered. "Not that *I* think you're hot, but my friends certainly do."

He felt a rush of gratitude. "That means a lot. But Dad will be pissed if you help me."

She rolled her eyes. "I've done worse, and he still hasn't cut me off."

"That's different. And it wasn't your fault."

"Not the way he saw it." She looked behind her to where the two men remained seated. "Dad might come around eventually. I think you should send him your five-year plan, like you told him."

As much as he appreciated her optimism, he couldn't share it. Even if Victoria had screwed up once before, she'd spent years playing the role of the perfect daughter. "Why? He's not going to read it."

"He might. I can try talking to him tomorrow. Or I'll get Mom to talk to him." Victoria gave him a sweet smile. "You know Mom's always had a soft spot for you."

That might be true, but she'd never gone out on a limb for him. Not publicly, at least.

"I'll think about it." Right now, he wanted to get as far away from his family as humanly possible.

Only after he said good night to Victoria and headed back toward the lobby did he remember Jess. With all the shit his father had dished out, Connor had forgotten about the sweet reward waiting for him. Not that he had any guarantee she'd still be up. He pulled out his phone and saw he'd missed three texts from her.

Jess: Where are you?
Jess: Are you still coming to my room?

Jess: I'm going to bed soon. Alone.

Her last text was sent ten minutes ago, which meant he still had a chance. He was about to reply when his phone beeped with a voicemail notification. Tom Bartolli had left him a message. "Connor? I have no idea what time it is in Maui, but call me when you get this. We have a problem."

Whatever the problem was, he couldn't leave it until tomorrow.

In the elevator, he sent Jess a text. *Don't think I can make it tonight. Sorry. I'll be there tomorrow at 3:30 am.*

Her reply was immediate. *Good night.*

Ouch. She was mad, all right.

As he passed her door, he was tempted to knock and explain the situation. But once he was alone with her, he wouldn't be able to resist temptation. If he shared his tale of woe, she'd be sure to listen and empathize. And offer him fantastic sex to make up for it. He wouldn't want to leave. And postponing the problem wouldn't make it go away.

Instead, he opened the door to his room and let himself in. He eased down on the bed and returned Tom's call. The news was worse than he imagined. One of their potential investors—an up-and-coming actor from Los Angeles—had pulled out, citing financial issues. Tom was so riled up that Connor didn't have the heart to mention his disastrous conversation with his father.

After he ended the call, he rubbed his hands over his face, trying not to lose his shit as his father's words echoed in his head.

You've never shown any initiative.

If you weren't my son, I would have canned your ass three years ago.

You're an embarrassment to the family.

Maybe his father was right.

Maybe he wasn't cut out for more.

But you won't know if you give up now.

Jess believed in him. Victoria, too. Hell, Brody had offered to build him a website, and the guy was a computer genius.

Even if his dad was pissed right now, he might come around. The least Connor could do was send him a five-year plan. *No.* He'd send him a *ten-year plan.*

He glanced at the alarm clock on the nightstand. Eleven thirty. If he went to bed now, he'd be lucky to get four hours' sleep. He'd be better off pulling an all-nighter. Sure, he'd be dragging on the volcano excursion, but he could load up on caffeine.

Rather than set the alarm, he went over to the work desk and booted up his laptop.

Crunch time.

For the first two hours, he was on a roll. Until a wave of fatigue crested over him. He closed his eyes and laid his head on the desk.

A quick catnap and he'd be good to go.

CHAPTER 18

ess stumbled down to the hotel lobby at 3:25 a.m. Five minutes early, which was a miracle, given how little sleep she'd gotten. She'd stayed up far too late, waiting for Connor to show. When he finally told her he couldn't make it, she spent another hour agonizing over her decision to trust him. Then she slept poorly, plagued by anxiety-prone dreams. The kind where she was lost, with no hope of finding her destination.

And now she was getting up in the dark to traipse around a volcano.

Gabi was already in the lobby, pacing restlessly. She scowled at Jess. "About time. I'm afraid no one's going to show."

"Calm down," Jess said. "I'm five minutes early."

Marc was slumped on a chair, eyes closed. By contrast, Brody appeared cheerful and alert. Jess couldn't believe how much he'd changed over the past five years. He was no longer the gawky, skinny kid she'd known at Big Bear. His upper body had filled out nicely, his disheveled mop of ash-brown hair had been tamed into a stylish do, and his old-school glasses were ironically vintage.

Brody looked up from his phone. "Hey, Jess. How's it going?"

She made no attempt to hide the irritation in her voice. "How do you think? It's three in the morning. Why are you so wide-awake?"

"I'm used to staying up all night, working on coding projects."

She scanned the empty lobby. "I thought more people were coming. Like Connor, and…"

Damn. Had *anyone* else volunteered to come?

"I doubt Connor's getting up to see a sunrise. His dad was pissed about the winery. He probably dragged him over to the bar and gave him a long lecture on family loyalty."

Maybe that was why he hadn't shown last night. Still, she deserved a better explanation than a one-line brush-off. "I just… thought he'd be here," she said.

Brody lowered his voice. "Please tell me you're not pining over Connor anymore."

She tensed up. "What if I am?"

"He might be my favorite cousin, but he treated you like crap."

Her face prickled with heat, making her uncomfortably warm. She took off her hoodie and tied it around her waist. "Maybe he's not like that anymore."

Brody groaned. "You're sleeping with him again, aren't you?"

"Do we have to talk about me? I want to hear more about your girlfriend. Taylor, right?"

He crossed his arms. "Don't change the subject. What's up with you and Connor?"

"Shhh. I'll tell you later." She turned to face her sister, who had walked over to join them. "Hey, Gabi. Everything okay?"

"We're missing half the group," Gabi said. "The van will be here soon."

"I assume Mama and the senior Blackwoods aren't getting up this early," Jess said. "Victoria and Ben already opted out. Connor was up late with his dad. Luisa was thinking of taking surf lessons. That leaves Lance, Darren, and Melanie. Unless any of your friends decided to join us."

"Darren's out," Brody said. "He and Melanie are doing a private fishing charter this morning. I heard them mention it last night."

"A fishing charter?" Gabi said. "Are you serious?"

Marc approached her and slung his arm around her shoulder. "Relax. Even with a small group, we'll have fun."

"Should we wait for Lance?" Gabi asked.

Please no. Jess couldn't face him this early in the morning.

"If he wanted to come, he'd be here by now," Marc said.

Gabi clenched her hands. "This is great. No one cares that I put all this time and energy into arranging these outings."

"I'm here." Jess forced herself to sound enthusiastic. "That counts for something, right?"

"You're only showing up because you felt guilty about spending yesterday with Connor."

Ouch. Even if Gabi was partly right, the accusation stung. "Not true. I wanted to come. I've never seen a real-life volcano." She turned to Brody. "Have you ever seen one up close?"

"Nope. Just in movies." He placed his hand over his heart. "If only I had a ring to dispose of, our outing would be even more meaningful." When Gabi stared at him blankly, he grinned. "Sorry. Nerd humor."

Jess removed a gold filigree ring from her index finger and handed it to him. "Here you go, Mr. Frodo. Don't let Gollum take it."

"How come I have to be Frodo?" Brody said. "He's such a whiner. Sam's more of a stand-up guy."

"Exactly. That's why I get to be Sam."

"Will you stop it!" Gabi's voice carried over the empty lobby. "This isn't funny. Everyone abandoned me, and you're turning it into a big joke."

"They were just teasing," Marc said. "And you can't get upset with our family if they choose to do their own thing. These events are optional."

"Oh, fine, stand up for them," she snapped. "I'm the one who organized everything!"

"Because you wanted to," Marc said. "No one forced you. Stop acting like a martyr."

Jess took a few steps back. She needed to get out of the danger zone—stat. "I'm going outside to see if the shuttle van is here yet."

Brody leapt out of his seat. "I'll go with you."

They left the lobby and checked the hotel's drop-off area. No sign of the shuttle van. No sign of *anyone*. Not surprising since it was still dark outside.

"I wish we could go back to bed," Jess said. "Gabi's in full Bridezilla mode, and I'm getting caught in the crossfire. Never mind that I'm *actually* trying to be a supportive maid of honor for once." She understood why Gabi was upset with the others, but her sister didn't need to take it out on her.

"She'll be fine once we get going," Brody said. "And we can catch up on the drive. I haven't talked to you in ages."

No one had. For months now, she hadn't opened up to anyone except a couple of friends in Chicago. She'd even kept her conversations with her mom and Gabi at a superficial level, out of fear she might reveal the truth. It was a miserable way to live.

The loud blast of a horn made her jump. The driver of the shuttle van opened the door and peered out. "You two waiting for the Haleakala tour?"

"Yeah," she said. "There are two others inside. I'll go get them."

As Gabi had promised, the tour came with thermoses of coffee and hot chocolate, as well as trays of delicious Hawaiian banana bread. Jess and Brody took a couple of thermoses and a tray of bread to the back of the van. They left Gabi and Marc up front, where they could snipe at each other. Though Jess was bone-tired, she perked up after her second cup of coffee.

"About you and Connor...?" Brody asked.

"Lower your voice. I don't want Gabi to hear us."

"Sorry," he whispered. "But I want to know what's going on. We used to talk all the time."

Though his persistence was maddening, he genuinely cared about her. "You never give up, do you?"

"Nope. And don't try to bullshit me. Last time we talked, you were upset you'd have to see him again."

"I *was* upset. But Connor and I have such a long history together. And he bailed me out of a bad situation; actually, he bailed me out twice."

Between sips of coffee and bites of banana bread, she told Brody everything. A few times, she glanced toward the front of the bus to make sure Gabi wasn't listening in, but her sister was too busy arguing with Marc.

When Jess was done, Brody was quiet for a moment, and then he refilled his coffee cup from the thermos. "Connor's a great guy. But I remember how much he hurt you. You think it won't happen again?"

She sighed. "I hope not. At least we set ground rules this time. I told him all I wanted was a fling, and I didn't ask for a commitment. As far as he knows, I'm going back to Chicago, and we won't see each other again."

"Wait. Aren't you going back to Chicago?" Brody asked. "What's going on?"

Damn. She'd said too much. She was tempted to feed Brody the same line she'd given the others, but she was desperate to confide in someone. And she'd missed sharing her life with him. Up until she moved to Chicago, they'd texted each other on a regular basis.

"Don't tell anyone, but I'm moving back to Southern California in August. To my mom's apartment in Riverside. Things in Chicago didn't exactly work out."

"That's too bad. I thought you liked it there."

"I did at first, but—"

With an ear-splitting shriek of feedback, the driver turned on his microphone and addressed them. As the shuttle van barreled through the darkness, he regaled them with stories of Hawaiian lore and culture, which Jess found fascinating.

When they reached the top of the mountain, the parking area was crowded with shuttle vans, buses, cars, and motorcycles. Groups of people stood around, wrapped in blankets, wearing sweatshirts and knit caps to ward off the chilly morning air, some holding thermoses or travel mugs. Brody grabbed a couple of fleece blankets from the back of the van and passed one to Jess. They followed Gabi and Marc outside to take pictures of the sunrise.

Brody placed his arm around her shoulder. "This is a great view. I wish Taylor were here to see it."

Jess was curious about her, especially after Brody had shown her a few photos. Though he always chased after beautiful women, he'd never dated anyone that striking before. "She's coming on Friday, right? I'm excited to meet her."

"I still can't believe I'm dating her. She's so freaking gorgeous." Brody smacked his forehead. "Sorry. I'm not obsessed with her looks. Or maybe I am. Girls like her never fall for guys like me."

"Stop knocking yourself. You're an awesome guy. Funny, smart, always one step ahead of the pack."

"And yet, despite these admirable qualities, you've been able to resist me?"

She rolled her eyes. "Because of Connor. I've been fixated on him since I was twelve."

"Kidding. But seriously, Taylor's so far out of my league it isn't funny. Unlike me, she has zero self-esteem issues. She's confident, driven, and ambitious as hell."

Taylor sounded like an odd match for Brody, who was mellow and easygoing, but if he was happy, Jess wasn't going to judge.

The sun rose until it was a fiery ball, high above the blanket of clouds below. As an orange glow filled the sky, a few people around them murmured in appreciation. But Jess and Brody stayed silent, absorbing the breathtaking view.

After the sunrise, Gabi suggested hiking a few miles into the crater on one of the trails marked by the National Park Service. Jess would have preferred to curl up in the shuttle van and take a nap, but she wanted to be a good sport. Within minutes, Gabi and Marc had outpaced her, though Brody lingered behind to keep her company.

"You can go on ahead," she said. "I don't have much energy."

"I'll stay back here with you. Now that those two have made up, I want to give them their space."

True enough. Marc must have talked Gabi off the ledge because they were holding hands. Every few minutes, they'd stop to kiss. Their PDA was a bit much, especially at six in the morning.

"Out of curiosity—what happened in Chicago?" Brody asked. "You don't have to tell me if you don't want to, but…"

Jess paused to photograph the reddish-brown cinder beneath their feet, which looked like it belonged on an alien landscape. "I don't mind talking about it. The only reason I'm keeping it quiet is to avoid stealing the spotlight. I don't need anyone fussing over me, so I'm waiting until after the wedding."

She kept telling herself that. But the more lies she spun, the more she suspected she was making things worse.

"I won't spill the beans, I promise," he said.

"When I first went out there, I was excited to live somewhere new. *Chicago Live* was a fun place to work, and they paid me to go to plays and restaurants and festivals." She stopped to catch her breath. The temperature had risen considerably in the past two hours. She was glad Gabi had suggested bringing water bottles.

"I read some of your articles," Brody said. "They made me want to visit."

"Thanks. For eight months, everything was perfect. Well, not entirely perfect, because Simon wasn't easy to live with. But in

March, I caught him with someone else, and he told me he'd fallen in love with her. Totally cliché, right?"

"What an asshole. I hope you kicked him out."

"I wish. The lease was in his name, so he got to keep the apartment. He gave me two days to pack up my stuff and move out."

Recalling that terrible month hurt less now than it had in April or May. But the pain still ate at her.

"Sorry. That's terrible." Brody slowed to let a group of hikers pass them. They looked hard-core, with sturdy boots, wide-brimmed sun hats, and strap-on Camelbak water bottles.

"Yeah, Gabi put up with a lot of tearful calls," she said. "If it hadn't been for my job, I would have considered coming home. One of my friends said I could crash on her couch so I wasn't out on the street. Two weeks later, *Chicago Live* had a major shake-up. A couple of their sponsors pulled out, plus they weren't generating enough ad revenue. They couldn't afford to keep all their writers, so…last hired, first fired. That was me."

"And you didn't tell anyone?"

"Nope. The Simon thing was bad enough, but this was worse. I figured I'd look for a new job instead. Once I had one, then I'd tell everyone I was working somewhere new." She stopped and blinked back tears. "I applied all over, but I couldn't find anything except temp work—office stuff like data entry and customer service."

Brody put his hand on her arm. "You should have told me. I would have been happy to listen."

"I know, but I was sick of feeling like a needy, miserable screwup."

"It wasn't your fault you were laid off."

In her heart, she knew he was right. But losing her job, after less than a year, had been a huge blow. "It's still debilitating. I'm done with Chicago. If I'm going to be unemployed, I'd rather be in Riverside. The winter isn't brutally cold, and I can save money by living at home."

Ahead of them, Marc and Gabi had stopped to take pictures. By now, the sun was beating down with a fiery intensity. Jess took another swig from her water bottle.

"Does Connor know?" Brody asked.

"Nope. I figured he wouldn't be up for a fling if he thought I was moving back home. The last time he bailed, it was partly because I was too close for comfort. By telling him I'm going back to Chicago, I'm giving him the perfect out." She sighed. "No one knows we're sleeping together either, because Gabi asked me to stay away from him. She didn't want us causing any drama at her perfect wedding."

Brody wiped his forehead. "That's a lot of secrets."

"I know, but I can handle it."

Three days remained until the wedding. Three more days of lying and sneaking around.

Not ideal, but infinitely better than revealing the truth.

CHAPTER 19

Connor groaned and opened his eyes. He lifted his head and winced at the crick in his neck. His laptop had gone into sleep mode, which meant he'd crashed out longer than he expected.

He cast a wary eye toward the clock on his nightstand. 6:30 a.m.

Shit.

He'd missed the van to Mt. Haleakala by a full three hours.

He checked his phone. No new messages from Jess. She was probably furious. Who could blame her? She'd expected him to stop by last night, but he'd ditched her without offering a full explanation. Then he compounded his assholery by failing to show up for the volcano excursion. Not only that, but he let down Marc and Gabi, after promising to be there. After all his declarations about being responsible, he'd already disappointed three people this morning.

Not a great start to the day.

He rubbed his eyes and woke his laptop out of hibernation. As he scrolled through his proposal, he was pleasantly surprised at how much he'd accomplished. Granted, his work needed editing and was rife with typos. But it was all there. Ten years' worth of projections.

In your face, Darren.

He owed Jess a major apology, but he'd do it in person once she got back from Mt. Haleakala. In the meantime, he could polish up his proposal. But first, he needed to clear his head.

He changed into his swim trunks and left the hotel. After a quick jog down the beach, he spent the next hour bodysurfing. The bracing surf revitalized him. When a rogue wave churned him up, he spat out salt water and cleared his sinuses. Now he was awake.

By the time he showered and dressed, he was ready to dive back into his proposal. On the chance his father still refused to support him in any way, he could look for other investors. And if he needed a loan from the bank, he could offer his condo as collateral.

Or...

He could minimize his risk by apologizing to his father, promising to do better, and dedicating himself to Blackwood Cellars. If he put in the effort, the old man might come to trust him in a few years.

But even if Connor busted his ass trying to be a model employee, he'd never succeed, not as long as he worked directly under his older brother. Darren wanted to keep him in his place, which meant he'd undermine him at every turn. As long as their father kept believing Darren's bullshit, he'd never come to respect Connor.

Better to take the risk and live with the consequences. Wasn't that what Jess had done with her life?

He went down to the coffee bar and ordered an extra-large cappuccino. For the next three hours, he reviewed the document and gave it a final polish. He emailed it to his father, then sent a copy to Victoria, along with a brief note: *Thanks for the support last night. Let me know what you think. If you can come up with any investors, I'm open to suggestions.*

He stood and stretched. When he popped into the bathroom to shave, he heard the shower in Jess's room running.

He hesitated. While he was grateful to have her friendship back, he was having second thoughts about their fling. Even if the sex was amazing, he wasn't entirely convinced she could adhere to the no-strings rule. The more time they spent together, the greater the chance she'd get hurt. And he didn't want to hurt her.

But then he imagined her in the shower. Naked. And all thoughts of being responsible vanished.

He picked up the phone and called room service.

AFTER A TWO-HOUR NAP and a lengthy shower, Jess had regained her energy. Though she hadn't appreciated waking up at 3:00 a.m., the sunrise had been spectacular. She'd enjoyed getting the chance to talk to Brody. And she'd proven to Gabi she could be trusted to show up when needed. Though her sister had ignored her for most of the trip, she came around at the end, when she thanked her for coming.

Now that Jess was back on a firm footing as a model maid of honor, she was hoping for a few hours off, with no planned activities. She wanted to snag some alone time with Connor before the luau. But when she peeked at her phone, her stomach clenched into a knot.

No new messages. *Bastard.*

She'd been a fool to think he would treat her differently than any of his other women. This was the last time she'd fall for his charm. Once she saw him, she was giving him hell. And she was *not* inviting him back into her bed.

A knock at her door sent her adrenaline racing. Bracing

herself for a confrontation, she flung the door open, only to see a uniformed waiter standing in the hallway.

"Yes?" she said.

"Sorry to disturb you, miss, but your order has arrived." Beside him was a metal room service cart.

"I think you have the wrong room. I didn't order anything." She wished she had. The smell of french fries made her mouth water.

"Jessica Chavez, room 945? It's already paid for."

Had Gabi had sent the food to thank her for going to Mt. Haleakala?

She gestured for the waiter to come in and grabbed five bucks out of her wallet to give him a tip. When she opened the silver domes, she drooled at the sight of all the food: barbecue pork sliders, fish tacos with grilled mahi mahi, Parmesan-dusted french fries, fresh pineapple spears, and two bottles of Snapple iced tea. This meal couldn't be from Gabi. She would have sent something healthy, like a spinach salad or a papaya smoothie.

As the waiter was leaving, Connor poked his head out of his room. "Hey, Jess."

She was tempted to hurl a few choice expletives at him and slam her door for emphasis, but he was at her doorway before she could make a move.

He rubbed his hands together. "Excellent. Lunch is here."

"You sent this?"

"I did. Sorry about last night. And about missing the volcano. The food is my apology."

She crossed her arms. "You're on my shit list right now. Not only did I go to bed alone, but if Brody hadn't shown up, I would have spent all morning with Gabi and Marc, who alternated between bickering and making out."

He gave her a sheepish look. "For what's it worth, I wanted to visit you last night, but Dad insisted I join him at the bar. He wasn't done lecturing me. Naturally, Darren and Victoria chimed in."

Guilt lodged in her throat. She should have trusted him. He hadn't chosen to avoid her. Instead, he'd been stuck at the mercy of his father and his hypercritical siblings. Her voice softened. "Was it bad?"

"There wasn't enough scotch in the world to make it bearable."

"Why didn't you come see me after? I would have listened." She didn't want to make this about her, but she was hurt he hadn't thought to confide in her.

"I got some bad news about one of my investors, and then I had to revise my plan to fit my dad's demands." He raked his hand through his hair. "I made the dumb mistake of trying to pull an all-nighter, thinking I could stay up until three. But I was wrong."

She gave him a small smile. "You're not a college kid anymore."

"Nope. Those days are over."

She twisted her hands together. "I know the winery is your first priority. It's just...I thought you didn't want to spend the night with me. Like you'd gotten what you wanted, and you were done."

He frowned. "I thought you were starting to trust me."

"I'm trying to. Sorry." If she really trusted him, she would have shared her plans to move back home.

When she found the courage to look him in the eye, he wasn't angry. "I'm sorry, too," he said. "Last night was a disaster. But we still have three days left, and I'd rather spend them with you than anyone else."

"Are you sure?"

His eyes took on a teasing glint. "I spent a lot of time in the shower thinking about you, and I'll be really frustrated if I can't carry out any of my fantasies."

Now he was playing dirty. Her traitorous lower regions tingled in anticipation. "You fantasized about me?"

"You'd better believe it." He gave her a naughty grin. "Do you want details?"

"Later. I'm not letting this food go to waste." She motioned for him to come in. "You have to help me eat it. There's enough for two."

After she wheeled the tray up to the edge of the bed, Connor pulled the desk chair over and sat across from her. Though she was glad he'd come back, and excited at the promise of more sex, right now, nothing was more appealing than fish tacos and pork sliders. She loved that Connor knew what to order—and that he'd ordered a lot of food.

She licked a speck of barbecue sauce off her fingers. She didn't want to push him about his meeting with his father, but she was too curious to keep quiet. "Can I ask what happened last night? If you don't want to talk about it, I'll understand. But I'm happy to listen."

"Sure. There isn't much to tell."

After Connor filled her in, she couldn't help but sympathize. He had so much potential, and he was squandering it, working for Blackwood Cellars. He was the kind of guy who liked to think outside the box—something his family had never appreciated. She couldn't understand why his father wouldn't give him the benefit of the doubt.

"What if Victoria doesn't come through?" she asked. "Are you still going to invest?"

"What do you think?"

"You're asking me? I'm not exactly a poster child for making smart decisions."

"Unlike my family, you don't have a hidden agenda. You've always been open about your feelings."

Until now.

More than ever, she wished she could be honest with him. But if she told him the truth now, she might lose him. She didn't want to take that risk.

"It sounds like you've been miserable at Blackwood Cellars," she said. "If you hate it now, think how you'll feel in another five years after putting up with more of Darren's garbage. Do you really want to live that way?"

When he didn't reply right away, she feared she'd overstepped. How could she presume to know what was best for him? Especially when it involved such a huge risk?

But he nodded, as though her advice resonated. "You're right. I've already wasted five years there. An opportunity like this might not come up again for a long time."

"Exactly." She held up her bottle and clinked it against his. "Here's to your success."

"I'm going for it. Look at how well things turned out for you, all because you took chances. A new job, a new city, a new life. You're an inspiration."

"Right." She looked away, for fear her face would betray her.

The longer she let Connor believe her lies, the harder it would be to confess the truth. But she was still afraid to tell him she was moving close enough for them to consider a *real* relationship. Better to have him believe they'd gone their separate ways.

In the fall, she could let him know she'd decided to return to California. By then, he'd have his new winery to keep him busy.

Though lunch was delicious, she was so full afterward she couldn't imagine getting naked—not even with Connor. But he didn't have sex on the brain either.

"How about a drive up the coast?" he said. "I was thinking we could find a private beach, do some snorkeling, and then get ice cream."

"I'd love some beach time, but I should talk to Gabi first. She wasn't thrilled I missed yesterday's golf outing." She tensed up as she waited for his reaction.

He chuckled. "Same with my family. Being responsible is the worst."

"You said it. I'll call Gabi, and you can check in with your family." She stood and walked out to the balcony. Gabi answered after the third ring.

"Jess? Everything okay?" She sounded slightly breathless.

"Sorry. Did I wake you?"

"No, I'm…hanging out. With Marc. We were pretty tired after Mt. Haleakala, and…"

And you were banging. Because there's nothing quite like make-up sex.

"I won't keep you," Jess said. "There's nothing listed in the calendar app, so I wanted to make sure I wasn't missing out."

"I was going to suggest a shopping expedition in Lahaina, but I'm wiped out. Is that okay? I think Mama and Luisa are going if you want to join them. They might have left already, but you could meet them there."

Jess let out her breath in relief. "I'll pass. Shopping's not in my budget right now. And I'm still kind of tired. But the volcano was great. I took a ton of pictures."

"You liked it?" Her sister's voice brightened. "Thanks for coming. I know I was grouchy at first, but I'm so glad you and Brody showed up. Despite the dumb Hobbit jokes."

"You know how it is when Brody's around. We always default to our nerdiest settings."

"Right. Don't forget the luau's at six."

"I wouldn't miss it." As Jess hung up, Gabi's words of gratitude filled her with a warm glow. She'd done her due diligence. And now she could take the afternoon off, without feeling a shred of guilt. When she peeked back inside, Connor was on the phone.

"You sure?" he said. "The last thing I want to do is piss off Dad again. Or have Darren claim I'm not paying attention to the family."

Jess waited, her hands clasped tightly, as he continued his conversation. From the sound of it, he was talking with Victoria.

But when he got off the phone, he smiled. "It's all good. The others left at noon to visit the Ulupalakua Vineyards. They're getting a private tour of the estate, followed by a VIP tasting at MauiWine. Victoria assumed I was going to Mt. Haleakala. That's why I wasn't invited."

"Sorry. Visiting a vineyard in Hawaii would have been a cool experience."

"Yeah, but not with my dad. After last night's conversation, the last thing I'd want to do with him is visit a winery." He frowned but shook it off. "Forget it. The thing is—we're both free. So, how about a little beach time?"

She grinned in anticipation. "Perfect. I'll bring my bikini."

Maybe she'd been right.

Maybe she *could* balance everything and have it all turn out perfectly.

CHAPTER 20

Connor found a quiet, secluded bay, twenty miles from the hotel. Then he and Jess rented snorkeling gear and spent hours in the water. With no one else around, they were free to act like a couple. All too easily, they slipped back into their old patterns—teasing each other, talking about movies, and making jokes about their families. He had such a relaxing afternoon with her that he lost track of time. They had to rush back to the hotel in order to fit in a quick romp, followed by a steamy shower. When he took her up against the tiled wall, with the warm water cascading around them, the sex was every bit as good as his fantasies.

With a half hour to spare, they went their separate ways to change for the luau. Connor hadn't planned on leaving at the same time as Jess, but she emerged from her room seconds after he did. She looked drop-dead gorgeous in a tropical-print sundress that bared her shoulders and fell above her knees, revealing her shapely legs.

She tossed her hair and flashed him a sultry smile. "Don't disappoint me tonight."

"I won't. After the luau, we'll head back to your room. Discreetly, of course."

"Of course. But don't keep me waiting too long."

In the elevator, she pressed up against him and captured his mouth in a deep, passionate kiss. He cupped his hands around her butt and pulled her closer, aware that any moment, the elevator could stop, and the doors could open. That didn't stop him from trailing kisses along her neck and shoulders, making her gasp. He caught a whiff of something flowery. Like jasmine. Her perfume? Whatever it was, the smell turned him on.

"Let's go back to my room," he said. "Just for a little while longer."

She pulled away. "Are you kidding? Gabi and Marc would ask too many questions if we both showed up late." She smoothed the front of her dress. "We need to behave once we're out there. No one can suspect what we've been up to."

Easier said than done when he could barely keep his hands off her.

The luau was held on the Makai Terrace, the oceanfront lawn where the wedding would take place in three days. Bright tiki torches ringed the perimeter, adding to the ambience. Facing the beach, a low stage showcased a trio of guitarists, who serenaded the guests with Hawaiian melodies. Unlike the other activities Gabi and Marc had planned, the luau was one of the resort's regularly scheduled events, open to all guests, and the area was thronged with people.

As Connor approached the party with Jess, Brody intercepted them. He was wearing a bright yellow Hawaiian shirt and had three leis strung around his neck.

"Hang on, you two. We need to split you up." He raised his eyebrows. "Unless your dirty little secret is out in the open."

Connor turned to Jess, making no attempt to hide his irritation. "You told him about us?"

"She didn't have to," Brody said. "I guessed it earlier. Even now, it's painfully obvious." He took Jess's arm. "You—come with me. And you—Connor—go be your flirtatious self."

"But not too much flirting," Jess called out.

Frustration gnawed at Connor as he watched them leave. He had no desire to flirt with *anyone*, even in the guise of fooling their families. All he wanted was Jess. But keeping things quiet was for the best, especially after Darren had accused him of blowing off the family to spend time with her.

He went to order a beer and ran into Marc and his father, Rob Blackwood, in line at the bar. Marc insisted Connor try one of the luau's signature drinks, which came in a giant coconut, then they found a place to watch the show. The master of ceremonies held the crowd spellbound as his assistants unearthed a huge roast pig from under a pile of coals and leaves. Connor, however, could barely focus. Across the terrace, Jess stood beside Brody, her head tilted back in laughter. Was Brody hitting on her? His cousin better not be putting any moves on his woman.

His woman? Where did that come from? And how could he be jealous of Brody? Jess and Brody had been friends since they were kids, and there had never been any sparks between them. Besides, his cousin was in deep with Taylor.

Connor forced himself to breathe. Even if he couldn't spend the entire evening with Jess, he could still enjoy himself. He hung out with Marc and Uncle Rob, watched the breathtaking performances, and let himself get pulled onstage during the "audience participation" part of the show. But something was missing. When he caught a glimpse of Lance, talking with Jess, his hackles rose. If that overgrown frat boy thought he had any claim over her, he was sadly mistaken. And if he tried anything, Connor would be all over him like—

Stop. Enough with this caveman shit.

He drained the last of his tropical drink and shuddered. Fruity drinks served in a coconut were not his style. He set the empty coconut shell on the bar and wandered away from the crowd, past the hedge separating the grassy terrace from the beach. Under the moonlight, the waves gave off an ethereal glow. He wanted to find Jess and steal her away so they could enjoy the rest of the evening together.

"Connor?" Gabi stood beside the hedge, holding an enormous coconut with a straw sticking out of it.

"Hey, Gabi."

"I'm surprised to see you here alone. I assumed by now you'd be off with one of the dancers. Or a waitress. Or pretty much any willing female."

From the slur in Gabi's voice, she'd clearly enjoyed too many loaded coconuts. He'd never seen her get drunk before—not even tipsy. The wedding stress must have pushed her over the edge.

He kept his voice even. "You don't have a very high opinion of me, do you?"

"For good reason." She advanced closer and jabbed his chest with her finger. "I know what you're up to. You played nice with Jess so she'd forgive you. Then you spent the day with her 'as friends.' What a load of crap."

He gave her a disarming smile. "We're good, now that we've put the past behind us." Despite the cool breeze, heat prickled the back of his neck.

Gabi's dark eyes were laser-focused on him. "And you've been behaving like a gentleman? Bullshit."

He shook his head. "Gabi, listen—"

"No, you listen. How dare you use my wedding to prey on my little sister? She's still recovering from her breakup with Simon, and you're taking advantage of her vulnerability. You act like all you want is friendship, but I know what you're up to. You're setting her up so you can fuck her again. Not on my watch, asshole."

He hadn't faced the brunt of Gabi's anger since they were kids. He'd forgotten how terrifying she could be. "You have me all wrong. I told Jess I was sorry, and we agreed to move on."

"So you could use her. Enjoy her for a couple of nights, then throw her away like garbage." Gabi's hands shook as she brandished the coconut. "If you break her heart again, I'll twist your testicles into a knot. Tied with a fucking bow."

He held his hands up. "No one's heart is getting broken. We're just friends." Good thing they were keeping their fling quiet. Otherwise, he might not escape the luau with his balls intact.

"You have no idea what you put her through. She blamed herself for being too pushy. But you're the one who led her on."

Gabi's words hit him with the force of a physical blow. "I'm sorry."

"Call me a bitch if you want, but I care about her. And I don't want you hurting her."

"Everything all right?" Marc approached them, sounding winded. He put his hand on Gabi's arm. "You okay, sweetheart?"

"I'm fine now." She glared at Connor. "I'm warning you. Stay away from my sister or you'll answer to me."

Marc gave him an apologetic smile as he led Gabi away. "Come on. The party's breaking up. Let's go say good night to our guests."

Connor took a moment to catch his breath.

Sure as hell didn't see that one coming.

He tried to shake off the encounter, but Gabi had gotten into his head, making him question his involvement with Jess. She'd told him she'd be fine with a no-strings affair, but what if she ended up wanting more, like she had when she was eighteen? He didn't want to break her heart again.

"Hey there, handsome." Jess slithered through an opening in the hedge. She tugged on his arm, pulling him along until they were standing on the beach. She kicked off her sandals and wiggled her bare toes in the sand. "That feels *so* good."

"What are you doing here?" He glanced back at the luau to ensure Marc and Gabi weren't standing nearby.

"The luau's about over, so I came to see you." She leaned into him, her voice a husky whisper. "Let's go have sex on the beach."

He groaned. "I didn't bring anything with me. Sorry."

She gestured to the large, woven handbag she was carrying. "No problem. I went up to my room and grabbed the supplies we needed. This Little Girl Scout is fully prepared."

Cupping his face, she claimed his lips. She tasted of rum and pineapple, and the intoxicating aroma of her perfume aroused his senses. The feel of her body, pressed against his, aroused him even more. When she smoothed her hands under his shirt and stroked his back, he lost all resistance.

He released her. "Let's walk up the beach. It's too public here."

"Good plan." She slipped her hand into his and squeezed it.

They walked along the sand, past other couples, some in clinches and others strolling along the oceanfront, as the waves crested and dissolved into foam. He blew out a long breath, releasing the pent-up frustration he'd held in all evening. Forget Gabi. He knew what he was doing, and so did Jess. This was their vacation, damn it.

"This is so romantic," Jess said. "I love it here."

The joy in her voice warmed his heart. He wanted to make her happy. To give her whatever he could, even if it was only for a few days. "Have you ever done this before?"

"Had sex on the beach? Out in the open? No way. What about you?"

"Nope." For all his carousing, he'd never been tempted. Not until now.

They ambled for another twenty minutes until they were far beyond the resort. Jess tugged on his hand, bringing him over to a secluded area, under a couple of palm trees. "Here. This is perfect."

If he'd had more to drink, he might have fewer inhibitions. What if someone saw them? Would they call the police? Was sex on the beach a crime? Or an offense worthy of getting ticketed?

He could only imagine his family's reaction if he got arrested for indecent behavior. They'd never let him live it down.

But when Jess took a folded-up towel out of her handbag and laid it on the ground, he couldn't bear to disappoint her. He'd just have to take the risk.

He laughed. "You planned this, didn't you? Naughty girl."

She gave him a flirty grin. "Let's just say I decided to plan ahead for once in my life. I brought condoms, too." She plopped onto the towel and reached behind her, giving a huff of frustration. "Can you help me with the zipper? I want to get this dress off."

As much as he wanted to see her naked, he didn't like the idea of her being so vulnerable. "Maybe just leave it on. Okay?"

"Okay. Good thing I'm not wearing any panties." She giggled. "That makes it easier for you, right?"

His last shred of resistance vanished. He knelt beside her and lowered her onto her back. She looked up at him with big dark eyes, her need evident. He undid her zipper, just a little, so he could free her gorgeous breasts.

"You are so damn sexy," he murmured as he swirled his tongue over one nipple. She moaned in response, tangling her fingers in his hair.

He hiked up her dress, but she gave a yelp and squirmed underneath him.

"You okay?" he asked.

She reached under the towel and pulled out a rock. "This was digging into me." Once she tossed it aside, she lay back down. "Much better. I'm ready whenever you are."

He hated to dispense with foreplay, especially since he loved the way she reacted to his touch, but a hotel guest could walk up the beach at any minute. He fumbled with his zipper, tugging his shorts and boxers down around his ankles. Despite his uneasiness at getting caught, his dick had no such fears. He was hard as a rock.

"Hang on." Jess reached over to her handbag and pulled out a condom. "I picked up some extras at the hotel gift shop."

Damn, but she was cute. And sexy. And incredibly eager, despite the risk of being interrupted. "You're not worried about getting caught?"

She smiled up at him in adoration. "Not when I'm with you. Sex on the beach has always been one of my top ten fantasies."

How could he deny her? He opened the packet and sheathed himself. "Sorry, but this is going to have to be quick."

"Don't apologize. You can make it up to me when we're back at the hotel."

He'd make certain of it. Once they were alone, in the privacy of her room, he could take his sweet time, lavishing her body with the attention she deserved.

He parted her thighs and stroked her slick folds with his fingers. She was more than ready. He wanted to go down on her first, to ensure her satisfaction, but he couldn't risk it. When he entered her, she wrapped her legs around him and moaned with pleasure. He placed his hand over her mouth and whispered into her ear.

"Shhh. We don't want everyone to hear us."

"Sorry. But you feel *so* good."

He wished they were both naked so he could feel her bare skin against his, but there was something erotic as hell about doing it on a public beach. He thrust deeper inside her, increasing his pace, but stopped before he reached the precipice. He caught her eyes and smoothed her wayward curls from her face.

"Connor?" she whispered. "What is it?"

"I want to remember you like this. So beautiful. So sexy. And all mine." Wanting to bring them closer, he captured her mouth with a searing kiss. She moaned again, and he picked up the pace, thrusting even harder.

"Yes," she said. "Don't stop. Please don't stop."

He tried to hold back, but within minutes she was clutching him harder and whimpering with pleasure. With a final surge, he let himself go, and a rush of sensation enveloped him. He pressed his forehead against hers, now damp with sweat. For a moment they said nothing as the surf crashed behind them.

She gave a little shudder. "That was amazing. Better than my fantasies."

He looked into her eyes, wanting to savor their closeness. "You're the one who's amazing." What was it about this woman that made him feel both protective and passionate?

The murmur of voices shocked him out of his stupor. "Someone's coming." He stood up, hating the rush of chilly air where there had been warmth before. After pulling up his boxers and his shorts, he offered her his hand and helped her to her feet.

She shook out the towel and adjusted her dress. "Let's go back to my room and take a shower. Does that sound okay?"

He placed his arm around her waist. "Sounds perfect."

CHAPTER 21

Jess curled up against Connor, enjoying the warmth of his naked body. A glimpse of sunlight, peeking through the blinds, made her suspect they'd slept late. But she couldn't make herself look at the time. Not when she was suspended in a blissful state of contentment.

She still couldn't believe they'd had sex on a public beach. While the act itself had been furtive and quick, the setting was undeniably romantic. But though she'd kept her butt firmly on the towel, she'd still gotten sand in unexpected places. The only way to get rid of all the sand was to take another shower. Then they curled up in bed and watched *Terminator 2* on cable before drifting off to sleep in each other's arms.

She could get used to this. The feeling that Connor wasn't just a lover who brought her to the heights of passion, but a friend she could snuggle with and share bad jokes. But their fling had a definite expiration date. Today was Thursday, two days before the wedding, which meant they had three more nights left. Most of the wedding party was departing on Sunday. Everyone was returning home except Marc and Gabi, who were flying to the island of Kauai for their honeymoon.

Connor stirred, then rolled over to face her. He looked as gorgeous as ever, his dark hair mussed from sleep. He brushed his hand against her cheek. "Have I ever told you how sexy you look first thing in the morning?"

"Maybe? But you can tell me again."

He ran his hand through her hair, tangling it in her curls. "For the record, you're completely irresistible." He lowered his head, trailing kisses along the hollow of her throat.

Even after a wild night of passion, she couldn't get enough of him. But her phone trilled with an alarm, startling her. She pulled away from him and shut it off. "It's nine fifteen. I have to meet the girls for a spa morning at ten."

Though she would have preferred to lounge in bed with Connor, she needed to revert to her role as Gabi's maid of honor. At least they'd gotten the chance to spend the night together.

"I need to run, too," he said. "I've got a tennis game at ten. Darren's going to kick my ass. He's been taking private lessons."

She smacked his bare butt. "All right, then. Time to get up. I need a shower, stat."

He grinned. "Sounds good."

"Not with you. If you and I get into the shower..." She shivered at the memory of their late-night shower, when she'd knelt down and taken him in her mouth, putting him at her mercy until he groaned in submission.

"Admit it, you're tempted," he said.

"No! Put on your clothes and go back to your room. I command you."

He laughed. "Yes, ma'am."

Once he left, she went into the bathroom to take stock. After last night's lengthy shower, she was clean enough. But because she'd gone to bed with wet hair, her curls were a crazy corkscrew mess. After *another* shower, she threw on a sundress and took the time to do her makeup properly.

Gabi's mini spa event was set up on the shaded lanai of the

Pink Orchid Spa, giving them a spectacular view of the ocean. Luisa and Victoria were already seated, as was Darren's wife, Melanie. The only one missing was Paige, Gabi's former college roommate, who was supposed to arrive on Friday. A table draped in pink and orange linens held a delicious breakfast spread— fresh fruit, croissants, mini quiches, cinnamon rolls, coffee, and a pitcher of mimosas.

Jess scanned the lanai. "Where are the moms at? Are they joining us?"

"They're spending the morning at the Spa at Black Rock," Gabi said. "Marc's mom wanted to treat them to a Poha Berry Body Wrap. I did it last time I was in Maui and it was incredible, but it was a little too pricey for all of us. Sorry."

Jess settled into a chair and sipped her mimosa. "Don't apologize. This is perfect. I can't think of a better way to wake up. Or a better place for a wedding."

"Don't say it's perfect," Gabi said. "You don't want to jinx things. After the ceremony, when Marc and I are finally married, then you can say it was perfect."

"Well, I'm loving it so far." Luisa gave a huge yawn. "My only complaint is my lack of sleep. Lance and I went out after the luau and found a great club."

Jess bit her lip, holding back a laugh. "How was it?"

Luisa's brow creased. "You're not upset, are you? He said you two weren't together."

"Nope. No chemistry." Jess still couldn't believe what a giant bullet she'd dodged.

"It was fun. Lance's a great dancer. But..." Luisa shrugged. "All I wanted was a night out. Nothing else. He's too much of a frat-bro for my tastes."

Thank God. Jess wouldn't wish Lance on anyone, not even her ultra-competitive cousin.

Three attendants began setting up the footbaths for the pedicures. Though Jess would have preferred to pick out her own shade of nail polish, Gabi insisted they all wear the same color. Jess agreed without question. It was hard to argue when her feet were being immersed in a warm bath and another attendant was bringing her coffee.

Luisa sighed. "I need to marry someone rich so I can have my own destination wedding. Maybe in Baja or the Caribbean."

"Did you consider it for your wedding?" Jess asked Victoria.

She scowled. "I wish. I wanted to get married somewhere romantic, like the south of France, instead of the Temecula Valley."

If Jess recalled correctly, Victoria had spent a semester abroad in Paris. And she spoke French. "Why didn't you go for it? Your family could totally afford it."

"My father said it was vital we didn't snub any of the Blackwoods. Not this time."

"I didn't snub anyone," Gabi said. "I invited all the Blackwoods."

"I know," Victoria said. "But not everyone could spare the time to jet off to Maui. That's why my father insisted I have my wedding at the Blackwood Cellars Estate."

Gabi's face fell. When she spoke again, her voice was small. Humble. "I never intended to leave anyone out."

Luisa arched an eyebrow. "And yet, you did. Mom's still upset she can't be here. I offered to let her share my room, but she couldn't swing the airfare and everything else. Not with the twins starting college in the fall."

"I realize that," Gabi said. "But Marc's family couldn't pay for everyone."

Jess counted herself lucky Marc had offered to pay her way. If she'd had to foot the bill, she would have limited her trip to a few days and stayed in a cheap hotel. Since Luisa came from a family of six, Gabi couldn't have asked the Blackwoods to pay for all of them.

But even if she wished more of her family could have

attended, Jess didn't want Gabi to feel guilty. Her sister had already dealt with enough grief after she announced her engagement.

Jess frowned at Luisa. "Gabi and Marc are throwing a big party in August for the whole family. We can all celebrate then."

"Sure," Luisa muttered. "Because a party in Riverside is no different than a beachside wedding in Maui." She rubbed her forehead. "Sorry. That was super bitchy. But Mom called me this morning, and she was in a *mood*. She acted like I had no business coming here when the rest of the family couldn't afford it. It's not my fault I have such a high-paying job."

With that attitude, no wonder Luisa's mom was pissed.

Jess turned to her sister, trying to hold still as one of the attendants placed spacers between her toes. "Don't stress about it. This is *your* wedding, not theirs. Besides, isn't this what Marc wanted? Didn't you say he fell in love with Maui when you were here two years ago?"

Gabi looked down. "He did. But...he originally wanted us to get married in Napa. I had to talk him into having our wedding here. And then, when we couldn't have a sunset wedding like we wanted, I had to convince him a brunch wedding was just as good."

"The brunch wedding was a great idea," Jess said. "What's not to love? Mimosas, pastries, a fully stocked coffee bar. Sounds like heaven to me."

She'd been on board since day one. She'd take breakfast fare over a boring plate of chicken any day.

"We didn't have a choice about the time," Gabi said. "Even though we started planning a year ago, the coordinator told us all the sunset weddings for Friday and Saturday night were booked for the entire summer."

Jess sought to reassure her. "After all the work you've done, it's going to be fabulous." She locked eyes with Luisa, who nodded.

"Thanks," Gabi said. "I just keep worrying that I'm forgetting some tiny detail."

Jess spoke up quickly. "If you have any last-minute errands, let me know. I'm glad to help."

"Since you're offering…" Gabi said. "I still haven't found the perfect shells for the table settings. Would you mind checking out the stores in Lahaina? I can send you pictures so you'll see what I had in mind."

"No problem. I can handle shell duty." If Jess sweet-talked Connor, she could easily convince him to drive her around.

"Great. That's one thing off my plate," Gabi said. "Don't forget the shuttle's taking us to the cacao farm tour and chocolate tasting at three. We'll meet in the lobby. And the bachelorette party starts at eight tonight. We're doing a bar crawl in Lahaina, but we have the shuttle all night, in case we want to go somewhere else."

"Please say you're not making us do something distasteful, like wearing glittery headbands or drinking out of penis-shaped shot glasses," Victoria said.

Gabi shuddered. "Never. We'll be wearing matching leis, but that's it. Just because we're going out drinking doesn't mean we have to lose *all* semblance of control." She gave Jess a pointed look. "Right?"

Normally, Jess might have chafed at her sister's tone. But she'd learned her lesson after her night at the Blue Lagoon. She gave Gabi her sweetest smile. "I'll be on my best behavior."

She could save the naughty antics for later, after Connor returned from the bachelor party. She'd promised him she'd wait up, no matter how late the hour.

After the spa treatment ended and the others went their separate ways, Jess lingered behind, waiting to catch Gabi alone. She approached her sister, who stood at the edge of the lanai, looking out at the ocean. "Are you okay? Luisa and Victoria were kind of salty about the destination wedding thing."

Gabi let out a lengthy sigh. "Do you think it was unreasonable asking everyone to come here?"

Squinting at the bright sun, Jess brought out her sunglasses. "No. Like I said before, it's *your* big day. They need to chill."

"I can see why Luisa would be pissed. She'd probably have more fun if the rest of her family were here. But Victoria doesn't have the right to criticize me for choosing a destination wedding. She's having a huge Winter Wonderland wedding with *twenty* Christmas trees."

"Twenty trees?" Jess giggled. "Even for her, that's excessive."

Gabi took off her sunglasses and wiped her eyes. "She's been kind of bitchy this whole trip. That golf outing was miserable."

Yet another reason Jess was grateful she'd missed it. She lowered her voice, even though no one was around but the attendants who were cleaning up the breakfast spread. "I'm not sure how much she told you, but she's having trouble with Ben. He cheated on her last month."

"Really? Now it makes sense. They were sniping at each other all during golf. I can't believe she's still marrying him. That would be a deal-breaker for me."

"Same. Not that I plan on getting married any time soon." For now, Jess was perfectly happy just to indulge in a tropical fling.

Gabi's voice tightened. "But you're having fun, right? You're enjoying Maui? I'm sorry it didn't work out with Lance."

When would Gabi understand she wasn't responsible for everyone's happiness? No wonder she could never relax.

"I'm having a great time," Jess said. "Maui is *glorious*. And I know you weren't thrilled about my Hana excursion with Connor, but I'm glad I got to see that part of the island."

"Hana's totally worth the trip. Though I made Marc do *all* the driving. Those narrow roads were terrifying."

"I know, right? A couple of times when we went over those bridges, I had to close my eyes because I thought we were going to have a head-on collision."

For a moment, Jess was tempted to tell Gabi everything. That Connor was different now. That she was having more fun with him than she'd ever had with Simon. That she was finally regaining some of the spark she'd lost after that horrible spring in Chicago.

But she couldn't. Because, on edge as Gabi was, there was no guarantee she'd be okay with it. For now, Jess would have to hold her tongue.

CHAPTER 22

On his way to the tennis courts, Connor stopped by the coffee bar in the lobby and ordered an espresso. Without a little pick-me-up, he wouldn't have enough energy for tennis. How much sleep had he gotten last night, anyway? Four hours? Five? Not that he had any regrets. Despite Gabi's threats, he was glad he'd spent the night with Jess. He'd slept amazingly well, sated and happy, with her naked body nestled against his.

Brody came up and gave him a friendly shoulder punch. "You look like shit. Didn't you get any sleep?"

"I'll be fine once I get some caffeine in my system." Connor downed his espresso, wincing at the bitterness.

"Up late?"

"Too late." He couldn't repress the shit-eating grin spreading across his face. "Worth it, though."

"I can't believe Jess forgave you. She was mad at you for five years."

He set his empty cup on the bar. "She's not mad anymore."

"Don't look so smug," Brody said. "Anyone can have great sex while they're on vacation. Maintaining an actual relationship is hard work."

"You don't have to lecture me about relationships. I was in one before, remember? That's eight months of my life I'll never get back."

"That was Natasha. By now, we've all agreed she was nothing but a gold-digger. What if you met the right woman? Wouldn't you want more than a week with her?"

Connor had thought he wanted a future with Natasha until she'd kicked his pride and his heart to the curb. At this point, letting someone into his life for longer than a week involved more trust than he was willing to give. "Nope. Can't see it happening."

Brody wouldn't be dissuaded. "What about Jess? Ever think about getting serious with her?"

"Not an option. She's going back to Chicago." Though he cared about her, he couldn't see himself making that leap. Long-distance relationships required a lot of patience and a major level of commitment.

"What if she wasn't?"

"I'm about to take the biggest financial risk of my life. I could end up flat broke. The last thing I need is a 'serious' relationship."

Victoria had texted him fifteen minutes ago. She'd read his new proposal and liked it, but when she tried to approach their father, he shut her down. No surprise there. But it also meant Connor had lost his potential safety net.

They headed out of the lobby, toward the west side of the resort, where eight tennis courts were set on a rise, overlooking the Pacific Ocean. The air was a perfect temperature—warm, with a hint of a sultry breeze.

He and Brody went into the pro shop located outside the courts, where they confirmed Darren's reservation and rented four rackets and a bucket of balls. In their assigned court, Connor practiced his serve, smacking the ball with more force than necessary.

Brody took his place on the other side of the net. "Serve me up a few. I need to practice my backhand." He assumed a ready stance. "I know it's none of my business, but I'm looking out for Jess. She's one of my closest friends. And maybe she didn't tell you this, but you broke her heart."

Connor's shoulders tightened. Even if Jess had forgiven him, he still regretted waiting five years to apologize. "I know. I'm trying to make it up to her."

"I'd be a wreck if Taylor did something like that to me."

"Don't worry about it. I doubt she'd ever treat you that way." He served the ball to Brody, who returned it easily.

They got in a few rallies before Darren swaggered onto the courts, with Marc a few paces behind. "Nice try, but getting here early to practice won't help. You're going to get your asses kicked." He set down his bottle of Voss Artesian Water. "We had a tournament at the country club last month, and I came in third."

Brody laughed. "Only third?"

"Better than you'd do," Darren said.

"Cut the bullshit," Connor said. "Let's play."

Darren regarded him with a measure of amusement. "What's the rush? Are you that eager for a dose of humiliation? Think how you'll feel when you're forced to come crawling back to Blackwood Cellars, begging for your job."

Typical Darren, trying to break him down, like he did when they worked together. He'd berate him for failing to bring new ideas to the table, and then, when Connor finally offered a few suggestions, he'd shoot him down in front of the entire team.

"That's not going to happen," Connor said. "With or without Dad's help, I'm going to make this winery work."

"Big talk for someone with the emotional maturity of a twelve-year-old," Darren said.

Brody glared at him. "What's your problem? If you hate working with Connor, then why do you care if he quits Blackwood Cellars?"

"Aren't you mad he's jumping ship and betraying our

parents?" Darren said. "Grandpa Dominic would be rolling over in his grave."

"No, he wouldn't," Marc said. "Grandpa was a huge risk-taker. Didn't he sink half the family fortune into the first winery? He'd be impressed the next generation was trying something new."

"Connor's never had a responsible bone in his body," Darren said. "He's going to crash and burn."

Connor advanced a step closer. Darren might be able to beat him in tennis, but he was stronger and more muscular than his older brother. He could take him in a fight. "You'd like that, wouldn't you?"

Brody pinched the bridge of his nose. "Can we play? We only have the court until noon."

For the next two hours, Connor played his heart out. Unlike the rest of the Blackwood clan, he wasn't a big fan of tennis or golf. He preferred solo sports like running, biking, and swimming, where he could set his own pace and push himself to the limit. But if he had to play his dickhead brother, he wasn't going down without a fight.

In the end, Marc and Darren won both sets, though Connor made sure the last few games weren't easy victories. They had just finished when Jess approached them, looking far too sexy in a white cotton sundress and sandals.

"Hey, Jess," Marc said. "Is Gabi looking for me?" He grabbed his phone from the bench. "I haven't checked my messages."

"We're done with the spa treatment, so Gabi sent me to fetch you," she said. "You're supposed to meet with the wedding coordinator at lunch to go over the final details for the rehearsal dinner."

"Right. I forgot about that," Marc said.

"She said you're meeting at the Banyan Tree—the restaurant on the east side of the resort," Jess said.

"Thanks for the reminder." Marc turned to Connor. "After

lunch, Brody and I are going to the airport to pick up Grandma Blackwood. Want to come with?"

Connor hated letting Marc down, but he'd been hoping to squeeze in a few hours with Jess. "I'm kind of busy. Sorry."

Darren pinned him in his gaze. "How could you *possibly* be busy?" He snorted in disgust. "You met someone at the luau, didn't you? Good thing Dad didn't fall for your bullshit the other night. You haven't changed one bit."

Of course Darren would assume the worst of him. But he couldn't tell him the truth, not if he wanted to keep his fling under wraps.

Jess crossed her arms and glared at Darren. "For your information, Gabi asked me to run errands for her, and Connor offered to help."

Darren gave her a skeptical look. "Since when does my brother know the first thing about weddings?"

"He knows nada, but he has a vehicle. And Gabi wants me traipsing all over West Maui, looking for just the right shells to decorate the place settings at the rehearsal dinner. They have to say 'tropical' without being too obvious. Not too big, not too small, not too generic. I'll know them when I see them."

Marc beamed at her. "Thanks, Jess. You too, Connor." He took off, half walking, half jogging, toward the hotel.

"What is it with women and all this DIY shit?" Darren said. "Melanie and her friends hand-painted twelve dozen wineglasses to give to everyone as wedding favors. What a pain in the ass."

"You're a real romantic, aren't you?" Jess muttered. "Anyway, Connor, you coming with? The clock's ticking."

"Yeah, but you're buying me lunch." He handed his racket to Darren. "Here. You can turn our stuff in. I've got places to go."

As they walked away, he whispered to Jess, "Nice save. But we don't *actually* have to look for shells, do we?"

"We do. Sorry." She grinned at him. "But the sooner we get it done, the sooner we can sneak back to your room."

As she led the way, putting a little strut in her walk, he watched her ass sway, his groin tightening in anticipation.

He could not *wait* to get her alone.

CHAPTER 23

$\mathcal{J}$ ess shuddered at her reflection in the bathroom mirror. Even with her newly acquired tan, the bags under her eyes stood out.

Serves you right for getting five hours of sleep last night. What were you thinking?

Since last night's bachelorette party had ended at two, she'd gone to bed at a semi-decent hour. But she'd waited for Connor to come back from his party. Then they stayed up for another two hours, indulging their naughtiest fantasies. Exhausting, to be sure. But totally worth it.

Though she desperately needed a shower, she planned to wait until Connor returned from picking up coffee. He'd promised her another round of shower sex, and she did *not* want to miss out. Especially since the resort appeared to have an unlimited supply of hot water.

After that, they both had the day free until the rehearsal at 4:00 p.m. Bliss.

When a knock sounded at the door, she was tempted to greet Connor naked, but she restrained herself, in case anyone else was out in the hallway. She grabbed one of the leopard-print robes and put it on. But when she opened the door, she came face-to-face with her mom.

"Mama. Hi! What…what are you doing here?"

"Do you have a minute?"

Jess stole a quick glance down the hall. No sign of Connor. She hoped she could deal with her mom before he got back. "Come in. Is everything okay?"

"I wanted to see if you needed any more pictures." Her mom pulled a zip drive out of her purse. "If not, I loaded a bunch onto this drive before I left home. There are more in the cloud, but these are my favorites."

Pictures? Jess stared at her in confusion. "What are you talking about?"

Her mom strode over to the desk, where Jess had left her laptop open. She'd brought it with her, thinking she'd use her downtime to work on her novel. So far, all she'd done was look up places on Gabi's list of recommendations.

"Is the video on your laptop?" her mom asked.

"What video?"

"The video for the rehearsal dinner." Her mom frowned again, deeper this time. "Carly told me about it before she left for Nepal. Haven't you been working on it?"

In all of Jess's conversations with Gabi, both in person and via text, her sister had *never* mentioned a video. Other than the videographer she'd hired to film the wedding ceremony. But that didn't involve Jess.

She grabbed the wedding binder from her tote bag and flipped through it until she came to the section entitled "MOH Duties." She'd reviewed it when Carly had first handed off the binder, but she didn't remember anything about a video. Maybe Carly had forgotten to make note of it.

No. There, taped to the second-to-last page of the binder, was a handwritten note.

Jess,

*This isn't in the list of duties, but don't forget to put together a
video for the rehearsal dinner. One of those photo-montage
things, with pictures of Gabi and Marc and their favorite songs
playing in the background. Gabi never asked me to do it, but I
know she'd love it! You'll need to pick out 5 or 6 songs, then edit
them down to smaller snippets. Give yourself lots of time to pick
out the photos, because you'll need around 120 for a 6-minute
video.*

Carly

JESS STARED AT THE PAGE, speechless. She'd watched similar
videos at various weddings, family parties, and graduations. Of
course Gabi would adore having a video tribute, complete with
meaningful music. Why hadn't Jess thought of it earlier?

And how was it possible she'd screwed up again? Yesterday,
she'd been on her A game. She visited eight different stores to
find shells for Gabi. She enthusiastically praised the cacao farm
tour, even when Darren and Melanie deemed it boring. And she
only imbibed two cocktails during the bachelorette party.

But today? She was back at square one.

"You haven't started it, have you?" Her mom's voice was
like ice.

"I'm sorry." Shame twisted her stomach into knots. She'd
considered reviewing the binder again to make sure she hadn't
forgotten anything, but she'd been too preoccupied with Connor.

Her mom let out a huffy breath. "You should have asked me to
help. I would have been happy to pick out all the photos myself."

But I messed up. Big-time.

Jess booted up her laptop. No way was she letting her sister
down. "I can do this. The rehearsal's at four, so I have until then
to get it done." She turned to her mom. "Your zip drive has
pictures, right?"

"It does. But this seems like a big undertaking. You don't want to do a poor job."

A knock at the door startled them. Before Jess could run interference, her mom went to open it. Connor stood in the hall, carrying a cardboard tray with two coffees and a paper bag. "Oh… Good morning, Mrs. Chavez."

"Connor. What are *you* doing here?" She made no attempt to hide her displeasure.

Jess flashed him a look of desperation.

He gave her mom one of his patented, lady-killer smiles. "It's so nice to see you, Mrs. Chavez. I brought coffee for Jess, because her room's right next door to mine, and…"

"And the Keurig in my room doesn't work," Jess said. "Can you imagine? I can't function without my daily dose of caffeine."

"Right," Connor said. "She was complaining about it on the first day. As for me, I prefer a good, strong cappuccino to regular, brewed coffee. And you can't have coffee without pastries." He held up the bag. "Would you like a cinnamon roll?"

Her mom shook her head. "Not if I want to fit into my mother-of-the-bride dress. Why don't you come in? We're dealing with a small crisis."

"A *video* crisis." Jess wanted to make sure Connor understood the crisis did not involve her mom finding out about them.

Connor set the coffees on the desk. "Maybe I can help."

Jess showed him the binder with the handwritten note. "I need to put a video together in time for tonight's dinner."

"Why don't I bring my laptop over?" he said. "I have lots of family pictures on it."

"You store your photos on your laptop? That's so…responsible."

"Let's just say I've broken one too many phones. I'll get it and we can combine forces."

"Perfect," she said. "Do you mind if we start now? I only have until four o'clock." She gave him her key card. "Here."

"Thanks. I'll be right back." He pointed to the paper bag. "Don't eat the pain au chocolat. That one's mine."

Once he was gone, Jess chewed on her lower lip, bracing herself for her mom's interrogation. The temperature in the room felt like it had jumped ten degrees. "So...Connor and I made up. We're friends now."

Her mom raised her eyebrows. "I remember how much he hurt you."

She twisted her hands together. "That was five years ago. We've moved past all that."

Before her mom could probe any further, Jess leapt from her chair. "I should get dressed. I can't work on this project with Connor if I'm still in my bathrobe."

"I hope you know what you're doing."

She wasn't sure if her mom was referring to Connor or the video. Best not to ask. At some point she'd have to endure a lecture, but not now, when she had precious little time to create the perfect tribute to Marc and Gabi. She grabbed a tank top and shorts from her suitcase and dashed into the bathroom to change.

Her mom called out to her. "Jessica? Gabi sent me a text. She needs me to come to her room."

Thank God. "Okay. I'll text you if I have any questions about the video."

After Jess changed, she brought her laptop over to her bed. She set her coffee on the nightstand, along with one of the cinnamon rolls.

Seven hours, 120 photos. No problem.

When the door opened again, Connor returned, carrying his laptop. He sat down with it on the couch. "Should we get started?"

Her heart swelled with affection. This was his free time, yet he was here, helping her. But she still wished she hadn't dropped the ball. "You're not going to ream me out for being irresponsible?"

"Nope. Because you weren't irresponsible. This is an *extra* duty, and it's one Gabi wasn't expecting. Right? Otherwise, she would have listed it in the binder."

"True. The note was from Carly."

"So, if we get it done—great. If not, Gabi will never know."

His words filled her with a reassuring warmth. Even if she wasn't perfect, she was doing her best to be a damn good maid of honor. "You're very inspirational when you want to be."

He stretched out his hands. "I have to agree with you. Now tell me—what should I look for?"

"We'll want pictures of Marc and Gabi when they were kids, plus any recent photos. The rehearsal's not until four, so we have seven hours."

"A little less since we'll need time to shower and change."

"Shit. This isn't going to be easy." She put her head in her hands. She was tempted to say, "To hell with it," and forget the whole thing. But she could imagine Gabi's reaction when the video started playing. She'd be surprised, and then pleased, and then grateful to Jess for stepping up. And Jess would feel like she was more than just Gabi's second choice.

"It'll be fine," Connor said. "We've got this."

"But we also need music. Five or six songs, preferably ones Gabi and Marc like. And we'll need to edit them down."

"No problem. I know how to do that."

Relief coursed through her, loosening the tightness in her shoulders. "You do?"

"I'm a man of many talents. And not just in the bedroom."

She wagged her finger at him. "No bedroom talk, or we'll never get any work done." She gave him a cheeky grin. "But if we *do* finish early, I'm all yours. Any way you want me."

"With an offer like that, how can I resist?"

For the next few hours, she looked through pictures, setting aside her favorites in a folder on her laptop. Fortunately, her mom had done a fantastic job picking out photos from key moments in Gabi's life—birthday parties, dance recitals, swim meets, and graduation ceremonies. Jess discovered other photos in the cloud from their cell phones.

One of her favorites was a photo taken at Christmas, back when she was nine. She stood next to Gabi, under a raggedy excuse for a tree. Her mom had gotten it for half-price because she'd bought it on Christmas Eve.

"This picture brings back so many memories," she said.

Connor stood and stretched, then ambled over to her. He peered over her shoulder. "You look so cute. Is that an American Girl doll?"

She raised her eyebrows. "I didn't realize you were familiar with the American Girl line."

"Victoria had four of them. Plus, a ton of those overpriced accessories."

"This one's a knockoff from Walmart. We were broke, so a real American Girl doll was out of the question. But Gabi borrowed Mom's sewing machine and made all these outfits for my doll. She gave them to me on Christmas morning." She let out a sigh. "She was always looking out for me."

He kissed the top of her head. "That's not a bad thing. It probably made her feel important."

"But I'm such a mess compared to her." She didn't know if she'd ever be as poised, as confident, or as successful as Gabi.

"That's how I feel next to Darren. At least Gabi cares about you. Darren would be a lot happier if he was an only child." He reviewed the photos Jess had assembled. "Do you have any pictures from Big Bear?"

"Not as many as I thought. Didn't Victoria go through a big photography phase back when we were teens? I can't find any of them."

Connor rubbed his forehead. "I think Brody put them on a

photo-sharing site. Why don't you call him?" He went back to the couch and grabbed his laptop. "See if he'll email us the link."

She called Brody's number. He answered right away, his voice upbeat. "Hey, Jess. How's it going?"

"Do you have a sec? I'm putting together a video tribute for the rehearsal dinner. Connor said you might have an online album of the Big Bear photos?"

"Because you're *with* Connor right now, aren't you?"

"That's not important. I need those photos."

"Have you told him the truth yet?"

The last thing she needed was another guilt trip. "I don't have time for that right now. Can you *please* help me? Please, Mr. Frodo?"

After a lengthy pause, Brody sighed. "Fine. I'll help. This works in my favor, because the photos will go with the speech I'm giving tonight."

"What speech? Doesn't the best man usually give his toast at the reception?"

"I'm still doing that. This is different. Marc asked me to write a speech highlighting our favorite Big Bear memories. He thought it would emphasize the connection between our families. We could show your video after I'm done."

She shivered in excitement. Gabi would be so pleased at the symmetry. "Sounds awesome. I can't wait to hear it."

"Thanks. I've been working on it for a while. I'll email you and Connor the link for the photo site."

After Brody ended the call and sent the email, Connor pulled up the site right away. "This is perfect. You have to see these."

She joined him on the couch. She laughed at a photo of herself at age eight, clad in a neon green Little Mermaid swimsuit, her hair in pigtails. "Oh, my God. Is that me?" Next to her in the frame was twelve-year-old Connor, whose scraggly hair nearly reached his shoulders. "Check out your hair. I can't believe how long it was."

"That was the summer I refused to get it cut. I had this misguided notion it made me look tougher."

As Connor clicked through each photo, she was overcome with memories. Even if they'd only spent two weeks of each summer together, they'd had so much fun. Swimming and kayaking. Hiking up to Castle Rock. Sitting around the firepit at night and telling ghost stories. Picnics and second breakfasts and endless s'mores.

We have so much history together.

That was why her two weeks of passion with Connor had meant so much to her, back when she was eighteen.

That was why she'd bonded with him so quickly once they established a truce.

And that was *exactly* why she was falling in love with him all over again.

She couldn't deny it. The more time they spent together, the more time she wanted with him. Not just another night or another week, but something that would last. A real, honest-to-goodness relationship, with all the joys and sorrows it entailed.

But she couldn't tell him. She'd be breaking the rules. And if she so much as hinted she was falling in love with him, he'd run screaming in the other direction, like he had the last time.

"Jess?" Connor asked. "What do you think? Should we use some of these photos?"

"Definitely." She gave him a bright smile, suppressing the ache building up inside of her.

She'd told him she'd have no regrets when they parted.

Now she realized she'd regret losing him more than she had the first time.

CHAPTER 24

*A*fter finishing the video, Connor and Jess watched it twice to ensure it flowed smoothly. While he was impressed at their editing skills, Jess's reaction was more emotional than he expected. By the second viewing, she was openly weeping.

"It's so beautiful. The music's perfect. Gabi's going to love it."

"She'd better be grateful," he said.

"I'm sure she will be." Jess gave a satisfied sigh. "I finally feel like a worthy maid of honor."

He wished she weren't so obligated to her sister. By now, she'd done more than enough to prove her worthiness. Other than Tuesday, when she'd played hooky with him on the Road to Hana, she'd been the ideal maid of honor. But his irritation melted away when she gave him a seductive smile.

"Since we have an hour to spare, I'm all yours," she said.

"You sure?"

"One hundred percent. How would you like me?"

He took her hand and pulled her up so she was standing beside him. "The first thing we have to do is get rid of all those clothes. Then I'll think of something."

"My pleasure." She pulled her tank top over her head in a slow, leisurely way. The sight of her luscious breasts, nestled in a lacy pink bra, was an immediate turn-on. Her shorts followed, revealing matching panties. Watching her strip without a hint of inhibition aroused him even more. Her boldness was a far cry from the anxiety she'd shown when he removed her robe two days ago.

He was about to ask her if she'd get down on her knees when his phone rang. Uttering a groan of frustration, he grabbed it. "Shit. It's Marc. I should answer."

"No problem." She plopped onto the couch, still clad in her underwear.

He looked away, rather than be tempted. "Hey, Marc. What's up?"

"Are you free?"

Hell, no. He had a gorgeous woman stripped down to almost nothing, waiting to give him a blowjob. But he was also one of Marc's groomsmen. "What do you need?"

"We're having a small crisis."

Which meant Gabi was losing her shit over some tiny detail. But even if the request was ill-timed, he wasn't going to let Marc down. "Tell me what you need."

"Thanks. Yesterday, I picked up the wedding programs from the printer, but Gabi discovered a few typos. She asked that they be reprinted. The print shop called and said they're ready now. I'd go get them, except Gabi needs me to help with some last-minute stuff for the rehearsal dinner. And Brody already left for the airport to pick up Taylor."

"We don't have much time. Why don't I go first thing tomorrow before the wedding?"

"Are you kidding?" Marc's voice rose. "Gabi can't wait that long. She wants the bridesmaids to help her decorate the programs tonight, after dinner."

"Okay. Text me the address and I'll go get them." After he hung up, he expected Jess to be upset, but she merely shrugged.

"I'll have to owe you one," she said.

"You're not mad?"

"How could I be? You spent hours helping me with Gabi's video tribute. Sure, I was ready to fulfill your fantasies, but I can wait until tonight. Let's go save the wedding."

He chuckled. "We're just picking up the programs."

"Which Gabi obviously needs for the wedding. Therefore, we are once more proving our worth as the most vital members of the wedding party." She stood and gave her clothes a withering look. "What a shame to put these back on so soon."

"Don't make me feel worse than I already do." He checked his watch. "We'd better hurry if we're going to get to Lahaina and back in an hour."

As they headed out, he didn't think to suggest taking separate elevators, so he was relieved they didn't run into anyone from their families. So far, only Brody knew about them. They'd come so close to pulling off their secret that he didn't want to blow it this late in the game. Above all, he didn't want Jess to catch any flak from Gabi.

Once they were in the car, with the radio on, Jess sat back and put her feet up on the dashboard. "To be honest, it's just nice hanging out with you."

Strange how such a simple phrase could hit home. It *was* nice. Jess was one of the few people he felt completely comfortable with, who knew him for his true self.

After he found a parking spot in front of the printers, Jess dashed inside and picked up Gabi's order. Once she got back, she opened the box and took out one of the programs.

She whistled. "Check out this calligraphy. These are fancy as shit. And detailed. Everything's listed—the bridal party, the wedding vows, the songs, the order of the toasts. Jeez, there are *six* toasts. That's gonna take a while."

"I'm not supposed to give one, am I?" A surge of panic gripped him. He hadn't prepared anything.

She passed him the program. "Nope, and neither am I. Which is odd, because I thought the maid of honor usually gave a toast, right after the best man." She let out a long sigh. "Gabi probably assumed I'd botch it up."

He placed his hand on her thigh. "Sorry. That seems shitty."

She gave a sad shrug. "I agree, but I haven't exactly been a model maid of honor."

"What do you mean? Other than Hana, you've done everything Gabi asked."

"Except the one thing that matters most. She asked me not to get involved with you. And here I am, breaking that promise." She flashed him a look of concern. "Not that I regret any of this. I just wish Gabi hadn't put me in this position."

Irritation flared up inside him. "I realize she likes to be in control, but she's being ridiculous. It's your life, not hers."

"She can be overbearing, but I get it. She doesn't want me getting hurt again."

That was still no excuse. "Did you know she confronted me at the luau? She threatened to bust my balls."

"What? Why didn't you tell me?"

His anger melted away as he recalled the way the night had ended. "Because you were too intent on sneaking off to have sex on the beach. I wasn't going to ruin the moment."

Her cheeks flushed. "Oh yeah. That." She grinned. "But it was fun, wasn't it?"

"It was incredible." If he had one memory he'd want to keep, long after the trip was over, it would be their passionate encounter on the beach.

Jess pulled out a packet of papers, tied with a ribbon. "Get this. Even the rehearsal dinner has a program. It's just one sheet, but same calligraphy and everything." She handed him one.

He read it over. "What's the 'Tribute to Big Bear'? Is that our video? I thought Gabi didn't know about it."

"No, it's the speech Brody's giving. Sort of a greatest-hits recap from all our summers there. We'll show the video right after." She put the programs back in the box. "Maybe I'm being cynical, but this seems like a ton of work. I can see why people elope."

"Or fly off to Vegas for a quickie wedding."

She set the box on the floor of the car. "Would you ever consider it?"

"What? Marriage?" He almost laughed, until he noted her serious expression. "I don't know. The only time I came close was with Natasha, but she totally screwed me over."

"Sorry. I shouldn't have brought it up."

He squeezed her thigh. "It's okay. It's hard for me to trust anyone. Except maybe you. When I'm with you, I feel like I can tell you anything. Sometimes I wonder…"

"What?"

"It's nothing."

She frowned. "It's not, or you wouldn't have mentioned it."

"It doesn't matter. You're going back to Chicago in a couple of days."

"And if I wasn't?" Her voice shook.

Shit. What was he doing? How could he possibly string her along when their fling had an expiration date? There was no way he could consider extending it. Even in the best of circumstances, relationships were a ton of work. Toss in a two-thousand-mile separation and things were bound to get complicated. Not to mention, he was about to jump off a cliff, career-wise. He couldn't allow himself a single distraction.

Still, he really cared about Jess. He was so grateful they were friends again. And he'd had more fun with her in the past few days than he'd had all year.

But, clearly, he'd said the wrong thing because she looked

decidedly uneasy. Before he could smooth over the awkwardness, his phone rang, startling them both. In his haste to reply, he dropped it, then fumbled to answer it in time.

Marc didn't even bother with a greeting. "Yo. Did you get the programs?"

"Done. I checked them over and didn't see any typos."

"Are you headed back? Rehearsal's in thirty minutes."

He started the engine, then switched his phone to the car's Bluetooth speaker. "Yep. On my way."

During the drive, Marc filled him in on every detail of the past few hours, which was more information than he needed, but better than dealing with the weird tension emanating from Jess.

Maybe tonight, after the rehearsal dinner, they could talk.

Or...

They could have a few drinks, engage in wild, uninhibited sex, and forget this conversation.

Option two was definitely the way to go.

ONCE THEY WERE BACK at the hotel, Connor let Jess go on ahead to avoid anyone seeing them together. He followed a few minutes later, carrying the box of programs. He went up to his room, changed, and downed a shot of brandy. A quick check of the calendar app confirmed the details of the rehearsal: *Wedding Rehearsal, 4:00 – 4:45 p.m., Makai Terrace, mandatory attendance for all members of the wedding party, casual dress.*

Since dinner wasn't until six, he could get away with wearing another Hawaiian shirt, which beat the hell out of a button-down and a tie.

When he reached the grassy lawn, most of the wedding party was milling around, chatting and taking pictures. He set the programs down on a table that held the original wedding binder and walked over to Marc, Darren, and Lance, who stood together, waiting for things to get started.

Darren, who was wearing his typical "casual" attire—a Lacoste polo and pleated khakis—regarded him with contempt. "Nice shirt. It's even more hideous than the one Brody wore to the luau."

Ignoring his brother's insult, Connor scanned the crowd. "Speaking of Brody, shouldn't he be here?"

"He told me he had to pick up Taylor from the airport around two," Marc said. "But he should be back by now. Maybe her plane was delayed." He cast a quick glance over at Gabi. "I hope he makes it back in time for dinner, because Gabi doesn't need any more stress. She already got into it with Paige."

"Who's Paige?" Darren asked.

"One of the bridesmaids. She arrived this morning." Marc sighed. "I won't go into details, but—"

"Please don't." Connor had heard the entire story on the drive back from the print shop. Once again, Gabi was freaking out, this time because her friend Paige had gained a few pounds and couldn't fit into her custom-made bridesmaid dress.

Marc checked his watch. "It's ten after. We'll have to start without Brody." He hesitated a moment, as if bracing himself for a confrontation. "I'll go inform Gabi."

Connor didn't envy him, not with Gabi looking tenser by the minute. Somehow, Marc got her on board, and the rehearsal went as planned, with Connor standing in for Brody. When they were done, the wedding party dispersed, except for Gabi and Marc, who pulled Jess aside to talk to her.

Connor sidled over to them, keeping his voice casual. "Everything okay?"

Marc shook his head. "Still no sign of Brody."

"Maybe he's waiting at the airport," Jess said. "For all we know, Taylor's plane could have been late. Look at what happened to me. I arrived eleven hours later than I planned."

Gabi pulled out her phone. "I already checked. Her plane arrived ten minutes *early*. They should have gotten back here by three thirty at the latest."

"They haven't seen each other in a week," Connor said. "Maybe Brody turned off his phone." He imagined the scorching encounter he could have shared with Jess this afternoon, if he'd let his phone go to voicemail.

Gabi let out an exasperated breath. "We need to find him ASAP. And I can't deal with it because I have to handle Paige."

"Why don't I go look for him?" Jess said. "I can check his room or see if he and Taylor went to the pool."

"I'll head up the beach," Connor said. "Maybe they went for a walk. For all we know, they lost track of time. It happens."

It easily could have happened to him and Jess this afternoon. When he was with her, he found it easy to lose sight of everything.

"Are you sure?" Marc said. "You both have to get ready for dinner."

"Dinner doesn't start until six," Jess said. "We have over an hour. I don't mind helping."

Connor expected Gabi to thank her sister, but instead, she gave a curt nod. "Fine. He's staying in room 655. Make sure he's prepared. He's supposed to give that Big Bear tribute tonight."

"Why don't you have him wait until the reception?" Jess asked.

"Not possible," Gabi said. "That's when he's giving his toast as the best man. Having him make two speeches in one day seems excessive. Besides, the Big Bear stories were meant for our families, not for all the wedding guests." Her gaze swept the area. "Damn it. Paige's gone. I'll have to track her down."

Once Gabi and Marc had left, Connor took Jess's hands in his. With so much going on, he didn't want things between them to be strained. "You sure you're up for this? You still need to shower and dress for dinner tonight."

She gave him a wry smile. "I have less than twenty-four hours left as Gabi's maid of honor, and I intend to own it like a boss. I'll stop by Brody's room, then check out the pool and the bar. Do you want to cover the beach?"

"On it." He gave her a quick kiss, then headed for the pathway that led to Ka'anapali Beach.

For everyone's sake, he hoped they'd find Brody, and soon.

CHAPTER 25

$\mathscr{A}$fter Connor left, Jess went into the hotel lobby. Once inside, she perched on a wicker chair and centered herself with a few deep breaths.

You need to tell him the truth.

When they'd been at the print shop earlier, Connor's words had caught her off guard. Though he'd spoken without thinking, he'd implied he might want more than a fling. That he might be up for an actual relationship.

All this time, she'd been lying to protect her heart and give him an easy out. But what if he didn't want one?

How was she going to walk back all the lies she'd told? More than once, he'd mentioned the importance of trust, especially after the way Natasha treated him. What would he think when he learned Jess had lied about her life?

She'd tell him tonight. After dinner and a few drinks. And a steamy session in bed. Then she could fess up and apologize. Even if Natasha had left him with major trust issues, Jess was equally vulnerable.

For now, she had a rehearsal dinner to save. When she reached Brody's room, she waited before knocking. What if he and Taylor were in the middle of a passionate reunion? If it was anything like her sizzling encounter with Connor last night, an interruption would not be well received.

Her phone buzzed with a text from Gabi. *Any luck? Is Brody in his room?*

She wished her sister would calm down. The more Gabi stressed about the tiny details, the more she overreacted when something didn't go as planned. Chasing perfection was an endless cycle—as soon as one problem was dealt with, another came to take its place.

She knocked on Brody's door and called out his name, but no one answered. She replied to Gabi. *Not there. I'll check out the rest of the hotel.*

Gabi responded instantly. *Thanks! Keep looking! I'm counting on you!*

She almost replied that Brody was *not* her personal responsibility, but she held back. If she could find him and potentially save the day, she'd score another win as the ideal maid of honor.

She searched the hotel lobby, the adjoining bar, and the Molokini Cafe but saw no sign of Brody. Her luck turned when she went outside to the Coral Cove. Brody was seated at a table facing the pool. Alone.

"Brody?" She sat down across from him. "You okay?"

He looked up, bleary-eyed, and pushed his empty glass away. "Can you get me another whiskey?" His breath reeked of booze, and his ash-brown hair was a disheveled mess.

"What's going on? Where's Taylor?"

"Not here." He looked away, his eyes focused on a group of teens splashing each other in the pool.

She wanted to shake him, but she forced herself to be patient. "Did she miss her flight?"

Brody wouldn't meet her gaze. "She wasn't on the morning flight from San Diego. You know why? Because she never bought a plane ticket in the first place. Turns out she's seeing someone else. *Pierce*. But she waited until today to tell me."

"Oh, Brody. I'm so sorry." Her heart ached for him. She waved over a waiter and ordered a glass of ice water for Brody and a Diet Coke for herself.

"Do you think I should fly home tonight?" Brody asked. "To see if I could win her back?"

"No!" Her voice was so sharp Brody turned to face her. At his wounded expression, she softened her tone. "Your brother's counting on you. Even if you rush home, you might not be able to change Taylor's mind."

If her experience had taught her anything, desperate pleas for attention rarely worked. Instead, they drove the other person further away.

"This sucks." He plopped his head down on the table. "I need another drink."

She could relate. When Connor had broken up with her, she'd gotten wasted and called Gabi in drunken misery. And she'd done it more than once. Watching Brody act the same way made her aware of how much weight she'd put on her sister's shoulders.

When the waiter came with their drinks, she pushed the glass toward Brody. "Have some water. Otherwise, you're going to feel like crap."

"I already feel like crap." He lifted his head and took a sip of water. "Love stinks. What's the point, anyway? All you do is get your heart broken. Isn't that what usually happens to you?"

"Yeah. My luck's been bad so far."

She was always the one who ended up getting dumped. But that didn't mean she wanted to give up on relationships. Or romance. Even if her fling with Connor wouldn't last, she'd had more fun with him in Maui than she'd had in a long time.

"You need to sober up and get through tonight," she said. "Gabi and Marc are expecting you to give your tribute to Big Bear."

"I can't do it." He pulled a wad of folded-up index cards out of his pocket. "Here. You can read it for me."

She took a deep, shuddering breath. "Sure. No problem." Those Big Bear summers were ingrained in her DNA. But she could barely comprehend Brody's messy scrawl. "Do you have a copy on your phone? You could email it to me."

When he shook his head, she decided to call for backup. She texted Connor and told him to meet her at the bar. They needed to get Brody out of sight, in case someone from the wedding party came outside to have a drink before dinner.

Connor arrived, and she filled him in. He patted his cousin on the shoulder. "Sorry, Brody. If Taylor wasn't going to show, she should have told you ahead of time."

Brody slammed his head back on the table. "I know. I hate that asshole Pierce. What kind of a name is Pierce, anyway?"

Jess caught Connor's eye. "Can you help me get him to his room? He needs to sober up and take a shower."

"Sure." Connor flagged down the waiter and told him to charge the bill to his room number. Then he slung Brody's arm around his shoulder and pulled him to his feet. "Come on. We're heading back to your room."

Brody looked from Connor to Jess. "You two are fucking, aren't you?"

She put her head in her hands. "I already told you, when we were at Mt. Haleakala."

He turned on Connor. "You broke her heart last time!" His voice rose. "Do you know what that feels like? It feels like shit!"

Around them, people were staring. Jess cringed. "It's okay, Brody. No one's getting hurt."

"That's what they all say," he muttered. "Someone always gets hurt."

They eased Brody away from the bar and toward the elevators. Jess tried calling Gabi, but the call went to voicemail. On the chance her sister didn't check it right away, she sent her a text. *Found Brody at the bar. Taylor didn't show. He's drunk, but Connor will make sure he comes to dinner. Could he postpone his speech until tomorrow?*

No answer. *Shit.* Jess was at a loss. Gabi wouldn't appreciate any deviations from her carefully planned schedule. But Brody was a loose cannon.

In the elevator, Connor kept Brody upright. "I'll make sure he takes a shower and gets dressed. If we're running late, I'll text you."

She handed Connor the index cards. "Here. This is Brody's speech. I'd offer to read it for him, but his writing's barely legible. Make sure he doesn't lose it. And don't be late."

"It'll be fine. I promise." Connor leaned in to give her a quick kiss. "Now go get dressed, like the sexy maid of honor you are."

Back in her room, she tried to focus. She didn't have much time. As she stood in the shower, letting the warm water run over her, the tension ebbed from her body.

She might have gotten off to a rough start as Gabi's maid of honor, but since then, she'd made every effort to support her sister. She'd trekked up to a volcano, scoured Lahaina for shells, made a kick-ass video montage, and found the runaway best man. All she had to do now was keep things under control until Saturday, and she'd prove herself worthy.

So why did she suspect it wouldn't be that easy?

CHAPTER 26

Connor headed for Brody's hotel room, half dragging, half supporting his cousin. He'd never seen Brody turn to booze before. The last time some girl had dumped him, he'd holed up in his apartment and worked on a coding project for forty-eight hours straight.

He set Brody on the bed, then went into the bathroom and turned on the shower, testing the spray under his fingers until it warmed up. "Time to get into the shower. After that, you need to get ready for dinner."

"Don't need a shower. Had one this morning."

"Come on. You smell like booze. It'll help you sober up."

Brody flopped back on the pillows. "Nope." He closed his eyes. "Not going. Start the party without me."

"Gabi's counting on you. So's Marc."

"They can have the dinner with or without me. Lemme sleep."

A valid point. Brody could easily postpone his Big Bear tribute until the wedding reception. No one would care.

Except Gabi. And Connor was already on her shit list. If she found out he'd allowed Brody to blow off the rehearsal dinner, she'd hate him even more. He could handle her rage, but he didn't want her to take her frustrations out on Jess.

"If you don't go to dinner, Gabi's going to be mad at Jess," he said.

Brody lifted his head. "Why?"

"She asked Jess to track you down. And Jess needs to stay on her good side, because—"

"Because she's fucking you?" Brody burst out laughing. "It's all your fault. Gabi would kill you if she knew."

"She doesn't know. No one does except you. Now do me a solid and get into the shower." He gritted his teeth. "Otherwise, I'll throw you in there with your clothes on."

"No way."

"Don't tempt me." He grabbed Brody's arm. "Water's running."

Brody pulled away from him. "I'll do it. Don't you have to get ready, too?"

"I can't leave you here. You might fall and hit your head. Hurry up."

Brody got up, stumbled across the room, and went into the bathroom, slamming the door behind him. Connor sat on the couch and slumped back against the cushions. So far, so good. He just had to keep Brody away from the hard stuff until after dinner. No easy feat when all his cousin wanted to do was drink away the pain.

He could relate. He'd been there after Natasha left him. It hurt like hell. Hours spent wallowing in misery, second-guessing the choices he'd made. In retrospect, he was incredibly grateful not to have ended up with Natasha. But for the first few weeks after she left, he spent more than a few nights drowning his sorrows in booze.

Fifteen minutes later, Brody emerged from the shower. While waiting for him to get dressed, Connor scrolled through his emails, flagging the ones from Tom and Reb to review later. He'd finally told them the loan with his father wasn't going to happen, so they were searching for other investors.

"I'm ready," Brody said.

Connor glanced up. Though Brody needed a shave, he looked presentable enough, dressed in an expensive shirt, a tie, slacks, and a sports coat. "Great. Let's head over to my room. I need to shower and shave before we go down to dinner."

"You don't trust me on my own?"

"Nope. Come on." He led his cousin into the hallway, and they took the elevator up to Connor's room. Once inside, he told Brody to wait on the couch and handed him the remote. "I'll be about twenty minutes, tops."

"Got it." Brody turned on the TV and flipped around until he settled on the History Channel.

Perfect. There's no way he can get into trouble in twenty minutes.

With that in mind, Connor took a quick shower and shaved. He wished he were taking his time, getting ready with Jess, watching her transform from adorably messy to incredibly sexy. In just a few short days, she'd woven a spell over him. Even when she wasn't around, he couldn't stop thinking about her.

It's the sex. That's all. You haven't had decent sex since Natasha, and you're making up for it.

But it was more than that. He liked being with Jess. He always had. He remembered warm summer nights at Big Bear when they'd sat out by the firepit, talking about movies. They spent two hours one night discussing the logistics of time travel and the eras they would visit if they lucked into the DeLorean from *Back to the Future*. Another night, they did a deep dive into their favorite Stephen King flicks, with Jess insisting *Children of the Corn* was an underrated classic. When he was with her, he didn't need to maintain his bad-boy image. She saw him for exactly who he was.

He hadn't realized until now how much he'd missed her during the five years they'd been out of touch. What would happen when they ended things this time? Would he get to see her again? Or would she abandon their friendship once she got involved with someone else? The thought of her with another man filled him with an inexplicable surge of jealousy.

You want more than a week with her. You are so screwed.

But falling in love was out of the question. Not when she was going back to Chicago. Besides, he was about to plunge into a business enterprise that would eat up all his time. How could he imagine—even for a minute—that he could have a real relationship with anyone?

When he emerged from the bathroom, Brody was still on the couch, watching a documentary about World War II spies. Connor did a double take when he saw the half-full glass in Brody's hand. Next to it was the bottle of Valois Brandy.

How could he have forgotten about the brandy? "What the fuck are you doing?"

Brody gave him a loopy grin and raised his glass. "Cheers!"

He snatched the glass away. "What the hell, man?"

"I tried calling Taylor again, but she wouldn't answer the phone. So, I texted her. You know what she texted back? *Leave me alone. It's over.* That's it. We were together for six months! Do you know how much that hurts?"

He did. More than ever, he regretted the dismissive text he'd sent Jess five years ago. "It's awful. But you can't think about it now. We have to go to dinner."

"Not think about it? It's all I can think about." Brody leaned back on the couch.

Connor set the bottle of brandy in the trash. It was completely empty, which meant Brody had downed at least two glasses.

Jess showed up at his door a few minutes later, looking far too alluring in a sleeveless dress made of a soft green fabric that accentuated her shapely figure. She smelled of the delicious floral perfume she'd worn to the luau. A perfume that immediately brought back memories of their passionate encounter on the beach.

He wanted to pull her into his arms and devour her sweet mouth, but not with his cousin watching. Instead, he gave her an appreciative smile. "You look stunning."

She tugged on his dark blue tie. "Thanks. You're not so bad yourself." She offered Brody an encouraging smile. "Hey, bud. How are you doing?"

Brody gave her a salute and collapsed back on the couch.

Jess leaned toward Connor and lowered her voice. "He doesn't look too good."

"No kidding. He was sobering up nicely until he found the brandy."

"Oh, shit."

"Oh, shit is right," Connor said.

"I can hear you," Brody said in a singsong voice. "I'm fine. A little drunk, maybe, but socially acceptable."

"Please behave yourself," Jess said. "Gabi's counting on me."

Brody responded with a totally fake smile. "Of course. Wouldn't want to let down ol' Bridezilla."

This wasn't going well. The odds of them getting through dinner without incident were not in their favor.

CHAPTER 27

Jess eyed Brody warily as they took the elevator down to the lobby. Although he no longer smelled like a distillery, his gait was shaky, and his eyes had a hazy, unfocused look. He was a far cry from the bright-eyed, cheerful friend who'd greeted her at three thirty in the morning when they went up to Mt. Haleakala.

She wished she didn't feel responsible for his behavior. All she wanted to do was relax and enjoy the rehearsal dinner. At least she didn't have to worry about Gabi's video. While she was getting dressed, her mom had stopped by to upload the video to her zip drive. She told Jess the AV coordinator planned to play it after Brody's speech.

Providing he was coherent enough to make a speech. The evening might go more smoothly if Jess took his place. Even without his notes, she could remember enough funny memories from Big Bear to entertain the crowd. But Gabi might be upset if she took over.

"You doing okay, Brody?" she asked.

He startled, as though waking from a trance. "Yeah. I'm good."

He didn't look good. When they got off at the lobby, she took his arm and guided him toward the Sunset Terrace. Although the rehearsal dinner was being held in the same place as the formal dinner they'd attended three nights ago, tonight's decor was more elaborate. Gabi had obviously spent a lot of time on Pinterest.

The four tables were draped in ivory cloths, accented by brightly colored place settings and napkins. The center of each table displayed a vibrant tropical centerpiece containing orchids, red ginger, and birds of paradise. Encircling the centerpieces were a dozen candle holders, filled with sand, tiny shells, and votive candles. Palm leaves and larger shells were artfully scattered around each table. Both sets of shells were courtesy of Jess, who'd sourced them from shops in Lahaina and Kihei. The place cards were done in gold calligraphy, secured by tiny golden pineapples. A program for the rehearsal dinner was set on each plate.

Jess found her place at a table with her mom, Gabi, and the other bridesmaids. Connor led Brody to the table next to theirs and seated his cousin beside Marc. The two sets of Blackwood parents were at another table, further away. As soon as Jess sat down, a waiter approached and offered her wine. She glanced over at Brody. Another waiter was at his side, filling his glass. Not good. If he started drinking again, he'd never sober up.

She texted Connor. *Don't let Brody drink any more!*

He replied quickly. *I'll try! You need to warn Gabi.*

She took a sip of wine, hoping the alcohol would ease the tension building up inside of her. Though Gabi was deep in conversation with Luisa, Jess swallowed back her nerves and approached her sister. "Can we talk for a second?"

Gabi let out a long breath. "Please don't tell me there's another crisis."

Jess had seen Gabi like this before, on the afternoon of her graduation. She'd been set to speak as valedictorian, but the cards for her speech had gone missing. Even though she'd committed the cards to memory, she worked herself into a state of panic until she found them.

Like then, she was now operating at her maximum stress level. If Jess didn't defuse the situation, a meltdown was certain to follow.

She spoke calmly, knowing she'd aggravate her sister more if she rushed. "Did you see the text I sent? Brody's kind of...wasted."

Gabi rubbed her forehead. "Because of Taylor? That sucks."

Was she annoyed on Brody's behalf or because he was inebriated? Jess chose to give her the benefit of the doubt. "The poor guy's miserable. And he's too drunk to be giving a speech." She gnawed on her lip. "Do...do you want me to say a few words about Big Bear? Otherwise, Connor could do it."

At the mention of Connor's name, Gabi scowled. "Not a chance. He'd tell a bunch of raunchy stories just to get a laugh." She stood up. "I'll go talk to Marc. He can do it."

As Gabi flounced off to Marc's table, Jess tried to rein in her growing irritation. She would have been happy to give the tribute, especially since she wasn't scheduled to give a toast at the reception. But Gabi hadn't even considered her offer.

Luisa gave her a sympathetic smile. "Don't take it personally. Gabi's wound up tight from fighting with Paige. She and Marc were arguing right before I got here."

"About Brody or Paige?"

"About everything. Marc was asking her to calm down, but you know Gabi. When she's like this, telling her to calm down is like pouring gasoline on a fire." Luisa lifted her wineglass in a salute. "If I were you, I'd have a drink and enjoy dinner."

Luisa was right. Jess had done all she could to salvage the situation. If Gabi wanted Marc to give the tribute, then so be it.

As the waiters brought out the appetizers, Jess put Brody out of her mind and focused on the delicious food in front of her: coconut-macadamia shrimp, sesame crab cakes, lomi lomi salmon, tropical fruit kebabs, and mango spring rolls with avocado. Caught up in the conversation and lulled by the wine, she allowed herself to relax. The food was excellent, and she got into a lively conversation with Victoria about mystery novels. Like her, Victoria was an avid reader with strong opinions about her favorite authors.

Not until dinner was almost over, when Marc stood and tapped his wineglass, did Jess's earlier anxiety return. She looked over at Brody but couldn't tell if the food had helped counter the effects of the alcohol he'd consumed.

"If I could have your attention, please," Marc said. "I want to thank all of you for coming. Having you with us, as we take this big step, means more than I can say." The guests broke into applause, but Marc held up his hand. "I also want to thank Gabi for accepting my proposal. I'm so grateful to have her in my life, and I can't imagine anywhere I'd rather be than here, in this idyllic setting, about to make her my wife."

Jess wiped tears from the corners of her eyes. She wanted to believe that someday, she'd be as lucky as her sister. She'd meet someone who would love her unconditionally and put up with her impulsive behavior. Who would treat her like she was worthy and special. She let her gaze drift over to Connor, who was focused on his cousin. Of all the men she'd dated, Connor was the only one she'd ever dreamed of marrying.

Marc cleared his throat. "My cousins and I thought it might be fun to pay tribute to Big Bear, since that's where Gabi and I met. We made some unforgettable memories, and I'd like to highlight a few of them, so—"

Brody stood and pulled his crumpled note cards out of his pocket. "I've got this."

Marc paled. "Um... Brody? It's okay. Gabi asked me to take over."

"Nope. I prepared a whole speech. With funny stories and everything." Brody swayed and clutched the table but straightened himself out. He gestured for Marc to sit. "If you don't mind, I'd like to take my shot."

Marc hesitated a moment and then sat down. When Jess caught Connor's eye, he shook his head ruefully.

Not good.

"My fellow wedding-goers," Brody said. "I'm so glad to see all of you. Even though it's a long trip across the Pacific Ocean, you all made it. Well, not all of you. Not Taylor, the woman who was supposed to be at my side. The woman who claimed she loved me. She decided it wasn't worth the effort to spend a few days in paradise, not if it meant she'd be stuck with me."

Jess sucked in her breath. Gabi's mouth was set in a grim line, as if she knew things would get worse.

Brody lifted his glass and took a long drink of wine. "Yep, Taylor screwed me over royally, but Marc's more fortunate than I am. Because Gabi is as loyal and faithful as a woman could be. Look at her, everyone. Isn't she lovely? A round of applause for the bride."

Gabi smiled and ducked in her head in false modesty, but Jess sensed she was seething inside.

"None of this would have been possible if we hadn't spent our summer vacations at Big Bear," Brody said. "Fortune favored us, fifteen years ago, when we met the Chavez girls, who were staying at the cabin next to ours."

Jess shot a nervous glance at the other tables. Everyone was listening intently, as if eager to hear more stories. Even if Brody was drunk, he'd gotten back on track.

He continued. "We created some incredible memories— swimming, boating, hiking, making bonfires, and occasionally getting drunk on Blackwood Cellars wine when the folks weren't around." He raised his glass in a salute to the senior Blackwoods. "Sorry, guys, but we pilfered a lot of wine."

"We figured as much," his father called out. "We may be old, but we're not completely oblivious."

Brody laughed. "I guess we weren't as sneaky as we thought. Anyway, I always knew there was something special between Marc and Gabi. Right from the day we met, when Gabi challenged Marc to that infamous swimming race, I could tell they were meant for each other. As we grew up, the two of them slipped away more and more, leaving us to wonder what they were up to."

Jess let out a sigh of contentment. She could look back on those days without regret, now that her memories weren't tainted by heartbreak.

"Of course, theirs wasn't the only romance going on at Big Bear. Everyone knew about Jess's childhood crush on Connor, but what most of you *didn't* know was that they finally hooked up once Jess turned eighteen." Brody chuckled. "And by the looks of it, they're having just as much fun in Maui as they did at Big Bear. I guess some habits never die, right?"

No. Jess's cheeks flooded with warmth. If she had to guess, she'd say this revelation had *not* been part of Brody's original speech. She wanted to vanish in a puff of smoke, but instead, she had to endure the shocked looks of everyone at her table.

Brody gestured toward her. "Don't worry, Jess. I'll make sure Connor doesn't break your heart again. Good old Brody has your back."

Oh God. "Thanks, Brody," she said weakly.

"I'm glad you're moving back to California because I've missed the hell out of you. Chicago's too far away." Brody swayed, then righted himself on the arm of the chair. "Whoa. Why is the ground moving? Was that an earthquake?"

He stepped back unsteadily, sending his chair flying backward. His leg caught on one of the rungs, and he stumbled over it, collapsing onto the grass. Connor sprang up to help him and half led, half dragged him away from the terrace.

No one spoke. Then Marc stood and addressed the guests.

"Sorry, everyone. I'm going to make sure my brother's okay, but I'll be back in a few minutes. Please, enjoy dinner."

As Marc left, Jess wished she could follow him. All she wanted to do was hide in her hotel room and escape the inevitable questions.

But it was too late.

CHAPTER 28

*J*ess swallowed back the painful ache in her throat. Not only had Brody exposed her lies, he'd done it at a time when Gabi was stressed to the breaking point. Just like that, all the attempts Jess had made to support her sister no longer mattered. Not when her deception had been outed in such a public fashion.

"You're moving back home?" her mom said. "How long have you been planning this?"

Gabi was right on her heels. "What's going on with Connor? You said nothing happened."

"You slept with Connor?" Victoria said. "I thought you were over him."

Jess hoped the Blackwood parents weren't listening in, but they seemed immersed in their own conversation, probably discussing Brody's epic fall from grace. She spoke quietly, hoping her family would do the same. "One question at a time."

"Me first," her mom said. "Why are you leaving Chicago? What about your job?"

"I got laid off at the end of March after Simon dumped me,"

Jess said. "I've been working at temp jobs, but I can't afford to live in Chicago anymore."

"Why didn't you tell us?" her mom asked.

Jess tried to control the waver in her voice. Bursting into ugly tears would only add to her humiliation. "Losing Simon was bad enough. But losing my job made me feel like a total failure. I thought if you found out, you'd expect me to come home, and I still wanted to give Chicago a chance. I tried to find something else, but I failed. I hope it's okay I'm moving back next month. It's only temporary—until I get a job and a place of my own."

"Of course it's okay." Her mom stood up. She walked over to Jess and held out her arms.

She stood, surprised her mom was offering a hug, rather than a lecture. She leaned against her, inhaling the familiar scent of roses. "You're not mad?"

"How could I be mad? It's not your fault. I'm sorry Chicago didn't work out."

"Thanks, Mama." After all this time, telling the truth was like lifting an enormous weight from her shoulders.

Gabi's voice cut razor-sharp. "What about Connor? When did that start?"

"A couple of days ago." Jess stepped back from her mom's embrace. Telling everyone about Chicago was one thing. Fessing up about Connor was a much greater level of mortification.

"You told me you were just friends," Gabi said. "Was that a lie?"

She bowed her head in shame. "Sort of. You said you didn't want any drama."

"So, you saved your big reveal for tonight?" As Gabi stood to face her sister, her voice rose above the buzz of conversation, capturing the attention of the other guests. "Why not announce it at the wedding before Marc and I were about to exchange vows? Wouldn't that have more impact?"

Jess forced herself to meet her gaze. The fury in Gabi's eyes made her recoil. "I didn't mean for everyone to find out tonight. That was Brody, not me."

Over at the far table, the Blackwoods were now watching the Chavez women as if they were a trashy reality show.

"But Brody knew, didn't he?" Gabi said. "And I didn't. I'm your sister. How could you tell him everything and leave me out?"

Was that why Gabi was so upset? Because Jess hadn't confided in her? Though she thought her sister was overreacting, she kept her tone humble. "Sorry. I didn't think you'd understand."

"I'm the one who stood by you after Connor dumped you five years ago. I was there for you, no matter what. I deserved to hear the truth."

Her mom frowned. "Shh. People are staring."

Gabi clenched her hands. "I don't care! What I care about is the fact that, once again, Jess has taken center stage! Why does it always have to be about you? Can't you let me enjoy the spotlight for once?"

Jess took a deep, calming breath. She told herself Gabi was under a lot of pressure. But it didn't matter anymore. She was *done* letting her sister push her around. "Stop treating me like crap! I've tried to do everything you asked, but you always make me feel I'm not worthy."

"You're not. I never should have asked you to stand in as my maid of honor. All you care about is yourself."

Jess blinked back tears. She'd tried to do better. But Gabi didn't care. All she did was pass judgment. Bile rose in her throat. "If anyone's selfish, it's you."

"How can you say that?" Gabi said. "This week is *supposed* to be about me."

Marc and Connor had returned, and they approached the table cautiously. Marc placed his hand on Gabi's arm. "How about you ease up a little? Let's not ruin dinner."

Gabi wrenched away from his grip. "If dinner is ruined, it's because of Jess!"

"The only one who ruined things was Brody, and you don't see me yelling at him," Marc said. "If anything, I feel sorry for him. Not everyone can achieve your level of perfection."

"What's that supposed to mean?" she said.

"You set unrealistically high standards for all of us. Cut your sister some slack, for once."

Gabi glared at Jess. "I hope you're happy. Now you've turned my fiancé against me. I am so done with you!" She stormed away from the terrace.

Marc waited for a beat, then addressed the crowd again. "Just a last-minute hiccup. Nothing we can't work out. Why don't you finish dinner? The waiters will be bringing dessert soon."

How could he be so calm? Jess's heart was beating a million miles a minute. "Aren't you going after her?"

"If I know Gabi, she's too mad to listen right now," Marc said. "I'll let her cool off."

She could barely meet his eyes. "I'm sorry. I told Brody that stuff in confidence."

"Don't worry about it. I'm not upset with you or Brody. The poor guy. He was crazy about Taylor."

After he returned to his table, Jess sat down. Her hands trembled so badly she could barely hold her wineglass. Though she hadn't finished all her dinner, the thought of food no longer held any appeal. She pushed her plate away.

Her mom rose from the table. "I need to talk to the AV coordinator. Maybe he can arrange to have Gabi's video playing during the wedding reception."

"Sorry." Jess felt tinier than a speck of dust. She'd not only ruined her sister's rehearsal dinner by getting into a catfight with her, she'd forgotten about her video.

Even with the bride now absent, the waiters proceeded as if nothing was amiss, whisking away the dinner plates and bringing out the final course. Dessert presented an array of delicious choices: key lime pie, mango coconut cheesecake, passion fruit tartlets, and mini pineapple upside-down cakes. But Jess was too upset to eat. She glanced toward Connor's table, hoping to catch his eye, but his stormy expression gave her pause.

As the waiters cleared the dessert, Connor was the first one to rise from his table. Before Jess could call out to him, he was already on his way out.

She excused herself and went after him. "Connor, wait!"

He ignored her, his stride so brisk she didn't catch up until he reached the stone pathway leading back to the hotel. "I'm sorry," she said. "I didn't know Brody was going to expose us."

Connor turned toward her, his face as hard as flint. "Why didn't you tell me you were moving back to Riverside?"

She swallowed. "I was going to, but—"

"Bullshit. If you found the time to tell Brody, you could have told me. You had plenty of chances."

"I'm sorry. I shouldn't have lied. But I was afraid."

"Afraid of what?"

Anguish welled up inside her, making her stomach churn. "Afraid you'd feel pressured because I was moving back home. I didn't think you'd want to get involved with me if you knew I'd be living so close by. By telling you I was going back to Chicago, I gave you an easy out."

Connor pulled open the door to the hotel lobby. "What makes you think I wanted an easy out?"

She followed him but stopped short when they got inside. Bracing herself on an end table, she responded in anger. "Isn't that what you always want from your hookups? No-strings sex? No romance, no tears, no commitment?"

"*You're* the one who made those rules, not me. And if you thought I was such a dick, then why'd you come after me?" His jaw tightened. "Oh, wait. I know. For the sex. That's all it was to you, wasn't it? Just sex."

"So what if it was? You think I'd let myself fall for you again after the way you ended things last time?"

When he flinched, she knew her words had struck home. He spoke softly, with none of the fury he'd shown earlier. "I thought you trusted me."

"I wanted to, but…" Tears burned her eyes, but she made no effort to wipe them away. The truth was, she hadn't opened up to him completely. She was so worried about frightening him off that she put up boundaries.

He let out a harsh breath. "Were you planning on moving back home without telling me? And hoping I wouldn't find out, even though you'd only be an hour away?"

When he put it that way, she sounded sneaky. Deceitful. But all she'd been doing was protecting her heart.

"I thought it wouldn't matter because you'd be over me. You wouldn't want me around. Not when you're about to start your own winery. After the way I threw myself at you last time, you should be grateful I gave you a guilt-free way to end things."

Even as she said the words, she cursed herself. All she was doing was pushing him away. By now, the bank of elevators loomed ahead. Her heart rate sped up. In a minute, Connor would go up to his room and she'd lose him. But before she could apologize, he turned on her.

"You're right. I *am* grateful. You've made it so much easier for me to cut you out of my life without a shred of guilt. So, thanks, Jess. The sex was great."

His words hit her like a gut punch. Before she could reply, he strode off toward the elevator. And she was left alone, in the wake of the devastation she'd wrought.

CHAPTER 29

A chill ran through Jess, prickling her skin with goose bumps. She couldn't move. Couldn't speak. All she could do was stand motionless, stung by the cruelty of Connor's parting remarks. He'd never been this mean before. Deliberately mean, like he wanted to hurt her. To make her experience the same pain he was feeling.

"Jessica?" Her mom came up behind her and took her arm. "We need to talk."

How much had she heard? "Do we have to?" she asked.

Her mom tightened her grip. "Let's go have a drink."

She led Jess through the lobby and into Jolly Roger's—a noisy, dimly lit bar with a nautical theme. The bartenders and waitstaff all sported some type of pirate gear: bandannas, puffy shirts, pirate hats, and red sashes. Jess shuddered. No matter how much she'd hated her temp jobs, none of them had required her to dress in costume.

Her mom found an empty table tucked into a far corner. "I think we could both use a tropical drink right now. They make a delicious Blue Hawaiian."

"Just a rum and Coke for me, thanks." She couldn't risk getting drunk, or even tipsy. She'd already made enough mistakes.

Her mom ordered the drinks but waited until after they arrived to start asking questions. Jess confessed everything: how she'd been laid off in March, how she'd spent days applying for work, and how she'd taken on low-paying temp jobs just to survive.

When she was done, her mom let out a long sigh, more in sympathy than in exasperation. "I wish you'd told me sooner."

"Sorry, but I was tired of calling you or Gabi every time I had a crisis. And I didn't want to admit I failed." Tears welled up in her eyes. "I'm sorry I'm such a disappointment."

"You're not a disappointment."

"Sure I am. Compared to Gabi, my life is one giant mess." Jess searched her purse for a Kleenex. When she couldn't find one, she had to wipe her eyes with a skull-and-crossbones cocktail napkin. *Pathetic.* "I'll never be good enough for you."

"Jessica Elena Chavez, I have never said that. Not once."

She prickled with irritation. "Then why do you compare me to Gabi every chance you get? You wish I were more like her."

"I wish we were *both* more like her."

"What are you talking about? You're great at your job. Zach thinks you're indispensable."

"I'm good at my job, yes, but I made some terrible decisions. I could have gotten a scholarship to college, all paid for. But I threw it away because a smooth-talking white boy took an interest in me. I was so afraid to lose him I didn't have the courage to say no. And then I paid for it when I found out I was pregnant."

Her mom rarely shared stories of the past. Whenever Jess or Gabi had asked, she'd deflected, saying the memories were too painful to share. For the first time, Jess wondered if her mom ever felt as inadequate as she did. Especially since her older sisters, Carmen and Elena, were both college graduates.

Jess sought to console her. "It was one mistake."

Her mom gave a bitter laugh. "It was a *huge* mistake. His parents hated me. He only married me because I was pregnant with Gabi." She narrowed her eyes. "You and Connor *have* been using protection, right?"

Her cheeks heated up. "Of course. I've been on the pill since college."

"And he always uses a condom, right?"

She did not want to be having this conversation. Not in this universe or any other. She looked down at her drink and focused on the red swizzle stick. "Yes."

"Good girl." Her mom finished her cocktail, then flagged down their waiter. "I'll have another. Jessica—what about you?"

"Sure." Another rum and Coke wouldn't kill her. A little buzz might lessen the pain. "Back to what you were saying about Dad. Do you think he ever loved you? I mean, you stayed together for four years. And you had me."

Her mom sighed. "He told me he loved me, but he wasn't faithful. I'm surprised he stayed as long as he did."

"Mama, I'm so sorry." For all the mistakes Jess had made, for all the lousy guys she'd dated, she'd never experienced that level of anguish.

"I'm glad he left. The hardest part was trying to provide for the two of you. I'm so grateful my sisters were around to help. If it weren't for Carmen and Elena, I would have been on my own." Her mom frowned. "That's why it bothered me when Gabi wanted her wedding here, because I knew they couldn't afford to come." She thanked the waiter as he set down their drinks, then gave Jess a slight smile. "It's a good thing your sister's having that party in August, or they might hold a grudge forever."

Jess considered how the family might react to her own news. "They're going to think I'm a loser, aren't they?"

"I doubt it. They've seen me go through much worse. Like you, I've made some bad decisions, so I understand how you feel. But you shouldn't hide things from me."

Jess didn't want to argue, but if she didn't speak up, she might lose her chance. "I won't. In return, you could go easier on me, once in a while."

"I'm sorry. But you're just like I was. You're so impulsive. When you went to Chicago with Simon, you weren't even sure if you loved him. But you wanted an adventure. You leap into relationships without thinking, and the men you choose treat you badly. I don't want you to suffer the way I did."

"I get that. But you have to stop comparing me to Gabi." Jess sniffed and wiped her eyes again. "It doesn't help. If anything, it makes me feel ten times worse."

Her mom blinked and looked away, as though fighting back tears of her own. "I'll try not to do it in the future."

Having her mother concede anything was a huge win. "Thanks. For what it's worth, I was going to tell you everything after the wedding, but I didn't want my news to ruin Gabi's big day." She sighed. "Obviously, I fucked up."

"Language. And you didn't ruin Gabi's wedding." Her mom clucked her tongue. "She's made this much harder than it has to be, always wanting things to be perfect."

Jess twisted the swizzle stick between her fingers. "But what if she calls off the wedding? I'll feel so guilty."

"Somehow, I predict it will still go as planned. Gabi usually gets what she wants. As much as I love that girl, she intimidates me. But I think you're the brave one."

"Me? I'm the one who breaks down whenever there's a crisis."

"You're also the one who moved to Chicago on your own. And you didn't fail. You had a good job, but things didn't work out. That's what happens when we take risks—we get hurt or have to start over. But taking risks is how we grow."

The words hit Jess like a smack upside the head because they also applied to her and Connor. She'd lied and said she wouldn't be available, because if she told him she was moving back to California, she'd be taking a huge risk. Rather than let him break her heart, she hadn't possessed the courage to tell him the truth.

What a coward I was. No wonder Connor was mad at me.

"Jessica?" her mom asked. "When did you say you were planning on moving back home?"

"In a few weeks. Is that okay? That way, I can help with Gabi's party in August."

"Of course. Whenever you're ready." Her mom's mouth quirked up in a smile. "I just need to move my sewing machine out of your bedroom. You're welcome to stay as long as you want, but I think you should consider taking a few classes to acquire some practical skills."

"I checked online and there's a UC Riverside extension class in basic accounting I could take." Not that she wanted to be an accountant. But it wouldn't hurt to have a backup plan, for once.

"Perfect. You might find accounting suits you." Her mom finished her drink and set the glass aside. "What about Connor? Are you two going to be together since you'll be living so close to him?"

If only. "I don't think he wants me back. I can't say I blame him, considering I lied to him about every aspect of my life."

"Maybe you're better off without him. He didn't treat you very well last time you were together."

"He's changed since then." Saying it made her realize it was true. He *had* changed. And she hadn't let herself see it, because she was so caught up in protecting her feelings.

Her mom pointed to Jess's cocktail glass. "Do you want another one?"

"Maybe just a Sprite, thanks."

Over the next round of drinks, Jess entertained her mom with anecdotes from her temp jobs and caught up with all the hot Chavez gossip. She couldn't remember the last time they'd had such a long, grown-up conversation. For once, Gabi wasn't around to hog all the attention.

As they got up to leave, her mom gave her another hug. "This was nice. We should do it more often once you come home."

"I'd like that," Jess said.

"I have to warn you—I've been trying a healthier lifestyle. Instead of coffee, I've been making smoothies for breakfast. Healthy ones, with kale."

Kale? She shuddered. "But you still have the coffeepot, right?"

"Of course. I could never abandon coffee completely."

Thank God.

After her mom went back to her room, Jess had to decide whether she wanted to track down Connor or Gabi. Though she suspected neither of them wanted to talk to her, she owed both an apology. She went outside to see if they were at the Coral Cove. No luck. Instead, she ran into Victoria, who was standing at the bar, waiting for a drink.

Victoria tilted her head to the side. "Are you doing okay?" Her voice lacked its characteristic snark. "That scene with your sister was rough."

Having Victoria—of all people—regard her with sympathy almost brought her to tears. *Again.* "I've been better. Sorry I lied about Connor. I didn't want you to think I was an idiot. Right from the first day, you told me he wasn't worth it."

Victoria gave a lengthy sigh. "That was just me being snotty. I shouldn't have said that. He's changed a lot this year."

Jess nodded. "I wouldn't have gotten involved with him otherwise."

"It's just—he hurt you before. He talked about it when he came back from Spain."

He'd discussed her with Victoria? Jess was about to ask for more details, but the bartender slid a cosmopolitan toward Victoria. "Here you go, miss."

"Put it on my bill. Room 962." She turned to Jess. "Do you want a drink?"

"I'd better not." She was almost afraid to ask but was too curious to let it go. Connor had never mentioned he'd confided in Victoria. "What...what did Connor tell you?"

Victoria sipped her drink. "After his trip, he moved back home for a few weeks. We had a lot of time to talk. I'd been through hell that summer, and I needed a shoulder to cry on. He told me what happened at Big Bear and how he ghosted you afterward. At one point, he was thinking of going to Irvine to talk to you. But it's better he didn't."

Jess's voice cracked. "Why? I would have loved an apology."

The bartender caught her eye. "Can I get anything for you, miss?"

She shook her head, keeping her focus on Victoria.

"Honestly? If Connor had shown up at your dorm, you wouldn't have gotten over him. You would have kept believing he was your one true love. Better to get your heart broken than end up with him."

"Why?" She hated how needy she sounded, but she was desperate for clarity.

"He wasn't in a good place. After he started working for Darren, he turned into a total asshole. He'd go out drinking with his friends and bring home a different woman every weekend. He wasn't the guy you grew up with."

Though Connor had told her almost the same thing, hearing it from Victoria hammered the message in Jess's brain. Maybe it was better he'd left her so abruptly. Since she'd assumed she had no chance with him, she was able to move on. She'd gone to college, dated other guys, and followed her dreams. She might have nursed a grudge for five years, but she hadn't put her life on hold because of him.

Victoria took another sip of her cosmo. "But if I were you, I'd forget about Connor right now."

"What do you mean?"

"I mean your top priority should be finding your sister. She might have been way out of line, but she still needs you."

CHAPTER 30

onnor paced in his hotel room. After he'd returned from dinner, he had every intention of making a few calls. With his winery plan in jeopardy, he needed to seek out more investors. But he couldn't concentrate. Not on his winery. Not on *anything*. He kept remembering the way Jess had reacted when he'd delivered his parting blow. She flinched in pain, which was exactly what he wanted.

So why did he feel like shit?

And why was he mad at her, anyway? She'd kept her word— she hadn't declared her love or asked him for anything more than five days of sex.

But she'd lied to him. From that first night, when she came into his hotel room wearing nothing but his t-shirt, she'd spun a web of lies about Chicago. Rather than admitting her bold move had failed, she'd encouraged him to take a similar risk with his own life.

What stung the most was that he'd tried to act like a decent guy. If she'd just been a booty call, he wouldn't have shared his winery plan with her. Or spent six hours helping her put together Marc and Gabi's video.

But she didn't think he'd changed. She might have slept with him, but she didn't trust him enough to let him into her life.

When his phone buzzed with a text, he was tempted to shut it off. He had no interest in hearing any of Jess's half-assed excuses.

His phone buzzed again. He forced himself to look at it.

Marc had sent him a text. *Need a drink? I'm on the top floor in the penthouse suite.*

Guilt surged through him, twisting his insides. By sleeping with Jess, he'd gone against Marc's wishes. But if his cousin wanted to ream him out, better to deal with it now than let things simmer. He changed into a t-shirt and shorts, then headed up the elevator to the twentieth floor. When Marc let him in, Connor stared in awe.

The suite had an enormous canopied bed, a huge Jacuzzi tub, a full wet bar, and floor-to-ceiling windows that looked out onto the ocean. Next to the bar was a six-foot-tall, freestanding aquarium.

"Holy shit." The aquarium was filled with colorful coral and tropical fish, like the kind Connor had seen snorkeling. "Is this for real?"

"Pretty wild, huh? Gabi loves it. *Finding Nemo* was her favorite movie as a kid. I realize this place is over-the-top, but I wanted to make her happy."

He couldn't stop staring. The Jacuzzi was big enough for six people. Same with the bed.

Marc made his way behind the bar. "What'll you have? I've got cab, beer, brandy, champagne, and bourbon."

"Bourbon. Neat." The stronger the booze, the quicker it would numb his feelings.

Marc poured them each a glass, then sat down on one of the leather-clad barstools. Connor eased himself onto a barstool and downed half the bourbon in one gulp, wincing as it burned his throat. He hadn't felt this bad since the night Natasha had walked out on him. Which was ludicrous, because he'd been with Natasha for eight months, whereas Jess…

What *was* Jess? A passing diversion? Or something more?

Definitely more. If she was just a passing diversion, her betrayal wouldn't hurt so badly.

He rubbed his forehead. Who was he kidding? In the short time they'd been together, he'd fallen back in love with her.

That was why he was so pissed. Not just because she'd lied, but because he'd never intended to get in this deep. He'd had his fill of relationships after his soul-crushing experience with Natasha. Clearly, his heart hadn't gotten the damn memo.

"Connor? You okay?"

Marc's voice brought him back to earth. As he met his cousin's eyes, he was hit with another surge of guilt, even stronger than the first. Here he was, moping over Jess, while Marc's fiancée was missing. On the night before the wedding, no less.

"I'm good. But what about Gabi? Shouldn't you be out looking for her?"

Marc waved the suggestion away. "Nah. When she's this mad, the best thing to do is give her some space. I'll wait a while, then I'll text her and apologize. She'll come back, and we'll talk it out rationally."

He could hardly believe how calm Marc seemed. "Does this happen a lot?"

"Only over the big stuff. The last time she walked out on one of our arguments was when we were planning the wedding. I didn't want a destination wedding. I wanted to have it at the Blackwood Cellars Estate in Temecula or at one of our Napa vineyards so more of our family could come."

"What happened?"

"Gabi left for a couple hours, drove around, probably called Jess. Then I texted her and said I was sorry. I asked if she could come back so we could talk it out. And we did. Like two rational adults."

"Why'd you give in?" He drained the rest of his glass and refilled it from the bottle.

"Because Gabi wanted it so badly. She's obsessed with having the perfect wedding, partly because her mom had a crappy courthouse wedding and her marriage ended in divorce. Gabi doesn't want the same thing to happen to her."

Connor kept quiet. A fancy wedding was no guarantee a couple would stay together. Or that they'd have a good marriage. He'd seen photos of his parents' lavish wedding, but he wouldn't call their marriage "good" by any stretch of the imagination. His father had been unfaithful to his mother for years and routinely cheated on her during his business trips. Connor suspected his mother knew about it but resigned herself to looking the other way.

"While you're here, you want to help me finish the wedding programs?" Marc said. "Gabi was going to ask Luisa and Jess to come up after dinner, but that's not going to happen now."

"Aren't the programs fine, as is?"

"Nope. We have to get them done tonight, as per Gabi's specifications." Marc walked over to a small table in the corner of the suite.

Connor topped off his bourbon, then joined Marc at the table, which held the box of programs he'd picked up from Lahaina.

Marc rifled through a shopping bag on the floor, then pulled out a large Ziploc bag filled with blue and purple ribbons. "I already punched holes along the edge of the programs. Gabi wants these ribbons woven through the holes. Like this." He held up a finished one. "Got it?"

Connor nodded. The bourbon was giving him a buzz, but he'd give it a shot. His first attempt was a disaster. As he looked around at all the wedding paraphernalia—menus, lists, photos of flower arrangements, bags filled with votive candles and bags of shells—his stomach curdled in shame. Marc was dealing with all this shit himself, and Connor was partly to blame.

"Hey, man, sorry if I fucked things up for you, even temporarily."

"Don't apologize. What happened at dinner was Brody's fault. Gabi overreacted."

He stared as Marc wove his ribbons flawlessly. "Yeah, but you asked me not to get involved with Jess, and I did it anyway. That's on me."

"I shouldn't have asked in the first place. It's your vacation. What you do with your free time is your business." Marc blew out a long breath. "The only reason I brought it up was because Gabi insisted on it. But, if you think about it, she wanted Jess to have fun on this trip, and obviously, she did. Right?"

"Right." He and Jess were both consenting adults. If Gabi hadn't demanded they stay apart, they wouldn't have gone to such lengths to hide their fling.

"I'm not even mad at Brody," Marc added. "Poor guy got his nuts handed to him on a platter. And I'm not mad at Jess either. She didn't want this."

"But she brought it on herself."

Marc gave him a look of genuine confusion. "You're mad at her? Why?"

He bristled with anger. "She lied to me. About everything. Fed me all this bullshit about her great life in Chicago."

Marc took Connor's program and unwound the ribbons. "Not good enough. Try again." He handed the program back to him. "Maybe Jess's lies had nothing to do with you. Maybe she was ashamed to be seen as a failure."

"I wouldn't call her a failure. She took a risk, and it didn't work out. That's not her fault." Like Jess, he'd made his share of mistakes, but he didn't want them to define him.

"I'm not so sure," Marc said. "Gabi was so excited when Jess got that job in Chicago because it seemed like her luck was finally changing. But instead of succeeding, she ended up with nothing. No boyfriend. No job. No apartment. Now she has to come home and start all over again. So, it wasn't about you."

Connor grunted. If Jess felt like a failure, she should have told him. She knew how much he was struggling, trying to decide whether to leave the security of Blackwood Cellars for the risk of starting a new business. Given all the hours they'd spent talking —not just fucking, but actually talking—he assumed she was comfortable sharing anything with him.

Obviously, he'd been wrong.

He finally got the ribbons to weave the correct way. He showed it to Marc. "Here. Nailed it."

Marc smirked and pointed to his pile. He'd already completed five.

Connor got up to pour himself another finger of booze. The way tonight was headed, he was going to need it.

CHAPTER 31

$\mathcal{U}$pon leaving the Coral Cove, Jess was tempted to retreat to her room. Few things sounded more appealing than changing into her pj's and watching a few hours of mindless TV. But she needed to set things right with Gabi. Even if her sister had been at her worst, Jess wanted her to be happy. And she wanted the wedding to go as planned.

She sent Marc a text. *Is Gabi back yet?*

He called her immediately. "I haven't seen her. I thought if I let her cool off, she'd be okay, but when I tried her phone fifteen minutes ago, she didn't answer. I'm getting worried."

"Did you call Luisa or Paige? Maybe she's having a drink with them."

"I tried. Neither of them has seen her since dinner." He sighed. "It isn't like her to keep me hanging this long. Even if she leaves in a huff, she always comes back. Then we talk things out until we reach an agreement."

Jess couldn't stop the snark from creeping into her voice. "Until you agree with her, you mean?"

"Pretty much."

Gabi always got her way. *That* was why she hadn't returned.

She wasn't mad at Marc. She was mad at Jess. And she'd only come around if *Jess* admitted she was wrong.

"I'll call her," she said. "If I beg for forgiveness, she'll probably talk to me."

"None of this was your fault. Brody's the one who messed up. I'd wake him, but he's sleeping off the booze."

"Let him sleep. Gabi doesn't want his apology. She wants mine. Not just for tonight, but for all the times I lied to her." And for failing to confide in her, the way she had before.

"Can you call me as soon as you've talked to her?" Marc said. "I won't be able to sleep until I know she's all right."

He was such a sweetheart. "Of course."

After ending the call, Jess braced herself and brought up Gabi's number. No response. Rather than leave a voicemail, she sent her sister a text. *Sorry I ruined your rehearsal dinner. Any chance we could talk???*

Gabi responded seconds later. *I'm walking on the beach. I've got nothing to say to you.*

Which was Gabi-code for "get your butt over here and prepare to grovel." Jess headed back outside, kicking off her heels and holding them in one hand so she could run on the sand. At night, the beach had a haunting, romantic feel, illuminated by the light of a full moon. When she passed a couple in the throes of a passionate embrace, she was overcome with memories. Two nights ago, she and Connor had done the same thing. When he'd held her in his arms, he'd looked at her with such tenderness she almost believed he loved her.

Stop it. You don't have time for this.

She ran down the beach, scanning the area for Gabi, until she found her sitting on a large rock, staring out into the waves.

"That was quick," Gabi said. "What'd you do—run?"

Jess leaned over, hands on her knees, gasping for breath. "Yeah. But...I'm out of shape." She gestured to a rock next to her sister. "Mind if I sit down?"

Gabi scowled. "It's not like I can stop you."

"I came here to say I'm sorry. I'm sorry for lying to you and Mama about Chicago. You told me no drama, so I thought it was better if I didn't say anything, but—"

"Bullshit." Gabi sprang up and loomed over her. "I meant no public meltdowns. Nothing that would embarrass me in front of the Blackwoods. But you could have told me and Mama privately."

"But if I told Mama, she would have worried about my future when she was supposed to be paying attention to you."

"Stop making excuses. This isn't about me. It's about you. Admit it, Jess. Just admit the fucking truth."

Jess's stomach pitched as the shame washed over her. She couldn't keep hiding behind her lies. It was time to be honest with everyone. Including herself.

She tucked her hands under her thighs to stop them from shaking. "You're right. Mostly, I hid the truth because I was ashamed. I didn't want everyone to know I failed, especially the Blackwoods."

"Especially Connor, you mean. You wanted to act like you had your shit together with your new life and your cool job. Right?"

As always, Gabi could see right through her. "Yeah. I didn't want everyone asking me questions, like what I was going to do with my life and how long I planned to live at home. But it's still no excuse for lying to you."

"You're right. It's no excuse. And it's certainly not my fault."

"Sorry." Jess hung her head and blinked quickly, willing herself not to cry again.

Usually, at this point, her sister would concede. But instead, Gabi's voice rose, reaching a new level of rage. "You think saying sorry is going to make up for it? You ruined my rehearsal dinner. Never mind I spent hours planning it, choosing the menu, and making sure everything was perfect."

Perfect. There was that word again. Aiming for perfection was admirable, but there was also something to be said for rolling with the punches when life didn't go your way. Like Jess had been doing for most of her life.

Her mood shifted from apologetic to irritated. It wasn't like she *planned* to fight with Gabi in a public setting. "In all fairness, if Brody hadn't said anything, dinner would have been fine."

"But—"

Jess stood up to face her. "Let me finish. Even after Brody passed out, we could have carried on like normal, and you could have confronted me after dinner, somewhere private, but instead you blew up at me in front of your guests." She clenched her fists as her guilt turned to anger. "You're the one who had a tantrum and stalked out of your own dinner like a five-year-old. That's on *you*."

Her sister's face crumpled. She started crying. "It's all ruined, isn't it? My perfect wedding is ruined!"

Now Jess was *done*. "Will you stop? Most people will *never* have a wedding like this. You don't get to make this incident into a big trauma because your rehearsal dinner wasn't perfect."

Gabi stared at her in shock. "God, Jess, I expected a little more sympathy."

"Then earn it. Stop yelling at everyone—me, Marc, Brody, Connor. We're trying to be supportive, but we're not perfect. No one is. And your wedding is *not* ruined. If I were you, I'd hold my head up, walk down that aisle, and act like nothing happened. You just need to keep swimming. You know—like Dory."

For a moment, Gabi said nothing. She sniffed and wiped her eyes, then gave Jess a weak smile. "I love that movie."

"I know. You've seen it—what—twenty times?"

"At least. Did you know there's an aquarium in my suite?"

"*An aquarium*? Do you know how lucky you are? Marc adores you. Everyone here loves you. All you have to do is pull off a beautiful wedding, and *that's* what people will remember."

"Easy for you to say." Gabi searched in her purse for a

Kleenex, then blew her nose. "You're not the one getting married."

"No, but unlike you, I've screwed up a lot, and I didn't have any choice but to keep going. I've been dumped multiple times, lost jobs, gotten in trouble at school, been publicly humiliated—and I've never let it stop me. That's one of the benefits of *not* being perfect."

As Jess said it, she felt proud of herself. Being perfect was one thing. But screwing up and having the courage to try again? That took a lot more guts. Maybe being an adult didn't mean she'd stop making mistakes. It meant she'd own up to them right away and try to do better.

Gabi wrung her hands together. "What if Marc doesn't want to get married? He's already gotten annoyed with me because of the way I micromanage things. And we argued right before dinner because I was mad at Paige and he took her side."

Jess wrapped her arms around herself. She was getting chilly, but she wasn't going to suggest leaving until Gabi was ready. "You were mad because her bridesmaid's dress didn't fit?"

"Because she's pregnant. She didn't tell me before because she wanted to surprise me. Some surprise! She gained thirteen pounds. Mom had to adjust the back of the dress so the zipper would close. Do you have any idea how stressful that was?"

Ouch. "Did you congratulate Paige? She must have been excited to share the news."

Gabi looked away. "Oh, God. I didn't. I'm a total bitch, aren't I?"

"Sometimes. You just need to relax. Everyone's having a great time. And if they didn't join in all the events you planned, then they had fun doing other things."

"I know, but I feel so much pressure," Gabi said. "I want this wedding to be perfect. I know a perfect wedding doesn't mean I'll have a perfect marriage, but I'm scared of ending up like Mama."

"You won't. Marc's never going to leave you. You're lucky to have someone who loves you that much." Jess's voice broke as she thought about Connor and what a mess she'd made.

"You're still in love with Connor, aren't you?"

She nodded, fighting back tears.

"I don't get it. What happened?"

Jess recounted the way Connor had come to her aid after the Blue Lagoon and invited her to explore the Road to Hana the next morning. "I didn't lie about that. When we spent the day together, we were just friends. After he offered me a *real* apology for the way he left me, I decided to give him a second chance. I'm the one who pursued him."

Gabi gave her a sly smile. "And was he worth it?"

"He totally was." She sighed. "But it's over. He was furious I didn't tell him I was moving back home. I shouldn't be upset, since I told myself this was a vacation fling and we'd end it when we left Maui, but I guess I never got over him."

A couple strolled by, arms around each other, no doubt seeking a place to be alone. Watching them, Jess ached with regret. If dinner hadn't turned into a complete debacle, she'd be with Connor right now, enjoying their second-to-last night together.

"Have you told him how you feel?" Gabi said.

"Nope. And it's too late now."

Jess's phone buzzed. Marc had sent a text. *Any sign of Gabi?*

"Marc's checking up on you," she said. "Can I let him know you're okay?"

Gabi smiled. "You can tell him. Thanks."

"Got it. Are we good now? I promise to behave myself tomorrow. No secret announcements. No scandals. Just support."

"We're good. Sorry I was such a bitch." Gabi moved in closer and gave her a hug. Jess hugged her back tightly. At least she'd mended one fence tonight.

She returned Marc's text. *Found her. On our way back.*

When they returned to the hotel, Marc was waiting in the

lobby, talking to Connor. Although Connor wouldn't meet her eyes, Jess was relieved he hadn't retreated to his room for the night. If she apologized again, he might be willing to listen.

Yeah, right. He looks like he'd rather be anywhere else right now.

"Thanks for finding my wayward bride," Marc said.

"No problem," Jess replied. "Sorry I caused so much drama."

"It's fine." Marc put his arm around Gabi and squeezed her shoulder. "What's a wedding without a little drama?"

Her heart swelled at the sight of them together. Gabi had nothing to worry about.

"I'm heading up for the night. Big day tomorrow." She kept her voice even, despite the churning sensation in her stomach. Would Connor follow her?

"Same. I'm ready to crash. See you in the morning." Connor turned and headed toward the bank of elevators.

When they reached the elevators, they stood in silence. Anyone observing them from a distance would assume they were strangers rather than two people who'd engaged in wild, passionate sex the previous night. As the seconds passed, Jess sensed her chances slipping away.

Say something, damn it.

She wiped her palms on the sides of her dress. "Umm... Connor? I know you're mad, and you have every right to be, but I'm really sorry."

"I know."

The elevator doors opened, and they got on.

She waited for him to say more. To accept her apology. But he stayed maddeningly silent as the elevator made its ascent. She wiped her hands on her dress again, trying to remove stubborn grains of sand from between her fingers. "If you want to talk, you can come by my room."

He kept his focus above the elevator doors, watching as the numbers rose. "There's nothing to talk about. I don't trust you, and it's obvious you feel the same way about me."

She fought back another round of tears. Connor was done with her, and she had to accept it.

They walked down the hall toward their rooms without speaking. Although Connor was giving off a dangerous don't-fuck-with-me vibe, she was tempted to hurl herself in front of him and confess her true feelings.

I don't want our fling to end. I love you as much as I did when I was eighteen.

But would he believe her after all the lies she'd told? Not anymore.

When she got to her door, she wished him good night and went into her room.

It was over.

CHAPTER 32

Though Jess hadn't planned to wake before sunrise, she couldn't fall back to sleep. Whenever she closed her eyes, memories of the disastrous rehearsal dinner came back to haunt her. She recalled the crushing guilt she felt when Brody exposed her lies. The pain she suffered when Gabi told her she wasn't worthy. And the gut-wrenching sensation she experienced when Connor said he couldn't trust her. His accusations hurt worst of all.

Stop. Enough with the self-pity.

Even if Connor hadn't forgiven her, she'd made amends with Gabi. And she'd been honest with her mom for the first time in years. It was time to stop wallowing in the past.

Besides, today was all about Gabi, and Jess wanted to support her in whatever way she could. Like a *real* maid of honor.

She brewed a cup of coffee and brought it out to the balcony. Though her heart had taken a pummeling, she could still enjoy the spectacular view. The steady roar of the waves infused her with a sense of tranquility, easing the tension from her neck and shoulders.

She took out her phone and checked Instagram. The first

photo on her feed was one from Gabi. She'd taken a picture of her veil, posed next to a cluster of hibiscus flowers, along with the caption, *Today's the big day!*

Jess sent her a text. *Happy Wedding Day! You're up early.*

She responded right away. *Marc's still in bed. But I'm too stressed to sleep. What if something goes wrong?*

Instead of bristling in irritation at her sister's constant desire for perfection, Jess's heart went out to her. She sent another text. *Call me if you need to talk.*

Seconds later, her phone rang. "Hey, Gabi," she said. "You doing okay?"

"Hang on," Gabi whispered. "I'm going out to the balcony so I don't wake Marc."

Jess sipped her coffee and waited until Gabi's voice came back on the line. "Everything good with you and Marc?"

"We made up last night. I'm…so lucky to have him." Gabi's voice trembled.

"Are you crying? What is it?" Jess set her mug to the side. "Do you want to come over? We could order room service and watch *Say Yes to the Dress*." It wasn't as though she had anything else on her agenda before the photo shoot at ten. Consoling Gabi would give her a sense of purpose.

"I'll be okay. I think it's bridal stress. Or the fear that everyone hates me because I've been yelling at them all week."

Jess wished she could take those words back. "I'm sorry I said that. No one hates you. We just want you to relax and have fun."

"Like you did with Connor?" Gabi's voice was more teasing than accusatory.

She let out a sigh. "It was nice while it lasted."

"You didn't make up last night?"

"Nope. No makeup sex. But I was fine." No need to tell Gabi she'd stayed up much too late, watching *The Princess Diaries* on the Disney Channel and bursting into tears at random moments.

"Hold on, okay?" Gabi said. "I'm getting another call."

"At this hour?"

"I'm not sure who it is. Can I call you back?"

"Sure. I'm not going anywhere." If Jess had to guess who was calling this early, her money would be on someone from the Chavez clan. Her cousins were probably oblivious to the time difference between Maui and California.

While she waited, she continued perusing Instagram. To her immense relief, the pictures Gabi and Victoria had posted from the rehearsal dinner were taken before Brody's speech. She liked all the photos but refrained from leaving comments. She couldn't exactly say, *What an amazing night!* when the night had turned out to be anything but amazing.

After twenty minutes, she was tempted to jump in the shower, but she didn't want to miss Gabi's call. She looked through her recent photos, swallowing back tears when she got to the ones from Hana. Why hadn't she told Connor the truth then? She'd had plenty of chances, especially since he'd been honest about his painful breakup with Natasha.

Her phone rang, startling her out of her reverie. She answered it quickly. "I'm here. Who was calling?"

"So…this isn't a big deal in the grand scheme of things. But… the bakery called. And…" Gabi's voice broke. "There was a problem with the compressor in one of their refrigerated units. It broke down in the middle of the night, and no one noticed until they showed up for work this morning. All those mini cheesecakes I ordered? They're not safe for human consumption."

"Shit. That's terrible."

When Gabi had come up with the idea of serving mini cheesecakes, rather than a wedding cake, Jess had heartily endorsed the idea. Who didn't love cheesecake? The photos Gabi had sent looked delicious, with flavors like mango margarita, piña colada, lemon blueberry, and white-chocolate raspberry. She and Marc had also ordered a large chocolate-truffle cheesecake for the cake cutting.

"I called the resort's catering kitchen to see if they could provide a last-minute cake," Gabi said. "But they're swamped because they're dealing with two weddings today. The one after mine is much bigger, with a full sit-down dinner."

Damn. The bakery snafu wasn't a huge crisis, especially since Gabi's brunch menu leaned heavily on sweeter options. But her sister had wanted a memorable dessert to cap off the reception.

"What did the bakery say?" Jess asked. "They're the ones that messed up."

"They can't make enough mini cheesecakes in time for them to cool and set. They suggested we go with something else. But I can't accept a substitution, sight unseen. Whatever I pick would have to go with my wedding aesthetic. And I don't have time to go down there. I mean, I could, but—"

"I'll do it." The words flew out of Jess's mouth before she had time to think them over. "I'm already awake. I'll go talk to the bakery and see what dessert options they have available. I can send you pictures. I'll even do taste tests, if need be."

It might be nice to help with someone else's crisis instead of focusing on her own problems.

"Would you? That would be wonderful. I'll call the bakery and let them know you're coming. It's Decadent Desserts on Front Street, in downtown Lahaina. I'm texting you the address. You can use the hotel trolley to get there."

"Okay. I'll text you once I know more." Jess went back into her room and grabbed a t-shirt and a pair of shorts from her suitcase. But when she called the lobby, the clerk told her the trolley didn't start running until 9:00 a.m. Not an option, considering she needed to be back for photos by ten. She was about to pull up her ride-share app when she thought of another solution.

One that was bound to be uncomfortable but made more sense than relying on an unknown driver.

After taking a deep, fortifying breath, she called Connor. The fact that he answered immediately made her suspect he'd already been awake.

"Jess," he grumbled. "What is it?"

His response was so off-putting she almost hung up. But she pushed past her anxiety and plowed on ahead. "Are you up and dressed? If so, I need a favor. Before you say no, it's for Gabi. And it's a legit wedding emergency."

A lengthy pause followed, making her regret reaching out to him. Maybe a ride-share was the best option. But what if she had to bring back a giant cake?

Connor sighed. "Fill me in. But it had better be a *real* emergency."

She gave him a quick rundown. Again, she had to wait for him to answer, and when he did, he prefaced it with another sigh. "Give me ten minutes and I'll meet you in the lobby."

Relief washed over her, allowing her to breathe freely. With no time to shower, she attempted to tame her messy curls but gave up after a troublesome snarl brought tears to her eyes. Makeup wasn't worth the effort. What did it matter if she looked like shit? Connor wouldn't care.

When she got to the lobby, Connor was leaning against the wall, next to the bank of elevators. Like her, he wore a t-shirt and shorts and sported a messy case of bedhead. Normally, she might have teased him or ruffled his hair, but his grim expression dissuaded her. Without saying a word, he gestured for her to follow him, and they headed out to the parking lot. The silence unnerved her, but she kept her mouth shut.

You're doing this for Gabi. Connor can suck it up and help.

Once inside the car, Jess pulled up the bakery's address on her phone and set it on the console. Rather than deal with Connor's grumpiness, she leaned against the window and closed her eyes.

If she was lucky, she might sneak in a ten-minute catnap.

CHAPTER 33

*A*fter a few minutes on the road, Connor couldn't take the silence. "Any idea what kind of dessert Gabi wants? Or are we supposed to wing it?"

When Jess didn't answer, he glanced over at her. She leaned against the passenger-side window, eyes closed, as if she'd already conked out. Either that or she was pretending to sleep. Not that he blamed her. He'd barely been civil when he answered the phone. And he acted like she was putting him out, when he'd been awake since six, too miserable to fall back to sleep.

Now that twelve hours had passed since the rehearsal dinner, he regretted the way he'd treated her. He shouldn't have blown up. Or left her looking so forlorn, all but begging him for another chance. After he went into his room for the night, he debated going back to her. But he let his stubborn pride get in the way.

As he struggled to fall asleep, his cousin's words echoed in his head. *Maybe Jess was ashamed to be seen as a failure.*

Was that why she'd hidden the truth? Out of shame? Connor knew what it was like to be the less spectacular sibling, the one who paled in comparison. How would he feel if he attempted his winery venture only to have it fail? Would he want to admit it at first?

He told himself to let it go. Even if their fling had ended a day early, they'd both gotten what they wanted—a fun, tropical affair with great sex and no strings. It wasn't as though they planned to continue seeing each other after the wedding.

Then why did he feel so conflicted?

Because, deep down inside, he wanted more.

Not going to happen. Your life's complicated enough as it is.

As Jess had instructed, he pulled up behind the bakery, next to a row of employee parking spaces. Since the place didn't open to the public until eight, Gabi had asked one of the morning bakers to allow them into the back of the kitchen.

He nudged Jess. "Wake up, Sleeping Beauty."

"Huh?" She blinked and rubbed her eyes. "Sorry. I didn't mean to drift off, but I barely slept last night. Thanks for driving us here."

"No problem. Let's go see what we're dealing with." He got out of the car, with Jess following behind. When they knocked on the door, a burly man with a shaved head answered. Given his muscular physique and the full slate of tattoos on his arms, he resembled a wrestler more than a baker.

"Morning," he said. "Are you two my bride and groom?"

In sync, Connor and Jess looked at each other and burst out laughing. "Hell, no," she said. "We're lowly members of the wedding party, dispatched on behalf of the couple. We're here to figure out a quick fix for the dessert situation."

"Come on in. The name's Kai. I'm one of the morning bakers."

As they walked inside, the aroma of baked goods made Connor's mouth water. His stomach growled, reminding him he hadn't eaten since last night's dinner. He might have to pick up a few donuts, since the wedding brunch was still hours away.

Kai led them to the bakery's storage area, which housed a couple of large standing refrigerators with glass panels. He pointed to the closest one. "We've been having trouble with the compressor on this unit, but we put off getting it fixed. Bad move on our part. This morning when we opened it, we discovered everything inside it was warm, including the mini cheesecakes your bride ordered. We had to toss them."

Jess chewed on her lip. "Good call. We can't have anyone getting food poisoning at Gabi's wedding."

"We can offer you a full refund, but I'm guessing your bride wants a substitution. How about a tower of donuts? We've done those for other brunch weddings, and they've been a hit. Kids love them."

Connor thought it sounded like an easy solution. "Perfect. What's not to love about a tower of donuts?"

Jess gave him a fierce glare. "Be serious. Gabi would never forgive me if I went with something so basic."

He scowled right back. "You have a better idea?"

"How about a cupcake tower?" Kai asked. "These days, a lot of brides prefer them over cake, since it allows them to choose multiple flavors."

Connor held back, waiting for Jess's reaction. This time, she bestowed a full-wattage smile on the baker. "That could work. Especially if you have a few tropical flavors, like the ones Gabi picked for her cheesecakes."

Kai pulled a binder from an overhead shelf. He opened it and passed it to Jess. "Here. These are the flavors we've baked today. We only have a few cupcake orders to fill this morning, so we can set aside enough for your wedding."

Jess motioned for Connor to join her. "Come help me choose."

He raised his eyebrows. "You sure you want my input?"

She rolled her eyes playfully. "Of course. You like dessert as much as I do. And for the record, there's nothing *wrong* with a donut tower. But it wouldn't be a good look for Gabi."

"Fair enough." He peeked over her shoulder and found it hard to resist her enthusiasm as she squealed over the cupcake choices: pineapple coconut, mango vanilla, key lime, red velvet, chocolate mousse, and salted caramel.

She took out her phone and snapped a few pictures. "I'll check in with Gabi." A minute later, she gave him a thumbs-up. "*Yes.* She's fully on board. And she'll contact the catering staff at the resort to ask if they'll arrange the cupcakes in a couple of towers, decorated with tropical flowers." She smiled at Kai. "I'll have the exact numbers for you in a minute."

"Sure..." Kai's enthusiasm seemed muted. "But before we go any further, remind me what time the wedding's taking place?"

"It's at eleven," Jess said. "But I'd rather take the cupcakes with me than have you deliver them later. The bride's kind of... anxious about everything going perfectly." She glanced at Connor. "Is that all right with you?"

He nodded. Knowing Gabi, she wouldn't relax until Jess confirmed she'd hand-delivered the cupcakes herself.

"There's just one problem," Kai said. "We haven't finished frosting them."

"Shit." Jess clapped her hand over her mouth. "Sorry. How long will it take?"

Kai paused before speaking. "Give me an hour. Maybe longer, depending on how the morning goes. We have a lot of orders to make up."

Connor pulled out his phone. Seven thirty. They still needed to drive back to the hotel, shower, and change. They'd be cutting things close. The last thing he wanted to do was show up late. He could only imagine his dad's reaction. But after Jess sent him a pleading look, he conceded. "It's fine. We'll wait."

Which was how they found themselves sitting at a wrought-iron bistro table outside the bakery, drinking coffee and sharing cupcakes. Jess had insisted on ordering a few, just to test them out, and he wasn't about to say no. Despite the early hour, a few tourists were already strolling along Front Street, drinking coffee and taking photos. A gentle breeze blew in from the harbor, and gulls swooped overhead.

Jess cut up the cupcakes and gave them each a sample of the four flavors Gabi had chosen. After a few sips of coffee and half a salted caramel cupcake, Connor had recovered from his initial fatigue. All things considered, sitting outdoors with Jess and drinking coffee in Maui on a gorgeous July morning wasn't a bad place to be.

As if sensing the change in his mood, Jess sought out his gaze. "Connor? I'm sorry you have to wait here with me."

He shrugged. "No worries. I didn't mean to snap at you earlier. Now that I've got some coffee into my system, I feel a little more human."

"I'm...also sorry I screwed up everything."

He was getting tired of hearing that. "You didn't screw up. Screwing up implies you tried and failed. Which is perfectly understandable. You *lied* to me. There's a difference."

She drew back as if he'd slapped her. "You're right. I'm sorry. I shouldn't have lied. It was a shitty thing to do."

At least she was owning up to her failings rather than blaming them on someone else. He drained his coffee and set the cup down. "I just wish you'd trusted me from the start."

"I guess I was scared after what happened last time." She blinked back tears. "I should have known you'd changed."

She should have. But in the clear light of morning, he could understand her reluctance. After the way she'd been hurt before —not just by him, but by that asshole, Simon—it was a wonder she trusted anyone. He'd been much too hard on her.

He reached across the table and entwined his fingers with hers. "I'm sorry, too. I reacted badly and said things I didn't mean."

"You don't have to apologize. You're not the one who lied."

"No, but I shut you down when you wanted to talk. I should

have given you a chance to explain. Then we both might have slept better."

A couple of cyclists pulled up and locked their bikes on a post outside the bakery. He waited until they'd gone inside to continue.

"The thing is—we both lied. Right from the start, we messed up by keeping this fling a secret from Marc and Gabi. We shouldn't have done it."

"Done what—had a fling?" Jess pulled her hand away, the hurt evident in her eyes.

Her vulnerable expression cut him to the core. "No. Our fling was the best thing about this trip. But we shouldn't have lied to our families. They asked too much of us. We're both adults. If we wanted to get involved with each other, that was our business, not theirs."

"You're right. And if we'd been honest with them, last night would have gone off perfectly, like Gabi wanted."

"True, but it wouldn't have been nearly as entertaining."

She burst out laughing. "We're the worst, aren't we?"

"Nah, we're just not perfect. Like ninety-nine percent of the population."

She gave him a shy smile. "You really think the fling was the best thing about the trip?"

He grinned. "Piña coladas are overrated. A beach is a beach. But being with you? That's unbeatable."

Even as he said it, he longed to take her back in his arms.

Good thing his flight was leaving in twelve hours.

If he stuck around much longer, he'd never want things to end.

CHAPTER 34

By the time the cupcakes were frosted, decorated, and boxed up, Jess had started checking her phone every five minutes. The last two texts she'd received from Gabi had been somewhat frantic, making her regret her offer to deliver the cupcakes personally. On the upside, the hour-long wait gave her time to reconnect with Connor. Once the ice between them had thawed, they eased into a comfortable conversation and enjoyed the beautiful summer morning.

After dropping off the cupcakes at the resort kitchen, Jess raced up to her room. She barely had time to shower, dress, and dry her hair before Gabi texted her with a ten-minute warning. She wanted all the bridesmaids to assemble in her suite before the photos so they could put the finishing touches on their hair and makeup together.

As Jess checked out her reflection in the bathroom mirror, she had to credit her sister's taste. The bridesmaids' dresses were not only beautiful but flattering as well. Her dress was a strapless lavender confection that fell to her knees in a series of layers. The design enhanced her figure, while the light color brought out her newly acquired tan. She slipped on a pair of nude heels, grabbed her clutch purse, and left her room.

When she stepped into Gabi's suite, she stood, transfixed. Her sister hadn't been kidding about the aquarium. It was easily six feet tall and filled with colorful tropical fish.

Gabi enveloped her in a hug. "I'm so glad you're here. I was terrified you wouldn't make it back in time."

"It's all good. The cupcakes are in capable hands. They're going to set them up in a couple of artfully decorated towers, as per your instructions." She gave her sister a teasing grin. "Chef Lani said you were *very* insistent."

"You know me. Even when things don't go according to plan, I need to take control."

"I can vouch they're delicious. Connor and I shared a few while we were waiting for them to get frosted."

Gabi arched her eyebrows. "I thought you two were at odds."

"We were. But the trolley wasn't running, and I needed quick, reliable transport, so I sucked it up and called him." She couldn't stop the sappy smile that spread across her face. "I'm glad we went together because it gave us a chance to talk. And we got to help you out. It doesn't make up for the shit storm we caused last night, but—"

"But you know I forgave you, right? You've been a huge help this week. I'd rather have you standing beside me as my maid of honor than a twenty-foot tower of cupcakes."

"Thanks." For the first time since she came to Maui, Jess no longer felt like the *second-string* maid of honor. Or the second-string anything. "Speaking of which, Connor thought you'd be satisfied with a tower of donuts."

Gabi's smile bubbled into laughter. "You're kidding." When Jess shook her head, Gabi laughed harder. "Thank you *so* much for talking him out of it."

Their mom showed up a few minutes later along with Marc's mom, and Paige, Luisa, and Victoria. Right on their heels were the wedding coordinator and her assistant. While the coordinator reviewed the details of the ceremony, her assistant pinned tropical flowers in everyone's hair. They were almost ready when a knock came at the door.

Jess answered it and found Brody in the hall, looking spiffy in his tux. His eyes were a little red, but otherwise, he gave no sign he was recovering from an epic bender.

"Hey, Jess. Marc wanted me to tell you the photographer's ready."

"Perfect," she said. "We'll be down in a few minutes."

He gestured for her to come into the hallway. "Can I talk to you for a sec?"

His hushed voice made her tense up. She went out with him and closed the door behind her. "Everything okay? Please tell me there are no last-minute emergencies."

"Nope. I wanted to catch you alone." He rubbed the back of his neck. "I feel terrible about what happened last night."

Poor Brody. He'd suffered even more than she had. "You remember all of it?"

"Unfortunately, yes." He winced. "I was a drunken asshole."

"I wouldn't go that far. You were upset about Taylor and got drunk. It happens."

"But I told everyone your secrets. That was a dick move."

Yesterday, she might have snapped at him, but she wasn't angry anymore. Especially after the morning she'd spent with Connor.

"It's partly my fault for not telling the truth to begin with," she said. "If I'd been honest, none of this would have happened."

"I screwed things up for you and Connor, didn't I?"

She gave a sad shrug. "It wasn't going to last. It was just a fling."

"Are you sure? Because it seemed like more."

If only. She and Connor might have come to a truce at the

bakery, but that didn't mean they had any hope of a future together. "Nope. Just a vacation romance."

The door opened and Paige poked her head out. "The coordinator said we need to get going."

Jess gave Brody a quick hug. "I'd better go. See you out there."

Gabi and the bridesmaids made their way to the Makai Terrace, the oceanfront lawn where the wedding was taking place. White wooden chairs and a matching canopy were already set up, and the grassy aisle was strewn with rose petals. Each row of chairs was festooned with lacy white bows, palm branches, and a cluster of white, pink, and lavender flowers. No other decoration was needed since the Pacific Ocean served as a backdrop.

When the time came to walk down the aisle, Jess couldn't resist sneaking a few glances at Connor. Although he was more the flannel shirt and jeans type, he looked completely swoon-worthy in his tux. Because it was his own tux and not some cheap rental, it fit his body perfectly. When he caught her eye and grinned at her, she couldn't stop the flutter that stirred inside her. Who was she kidding, thinking she could move on? She didn't know if she'd *ever* be over him.

To her enormous relief, the wedding went as planned. No one stumbled down the aisle, lost the rings, or interrupted the vows with an unexpected outburst. Her heart filled with love as she watched Marc and her sister tie the knot on a glorious morning in Maui. One day, she hoped she'd experience the same happiness. But for now, she could bask in the glow of Marc and Gabi's joy.

While the wedding party went down to the beach to take photos, the catering crew transformed the ceremonial setup into a dining area. Two heavily laden tables offered hot and cold brunch offerings: frittatas, honey-roasted ham, breakfast potatoes, fresh pineapple, lemon scones, and papaya parfaits. Uniformed waiters served juice, mimosas, and Bellinis.

Jess snagged a mimosa and took a long sip. Now that the wedding ceremony was over, she could finally relax.

When Connor came up to her and placed his hand on her shoulder, she couldn't repress the shiver that coursed through her. She smiled up at him. "Hello, handsome."

"Hello, yourself. You clean up nicely. That is a killer dress." His eyes swept over her appreciatively, making her toes curl in a familiar way.

"Thank you." She held up her mimosa. "Did you get a drink?"

"I will. The food looks great. Did you help plan the menu?"

"Naturally. Back when Gabi decided to do a brunch wedding, she called on my expertise. You know how much I love breakfast food."

He chuckled. "I remember you visiting the lodge for 'second breakfasts' whenever we had waffles. Though, sadly, I don't see a single waffle."

"Gabi nixed the waffle bar idea, but there's so much other deliciousness to enjoy—like baked brie with mango, smoked salmon, and cinnamon sugar crepes." She groaned at the thought of all the wonderful brunch offerings.

Now that Connor had forgiven her, she was tempted to bare her soul. To tell him she still loved him and wished they could find a way to stay together. But she didn't want to shatter their fragile peace.

When her mom took the mic, Jess assumed she was going to give a speech, but instead, she introduced the video tribute. In all the chaos that had ensued since the rehearsal dinner, Jess had forgotten about the video. She stood beside Connor, her heart swelling with pride as the pictures played on the screen to the tunes of Marc and Gabi's favorite songs. Even if she hadn't been the *perfect* maid of honor, she'd created a video her sister could treasure forever.

When it ended, Connor leaned toward her and whispered in her ear. "That turned out better than I thought."

"I'll say, considering we put it together in six hours."

He took her hand and squeezed it. "It was fun while it lasted, wasn't it?"

At least they weren't angry at each other anymore. But the thought of losing him made her ache. Even if the pain wasn't as sharp as the agony she'd experienced after the rehearsal dinner, it would still take a long time to heal.

She didn't want to come across as desperate, but she couldn't stop herself from making a last-ditch effort. "Any plans for tonight? We could have a farewell drink."

The pause that followed made her stomach lurch. Why was she pushing him? She should be grateful they'd talked at the bakery and leave it at that. When Connor had ended things the last time, her frantic pleas and desperate attempts to win him back had driven him further away.

But he gave her a tender smile, the kind that warmed her from the inside out. "One drink couldn't hurt. But we'll have to squeeze it in before six. My plane leaves at eight."

Which meant she couldn't entice him into her bedroom for a final romp.

Probably for the best if she ever hoped to get over him.

CHAPTER 35

Once the wedding had ended, Jess was so sleepy she holed up in her room and succumbed to a deep, drool-inducing nap. She awoke with scarcely enough time to freshen up and change for her meeting with Connor. She grabbed the one sundress she hadn't worn yet—a cute aqua number with colorful embroidery at the bodice—and slipped on a pair of sandals. As she rode the elevator down to the lobby, her heart started its wild dance. She took a few deep breaths, trying to center herself.

She had to get her emotions under control. Under no circumstances could she burst into tears or start begging. She wasn't eighteen anymore.

When she got to the Coral Cove and saw Connor sitting at a table in the shade, her chest constricted. Back in her room, she thought she would be brave enough to tell him what she really wanted. Now she wasn't so sure.

After ordering a margarita, she sat across from him. She took a sip of her drink, hoping the icy tequila would give her a rush of courage. But when Connor's ocean-blue eyes captured hers, she found herself at a loss.

What did you say to the man you'd loved since you were twelve, who'd broken your heart not once, but twice?

"You look serious," he said. "What's on your mind?"

She twisted the stem of the margarita glass. If she let him go without speaking her mind, she'd regret the chance she didn't take. "So…there's something I need to say."

"Go on." He gave her his full attention, which only heightened her anxiety.

"I wish we didn't have to end things. I know I asked for a fling and nothing else. And then I lied to you and didn't trust you, but…" She trailed off and gave a shaky laugh. "I'm really selling myself, aren't I?"

He took her hand. "We're good. I'm not mad anymore."

That was a start. But she needed to keep going. "Can I ask you something?" When he nodded, she continued. "If you'd known I was moving back to Riverside, would you have gotten involved with me?"

"Honestly? I don't know." His pensive expression gave her pause, until it melted into a sly smile. "Then again, you were awfully hard to resist when you came into my hotel room wearing nothing but a bathrobe."

"That was kind of sneaky, I admit."

"Like I said at the bakery, I had a great time with you. But I think we made a mistake when we assumed we could end it after five days without anyone getting hurt."

In theory, her no-strings plan had seemed like the perfect way to shield her heart. But despite the rules she'd insisted on, she'd fallen back in love with him. As the tears built up inside her, she blinked a few times and wiped the corners of her eyes. She didn't want Connor to feel guilty. Right from the start, she'd told him she didn't want any regrets.

He squeezed her hand, as if to bring her back to him. "But Jess? If my life wasn't so overwhelming…"

"What?" Her voice came out in a breathless rush.

"Then I might want more. But right now, it's hard for me to imagine getting in deep with anyone."

"Because of Natasha?" She hated that someone had hurt him enough to shatter his heart.

"Mainly because I need to focus all my attention on the winery. Especially since I'm not sure where we're going to find the funding. That's why I'm flying back a day early. Tomorrow afternoon, I'm meeting with one of Victoria's friends, who might be interested in investing. And I need to tidy up my condo, because a Realtor's coming over on Monday morning to assess it."

"You're selling your condo?"

"I'd rather not. But if I can't find more investors, I'd be willing to settle for a cheap rental and invest the money in the winery. I'm going all in."

She felt a swell of pride for him. He'd changed so much in the past five years. Instead of bemoaning his job at Blackwood Cellars, he was attempting to reboot his life. "I hope it works out."

"Thanks." He gave her a smile so genuine, so filled with affection, she almost believed she could reel him back in.

But she shouldn't be trying to reel him back in. At this point in their lives, neither of them had the time nor the energy to commit to a serious relationship. That didn't mean she had to give up. Instead, she needed to start thinking like Gabi. Planning ahead instead of making easy, impulsive choices.

"I know what you mean about needing to focus," she said. "Next month, I have to pack up my life in Chicago, move back home, and find a job. It'll probably be a good three months before I get my shit together. What about you?"

"In three months? With any luck, I'll be co-owner of a winery. And I'll have survived the sheer insanity of bringing in the harvest in August and September. But by October I should have a little breathing room. Why?" His mouth quirked up in a smile. "What's going on in that devious mind of yours?"

"What if we pressed pause?" She'd never approached a relationship with caution, but she found the concept strangely appealing. "What if we arranged to meet up, three months from now? Just to see where we're at."

She watched his reaction, her stomach churning. The waiting was agony, especially since he hadn't cracked a smile.

His brow furrowed. "Are we talking about another fling? Or something more?"

Admitting she wanted more had gotten her into trouble the first time. But she needed to be honest. "Something more. I know we have it in us. But we'd both have to want it."

To her surprise, he bestowed her with a slow, easy grin. "I like it. That actually sounds responsible."

"Imagine that. Us—responsible."

She held her breath as she waited for his decision. When he pulled out his phone, the tension played havoc with her heart. But he was still smiling. "Let's set a date. How about the second Saturday in October?"

Relief coursed through her, loosening the tightness in her chest. She wanted to leap out of her chair and hug him, but she kept her cool. "Works for me. Where should we meet?"

"Same place it started. The Blackwood Lodge on Big Bear Lake. I'll reserve it."

The thought of meeting up at Big Bear made her heart pound in anticipation. From the gleam in his eyes, she suspected he felt the same way. It was the perfect place for their reunion. She pulled out her phone and added the date. "Big Bear it is."

"But we need some rules." He gestured with his phone. "No communication before that. No social media. No sexy texts. Otherwise, I'll backslide too easily."

"You will?"

He shook his head in good-natured resignation. "Yes, damn it. You're too hard to resist."

She liked knowing she could still tempt him. But his rule made sense. If they wanted to put some distance between them, they shouldn't be sending flirty text messages. "Then how should we set up our meeting?"

"I'll plan on being at the lodge all day. If I've changed my mind before that, I'll send you a text. Same with you. Whatever you choose, I'll accept it."

He didn't sound impassioned, but this wasn't the time for bold, heartfelt declarations. It was time for them to be responsible and see if their passion had staying power. For once in her life, Jess liked the idea of taking control of her future rather than jumping into it headfirst.

When she nodded in agreement, he held up his cocktail. "Here's to October."

She tapped her glass against his. "To October."

Three months would be a hell of a wait.

But it was better than giving up completely.

CHAPTER 36

hree Months Later

Jess sat with Gabi on the patio of the Lazy Dog Restaurant, enjoying the comfortable October weather. She would have appreciated the setting more if she weren't so painfully aware of the minutes ticking by. For the last few weeks, she'd been counting the days until her reunion with Connor, intending to drive up to Big Bear Lake on the designated morning. If she arrived by noon, she figured they'd have all day— and hopefully all night—to be together.

But if experience had taught her anything, it was that her life rarely went according to plan.

A week before Jess was scheduled to meet up with Connor, Gabi decided to fly in from Napa for a few days to surprise their mom for her birthday. Though they'd had fun together, Jess was relieved her sister was heading home on Saturday afternoon. But when Gabi's flight was delayed, Jess suspected the universe was laughing at her.

They left for the airport two hours early, allowing them time to indulge in a glass of wine and share a flatbread platter with hummus. But a few minutes after they started eating, Gabi received a second text from Southwest Airlines with another delay. Though she accepted the change with uncharacteristic calmness, Jess's nerves were strung so tight she could barely relax.

Gabi took a sip of pinot grigio and let out a satisfied sigh. "I needed this. Mama was starting to smother me. I *just* got married three months ago. That doesn't mean I plan to pop out a kid anytime soon."

Their mom had been relentless, inviting her sisters over to help interrogate Gabi. After all the questions Jess had endured during her first week back home, she was happy to relinquish the spotlight to her sister.

"I don't know how you can handle living with her again," Gabi said.

"Most of the time, she's not that intense. Other than her new health kick. How can anyone stand kale smoothies?" Jess shuddered. "But she was great about finding me a job at her boss's company."

Zach Horton had not only hired her on a temporary basis, but he'd also offered to make the position permanent. Though she appreciated the offer, she turned it down, because she'd recently landed a job that would put her writing skills to use. Since her new job didn't start until November, she was staying on at Zach's office for another few weeks.

"The only time we clashed was when Mama insisted I show her boss's nephew around Riverside." Jess dipped a piece of flatbread into the sun-dried tomato hummus and took a bite. "Mmm. You have to try this one."

"Zach's nephew? You mean Ryan? I thought you liked him."

"He's all right. But Mama could have eased up a little. A week after I moved home, she started talking about him. Telling me how lonely he was, how he didn't know anyone in Riverside, how he needed a friend." She made a face. "We went out twice, but…"

Gabi set down her wineglass. "But what?"

"But nothing. He's a nice guy, but he didn't do it for me."

"Nice? That's the best you've got?"

She shrugged, hoping Gabi would move on. "Nothing to tell. Sorry."

For the past three months, she'd gotten used to reining in her feelings. No more tearful phone calls where she subjected Gabi to her inner turmoil. No more late-night wine-and-chocolate binges where she agonized over failed relationships. If Maui had taught her anything, it was that she needed to grow up and tackle her own problems instead of constantly crying out for help.

Rather than wallowing in regret for the mistakes she'd made, she channeled her energy into other pursuits. Building an adult relationship with her mother. Looking for work. Taking a night class in accounting. And writing her novel.

In all, her life was fairly balanced. Except when it came to Connor. The time apart hadn't diminished her love for him. If anything, her feelings had grown stronger. At night, when she was alone in bed, her thoughts drifted to him often, as she remembered the passion they shared in Maui. She still loved him as much as she had when she was eighteen. Maybe more because she was old enough to know what she really wanted.

Gabi narrowed her eyes. "What's going on?"

"What do you mean? I'm trying to act responsibly. I don't have to jump in bed with every guy I date."

"Jess?" Gabi's voice took on the nagging, "big sister" tone she hated. "Remember what we promised each other after my wedding? No more secrets."

Jess took another sip of wine to fortify herself. Ever since Maui, she'd tried to be honest with Gabi. But the one thing she hadn't divulged was her arrangement with Connor. She was afraid her sister would criticize her inability to move on.

"Don't judge me, but I'm still in love with Connor."

Gabi stared at her, clearly taken aback. When no advice or lecture was forthcoming, Jess forced herself to keep going.

"So...Connor and I made a deal before we left Maui. We agreed to a three-month break, where we'd try to get our lives in order. If we still wanted to be together after that, we'd meet up at Big Bear and attempt an actual relationship. Since we'd be living in the same state and all." Jess tensed up as she waited for her sister to tell her how delusional she was.

A noisy group passed by their table, laughing raucously over a shared joke. Once they'd moved on, Gabi spoke up. "Why didn't you tell me this earlier?"

"I thought you might be upset. I know you don't like Connor. And I didn't want you to worry about me or tell me I was making a huge mistake." Jess looked down, ashamed to meet Gabi's eyes. "Sorry. I should have told you. It's just, when I think about it, the idea seems ridiculous. Who puts their life on hold for a guy who might not be ready to commit?"

"Someone who's still in love," Gabi said, her voice dreamy.

"You don't think I'm being an idiot?"

Gabi dipped her flatbread in the garlic hummus. "I think you're being responsible. I know what it's like to wait for 'the one.' When I was at UCLA and Marc was at Davis, we dated other people, but I never got over him. Not completely. Then, when we met up at Stanford, I fell in love with him all over again."

"I remember. You were so excited." Her sister had been thrilled to learn Marc was still single. And that he'd never stopped thinking about her. If they could find love a second time, maybe she had a chance with Connor.

"When's the big reunion supposed to be?" Gabi asked.

Jess gnawed on her lip. "Today?"

"Today? It's after five. Why aren't you driving up to Big Bear *right now*?" Gabi signaled for the waiter. "Can we get the check, please?"

Jess placed her hand on Gabi's arm. "We don't have to leave for the airport yet. Your flight doesn't take off until eight."

"Then I'll check in early and treat myself to a book. I don't want you to miss out." Gabi set her Prada bag on the table and brought out an American Express Platinum card. "I'll pay. Marc got me a new card. Isn't it *shiny*?"

Though Jess could have done without the bragging, she appreciated the offer. Her job with Zach's office paid well, but most of her extra income went directly into her savings account.

Once they were back on the road, headed for the airport, Jess picked up their earlier conversation. "You don't think meeting up with Connor is a terrible idea?"

Gabi let out a long sigh. "Do you honestly think you can trust him?"

"He's changed a lot. At least, that's what Brody told me. He said Connor's been spending every waking hour at his winery. He's working hard and being responsible."

With every update, she grew prouder of Connor. Each time Brody passed along a tidbit of information, she wanted to send Connor a message to let him know how thrilled she was with his progress. But she followed the rules they'd set in Maui.

"Actually, Marc told me the other day he was impressed with Connor's efforts," Gabi said. "But that doesn't mean the guy's mature enough for an actual relationship."

"I know." Devotion to a business plan was a whole different animal than complete devotion to another person.

"If it doesn't work out with Connor, you can call me and cry on my shoulder. But after that?" Gabi's voice grew sharp. "You need to move on."

The same thought had crossed Jess's mind. She also told herself if Connor didn't want a relationship—if all he wanted was another fling or a friends-with-benefits deal—she had to be strong enough to turn him down. Otherwise, she'd be making the same mistakes as she had before.

"I'm not trying to talk you out of it. If you still love him, it's worth a shot." Gabi checked her watch. "But it's already five thirty. Once you drop me off, you should get going. The longer you wait, the harder it'll be to make your way up to the mountains in the dark."

Jess maneuvered into the departures lane and pulled over by the sign for Southwest Airlines. "If I leave now, I should get there by seven thirty. That's not too late."

"Just drive carefully, okay? And let me know how it goes. No leaving me out this time."

"Got it." Jess popped the trunk of her car.

Gabi got out, slung her carry-on bag over one shoulder, and hoisted her rolling suitcase onto the curb. She gave Jess a quick hug. "Thanks for the ride. It was great seeing you."

"You too. Thanks for coming to celebrate Mama's birthday."

Gabi turned to leave, but not without a parting shot. "No wimping out on Big Bear! I'm checking on you tomorrow!"

Jess laughed. She got back into her car and entered the address for Blackwood Lodge into her phone. Only then did she notice it had nineteen percent charge remaining. And she hadn't brought her charger. But if she went back and retrieved it, she'd lose valuable time.

The turnoff for the freeway was half a mile ahead. Decision time.

What if this was a big mistake? Three months was a long time to be apart.

What if Connor wanted a quick romp in bed but nothing more?

She had to stop overthinking things. At this point, she had nothing to lose but her dignity, and she'd lost that so many times it no longer mattered.

She pulled onto the 210 Freeway and headed east.

CHAPTER 37

Connor hadn't intended to call Tom Bartolli. He told himself he wouldn't obsess over the winery this weekend, that he would let himself enjoy a well-earned break. But by Saturday afternoon, he wanted to make sure nothing catastrophic had happened.

Tom laughed at him. "You've only been gone twenty-four hours. Everything's fine."

"But have you checked—"

"Don't worry about it. Reb and I have things under control. You need to get some sleep."

"I'm not tired," Connor said.

"Then you need to get laid. The sooner the better. Go out drinking, find a hot little number, and bring her home. I swear, you'll thank me for it." With that, Tom hung up on him.

Connor glared at the phone. Tom acted like it was so easy. Like all he had to do was head down to one of the bars in the village, have a few beers, and find a willing female.

Actually, for most of his adult life it *had* been that easy. But not lately. The last time he'd been with a woman was three months ago, in Maui. Since then, he'd experienced the longest dry spell of his adult life. And he'd done it willingly. Because of Jess.

At first, when he got back to Temecula, he was too busy to think about her. After meeting with a few potential investors, he'd secured enough funds to purchase the winery. He didn't even need to put his condo on the market. A week later, he and his partners made an offer, but when they were hit with a counteroffer, they almost lost the deal. Fortunately, he received a last-minute boost from an unexpected source. Marc's dad, Rob Blackwood, offered him a substantial loan.

With the loan in hand, Connor and his partners could up their bid and purchase the winery and adjacent vineyards. Closing the sale in August was sheer lunacy. They had barely taken ownership when they had to bring in the grape harvest. As a result, they killed themselves working sixteen-hour days. But no matter how hard Connor drove himself during the day, when he was alone at night and able to unwind, he thought about Jess.

Not just fantasizing about her but longing to talk to her. To tell her how his plans were going. To hear about her writing project. To confide in her when he was at his lowest, filled with fears he wouldn't succeed. A few times, he'd been on the verge of reaching out to tell her he couldn't wait another minute.

But he'd followed the damn rules. And as the evening drew near, he regretted not texting her to confirm the date. Now that she was under her mom's roof, she might have a harder time getting away for the night. Especially since Mrs. Chavez wasn't his biggest fan.

After agonizing for another ten minutes, he caved and called Jess. All he wanted to do was check in on her. What if her car was out of commission? Or she'd been in an accident? Entirely possible, given her propensity for bad luck.

His call went to voicemail. He followed it with a text but got no reply.

The crunch of tires on the gravel driveway caught his

attention. *Finally*. He couldn't wait to sweep Jess off her feet and carry her into the lodge. After dinner, he'd make a fire so they could recreate their unforgettable first night together. Heart pounding, he raced out to the porch only to see a sleek silver Audi. His stomach plummeted as his sister emerged from the car.

"Victoria?"

"Hey, big brother." Her voice held a weary tone. "Can you help me with my suitcase? It's in the trunk."

Having the universe send his younger sister instead of the woman he loved had to be the ultimate irony. But he wasn't about to turn Victoria away, even if he'd reserved this weekend at Blackwood Lodge for himself. He bounded down the stairs, grabbed her rolling bag, and carried it up to the porch. "Is Ben joining you later?"

"He's not coming. Quite honestly, I don't know when I'll see him again." She pointed inside the lodge. "Put my bag anywhere. And I could use a glass of wine. Red, not white. Then I'll tell you the whole sordid story."

"No problem." He set Victoria's bag in the great room and headed to the kitchen. Clearly, something was wrong since his sister was meant to be marrying Ben in two months.

Though Connor was curious about her situation, he knew better than to rush her. He poured them each a glass of pinot noir and assembled a tray of cheeses and baguette slices. He brought it out and set it on a rustic wooden table resting between two of the Adirondack chairs.

Victoria kicked off her heels and settled into one of the chairs. She flashed him a smile. "Wine *and* cheese. How civilized."

"Try the brie," he said.

She placed a wedge on a baguette slice and swallowed it down with a sip of wine. "Delicious. Where did you get it?"

"Casa de Cabras. It's a family-owned farm near our winery that makes their own cheese. Everything I've bought from them has been incredible. Now try the gruyère."

She took a piece and popped it in her mouth. "Mmm. That's sublime. You'll have to incorporate their cheeses into your tastings."

"That's what I was thinking." He sat on the chair next to hers. For a few minutes, he kept quiet, listening to the wind rustle through the pines.

Finally, Victoria gave a lengthy sigh. "Do you want all the gory details?"

He took a quick peek at his phone to make sure Jess hadn't texted. Nothing. He put it back in his pocket and focused his attention on Victoria. "Of course."

"When we were in Maui, did I tell you what happened with Ben?"

He shook his head. If she had, he couldn't recall their conversation.

"A couple of weeks before Marc's wedding, I caught Ben cheating," she said. "He'd reconnected with a woman he dated in college—Missy Cavendish—and they started up again. Their families have known each other forever. Old money, political ties, that kind of thing."

"That's terrible. I'm sorry."

"It gets worse." Victoria's hand shook as she sipped her wine. "Dad convinced me to forgive Ben. He's been hell-bent on this wedding because Ben's father is a state senator."

That selfish asshole. Yet another reason Connor was grateful to be out from under the old man's grasp. "This isn't *Game of Thrones*. You don't have to submit to an arranged marriage just to make Dad happy."

"I know. But I still owe him for that one summer when he bailed me out of trouble. Besides, Ben was a good match. Together, we made a total power couple."

Connor couldn't understand the appeal, but he'd never cared much about money or power. The only person he wanted was a woman who was so broke she'd moved back home.

"Did Ben behave himself after you went back to him?" he asked.

"For a while. Things were fine in Maui. But after we got home, he started working long hours. I thought something might be up, but I was too busy planning our wedding to pay much attention. We were supposed to go out to dinner tonight, but he called me this afternoon and told me he was done. The wedding's off."

She tossed back the rest of her wine and reached for the bottle. After she filled her glass, she continued. "He said he's in love with Missy. Whatever *that* means. He's giving me until next weekend to move out of his condo."

Connor stood and clenched his fists as a pulse of rage surged through him. "You want me to go kick his ass? Because I'll do it. I never liked him. Stuck-up prick."

Victoria laughed and wiped her eyes. "You don't have to beat him up, though I appreciate the offer. I wish Dad had responded the same way. Do you know what he said?"

Connor took a deep, calming breath and returned to his seat. "He must have been pissed. He wanted this wedding more than you did."

"He said I brought it on myself by getting so upset with Ben when he cheated on me the first time."

"Let me guess. He thought you should have looked past Ben's indiscretion? That it's perfectly all right for men to have something on the side?"

She put her head in her hands. "Oh, God. He's done it, too, hasn't he?"

"You didn't know?" Her reaction hit him like a physical blow. "I didn't mean—"

"It's fine. I'm not surprised. I've had my suspicions."

"Dad's a dick. He always has been."

"I'm supposed to meet with him on Monday morning to discuss the situation. With Ben canceling this late in the game, we won't get any of our deposits back. Which means I'll owe Dad more than ever."

His pulse pounded. What kind of a man cared more for the bottom line than for his only daughter's well-being? "Sorry. That sucks."

"It does indeed." She leaned back in her chair. "Right now, I want to drink and forget everything."

Given the ache he felt over Jess's absence, he wasn't the best person to console her, but at least he could offer her food. "Have you had dinner yet?"

"No. It all happened so fast. After Ben told me the news, I couldn't go back to his place. And I sure as hell wasn't going home to Dad. So, I headed for the only refuge I could think of. I haven't eaten since eleven this morning."

He went over to the table and picked up the tray. "Come on. I'll make us dinner."

"Fine." She got to her feet, collected her heels, and followed him into the lodge. "But you're cooking."

"Not much to do. Before I left yesterday, Tom Bartolli's wife brought me a pan of homemade lasagna. I heated it up last night, but there's a lot left, and I can whip up some garlic bread and a salad."

As he prepared dinner, he gave Victoria an update on his winery. The last few months had been so intense that he'd rarely made time for conversation. After they were done eating, they went into the great room to relax. While he started a fire, Victoria fetched another bottle of wine from the pantry and refilled their glasses.

She settled herself into an oversize armchair. "I'm not cramping your style, am I? If you want to go into town and pick up company, I can retreat to my room."

If he wanted company? Of course he did. But the woman he wanted had yet to make an appearance.

"I'm not interested. Not right now." He kept his voice neutral, hoping Victoria wouldn't push him on the subject.

"You're not interested in picking up women? In what universe?"

"In this one. I'm not the reckless asshole I used to be. I own a third of a winery and sixty-five acres of vineyards."

"Which means what? You're turning into a tight-ass like Darren?"

He repressed a shudder. No matter how big his winery got, he'd never turn into Darren. He set the iron screen across the fireplace and sat in the chair next to Victoria's. "I'm still up for a good time, but I'm done with mindless one-night stands."

She set down her glass and stared at him. "What's going on? You've been acting strange ever since we got back from Maui. And don't tell me it's because of the winery. I *know* you, Connor. It's more than that."

He looked away, but her piercing stare was hard to ignore.

"Wait." She laughed. "This is because of *her*. You're still fixated on Jessica Chavez."

Damn it.

She gave him a smug grin. "I'm right, aren't I? You haven't gotten over her."

"You win. I'm still in love with her."

"You're *in love* with her?"

How had he let that slip? Talk about rolling over and showing his underbelly. "Forget it."

"I will not forget it. My own brother, felled by another of those damned Chavez women. Why haven't you gone after her? Didn't she move back home two months ago?"

At any other time, he might have hesitated to share Jess's scheme with his critical sister. But Victoria could use a laugh. So, he told her everything. Sure enough, when he was done, her eyes danced with amusement.

"You two are the biggest idiots on the planet. Why make these absurd rules? If you wanted her, you should have told her right away. Forcing her to wait three months was a complete waste of time."

He raked his hand through his hair. "I realize that now. But in my defense, I wanted to get my life together. So did she."

Victoria gestured with her wineglass. "You know, everyone thought I had *my* life together. Rich fiancé, great job, extravagant Christmas wedding. And today it all exploded in my face. So, my point is..." She stared at her glass in confusion. "What was my point?"

"That life throws you curveballs?"

"Exactly. So, don't wait for the perfect time to tell someone you love them. Do it now."

"I tried calling her tonight. To see if we were still on. But she didn't answer. I'm worried something might have happened to her." He didn't want to torment himself with worst-case scenarios, but with Jess's luck, anything was possible.

"At least she wasn't flying this time. But you're not giving up. Right? Just call her tomorrow. I'm sure she'll have a good explanation."

When she put it that way, he felt like a tool. He was acting as though their entire relationship was riding on this one perfect reunion. But perfection wasn't something he or Jess had ever achieved.

"Right. I'll call her tomorrow. Unless you think a grand gesture would work better. I could rent a limo and show up at her mom's place dressed in my tux. Or track down a giant boom box and serenade her with her favorite song."

She held up her hand. "Stop. I'm not even going to ask why you're so well-versed in '90s rom-coms. But whatever you're thinking, don't do it. Grand gestures are obnoxious."

"But—"

"Trust me on this. Just tell her you love her. And that you

don't want to spend another minute without her. That's more than enough."

He gave her a grateful smile. "Thanks for the pep talk."

"You bet." She raised her wineglass in a salute. "*One* of us has to get their happy ending."

CHAPTER 38

By Jess's reckoning, the drive to Big Bear should have taken two hours. But when her phone's battery gave out, she had to pull over and retrieve the worn map her mom had stashed in the glove compartment. As she got back onto the freeway, an overturned big rig delayed her trip another hour. By the time traffic picked up, her check engine light came on.

Damn it.

Her bad-luck gene was kicking into gear.

She took the nearest exit and parked at a gas station. When she couldn't figure out the problem, she was tempted to turn back. But she didn't want to let Connor down.

That is, if he hadn't given up on her already. By now, he might consider her a no-show. Or be annoyed she'd failed to tell him she was running late. But she had no way to reach him.

At this point, all she could do was keep going.

She didn't make it to Big Bear until nine. Finding Blackwood Lodge was harder than she expected, because the roads leading to the cabins were dark, especially with so many places empty during the off-season.

When she found the sloping driveway that led down to

Blackwood Lodge, she almost cried in relief. She parked in the overflow lot—a wide, gravelly area near the main cabin—and brought her emergency flashlight out of the glove compartment. The cool mountain air made her shiver, and she put on the fleece jacket she'd stashed in the truck, glad she'd thought to bring it. At least she wasn't totally unprepared.

She made her way toward the lodge, guided by the beam of her flashlight. When she reached the parking area adjacent to the cabin, her light hit Connor's truck. Beside it was an Audi with California plates. She shone her light into the Audi's front window. On the passenger seat were a silver hairbrush, a tube of lipstick, and a metal water bottle with floral designs.

This was a woman's car.

For a brief, paralyzing minute, she stood frozen in place, staring at the car. Had she been played? If Connor had moved on without telling her, she'd be crushed. Especially if he was spending the weekend with another woman.

No. You need to trust him.

Wasn't that what their three-month separation had been about? Not just about rebuilding their lives, but learning to trust each other, even when they couldn't communicate. Connor would have told her if he'd found someone else. He wasn't the same guy who'd ghosted her five years ago.

She strode up the steps to the lodge, her feet crunching on fallen leaves. Taking a deep breath, she knocked on the massive wooden door, her heart pounding frantically as she waited for him to answer.

When he opened the door, his joyful expression swept away the last of her doubts. He pulled her into a crushing hug. "You're here. Finally."

She rested her head against his chest and inhaled his delicious pinewoods scent. Nothing could match the comfort of his arms. "Sorry I'm late. Once again, the travel gods were *not* smiling at me. I was hoping you didn't give up on me."

His lips grazed the top of her head. "I didn't. Not for a second."

A snarky voice cut into their reunion. "He totally did. The guy was whining like a baby. You could have thrown him a bone and texted back, you know."

She peered over Connor's shoulder, surprised to see his sister seated in an armchair by the fire. "Victoria?"

Victoria lifted her wineglass in greeting. "Sorry to crash the party. I had to get away, and this was the best escape I could think of."

"It's fine." She eased herself out of Connor's grasp. "I couldn't call because my battery ran out on the drive. I had to use a map to get here."

"See why I like them? They never let you down." He gestured inside. "Come on in."

She kicked off her shoes and left her fleece on the coatrack. Following him into the great room, she eased herself onto the overstuffed couch across from Victoria. The smell of woodsmoke brought back powerful memories. She and Connor had made love for the first time on the thick fur rug in front of this fireplace.

"Jess?" He waved a hand in front of her face. "You're spacing out on us. You sure you're okay?"

"Sorry. I was just...remembering." When he smiled knowingly, a warm flush heated her cheeks.

Victoria stood up. "Time for me to make my exit. I'll leave you two lovebirds alone, but don't even *think* about having sex out here in the open. And please keep the noise down because I need my beauty sleep." She hiccupped and wove out of the room.

"Is this okay? If Victoria needs you, I don't want to be in the way." After her epic trek up the mountain, Jess had no desire to head back so soon. But she didn't want Victoria to feel unwelcome.

Connor sat beside her on the couch, his thigh brushing

against hers. "Please stay. I thought we'd have the place to ourselves, but Victoria showed up a few hours ago. Ben broke off their engagement."

Her heart swelled with pity. "That's awful. I'm so sorry."

"I never liked the guy, but this is low, even for him. It's better you arrived late because Victoria needed to talk. But I have to admit, I was starting to worry you wouldn't come."

She pressed her hand against his cheek, rubbing the prickly stubble. "You gave up on me?"

He took her hand and placed a gentle kiss on her palm. "Knowing your luck, I assumed something had gone sideways. I was just disappointed. I've been thinking about this day for weeks."

Relief washed over her in a powerful wave. He'd been thinking about her. And he wasn't afraid to admit it.

"I wanted to get up here by noon. But Gabi flew in for a surprise visit on Thursday and didn't leave until now. Since I hadn't told her about our plan, she didn't know she was messing with our big day." She sighed. "I had to fess up tonight. Which is probably for the best since I'm tired of keeping secrets."

"Victoria knows, too. For the record, she thought we were being idiots."

"Do you think we were being idiots?"

He enfolded her hands in his. "Sometimes. There were nights when I wanted to call you so badly that I wished we'd never set those rules. But the time apart made me realize what I really wanted."

She tensed up but didn't break their gaze. "Which is?"

"You."

"Really?" She wanted to leap into his arms, but he held up his hand to stop her.

"Yes. But before we go any further, I want to be up-front about everything."

She drew back, scarcely daring to breathe, her heart thumping in triple time. But she stayed silent, letting him have his say.

"This winery business is more demanding than I ever imagined. My uncle's loan put us in a good place, financially, but the workload is intense. Right now, I have a small window to catch my breath, but this year's going to be all-consuming." He grinned. "Not that I'm complaining. It's the first time I've ever been in charge of anything, and I love it. Our winery is going to kick ass, but it'll take a lot of work to get there."

While she was proud he'd come this far, she couldn't envision how she could fit into his life. She blinked quickly, trying to stem the tears welling up in her eyes.

"So...maybe the timing's not ideal, but..." She stopped herself because she *still* hadn't let him finish. "Sorry. There's more, right?"

"There is. Because what I was trying to say is..." He squeezed her hand. "Even if my life's hectic right now, I can't think of anyone else I'd rather share it with. I love you, Jessica Chavez. I love that you're hopelessly jinxed when it comes to travel. I love that you wrote an eight-hundred-page fantasy novel. I love that you can be adorably cute and amazingly sexy at the same time. And I've missed you so much I can hardly stand it."

She wiped her eyes. "I love you, too. And I haven't stopped thinking about you. I've been dreaming about this reunion for weeks, and the waiting just about killed me."

Though she wanted nothing more than to tumble into bed with him and show him how much she'd missed him, she couldn't let her desire sway her. Not until she'd set out her terms.

"The thing is...this time, I want more than a week together," she said. "I want something lasting, even if we might get hurt. I trust you, and I hope you'll trust me back." She bit her lip. "Is that...do you feel the same way?"

"Absolutely. Now that we're finally together, I'm not letting you go." He gave her a sheepish grin. "But I'm kind of broke. So, until my winery takes off, I won't be able to lavish you with fancy gifts or expensive nights out. But I can promise you unlimited sex, unconditional love, and all the wine you can drink."

She couldn't imagine a better offer. "I'll take it. I don't care how broke you are. It doesn't matter if our lives are messy and uncertain. Perfection is highly overrated."

Their eyes met, and her body grew warm with desire. When his gaze dropped to her mouth, she leaned in to kiss him but stopped herself in time. She still hadn't told him everything.

"There's one more thing. I got a new job, starting on November first. It's in the Temecula Valley, about a mile from the winery district. I'll be commuting from Riverside for the first two months, but I'm hoping to get an apartment in Temecula in January."

"That's amazing. What kind of a job?"

"Brace yourself. I'm working for the Temecula Wine Growers' Association. Half the job is administrative, but the other half involves writing. They need someone to cover events, write PR copy, update their blog, that kind of thing. Like what I did in Chicago, except this time for the area wineries."

He gave her a sarcastic grin. "I had no idea you were such a wine expert."

She nudged him. "Shows what you know. When I saw the job listing, I called Brody. He invited me over to the Blackwood Cellars Estate and rounded up a bunch of experts to give me a crash course in all things wine related. Then he and his friends wrote me killer letters of recommendation. I asked him to keep it a secret because I wanted to tell you myself."

If she'd had any lingering doubts about Connor's feelings, they vanished at the look of joy on his face. "That's fantastic. It won't be a conflict of interest that you're sleeping with the owner of Maverick Winery?"

"Nah. But if the owner plays his cards right, I might feature his winery more than the others." She still couldn't believe she'd lucked into the job. She'd applied all over San Diego and Riverside County, but she'd never thought she'd find work in the same city as Connor.

"What about your own writing?" he asked. "Are you still working on your mystery?"

"Finished it two weeks ago. Now I'm muddling my way through my revisions. This time, I'm not shelving it under my bed."

His eyes shone with admiration. "I'm proud of you for sticking with it."

"Turns out writing a three-hundred-page mystery isn't quite as difficult as writing an epic-fantasy trilogy. But it's still a lot of fun." She gave him an adoring smile. "I can't wait for you to read it."

In all honesty, she couldn't wait to share every part of her life with him—the good, the bad, the stressful, the joyful. Even if the road ahead might be difficult, they'd be traveling it together. Supporting each other through every obstacle and victory along the way.

Connor leaned in closer and kissed her gently, his hand cupping the back of her head. He tasted of red wine and smelled of woodsmoke, and his touch made her tingle with longing. But she wanted more than kisses. She wanted to spend hours in his bed, reclaiming the passion they'd set aside for three months.

He broke away and gave her a wicked smile. "Can I entice you to spend the night, Miss Chavez?"

"If you'll have me."

"Oh, I'll have you, all right. I've spent a lot of nights thinking just how I'd like to *have* you." His blue eyes sparkled with amusement. "Three months is a long time to go without sex, you know."

"Tell me about it. Not that my fantasies about you weren't delightful, but they're no substitute for the real thing." She gave the fur rug a longing look. "I'd love to return to the scene of the crime, but we should go up to your room so we don't scandalize Victoria."

He picked her up in his arms. "As you wish."

As she placed her arms around his neck, she couldn't think of anywhere else she'd rather be than with the gorgeous, sexy man she'd loved since she was a teenager. "There's only one problem. I didn't bring pajamas."

"I don't think you'll need them."

He was right.

~

Thank you for reading *Blue Hawaiian*!
I hope you enjoyed Jess and Connor's story.
If you did, please consider leaving a review wherever you purchased this book.
Thanks! Your support is much appreciated!

Website and Newsletter Sign-up:
www.carlalunabooks.com

~

Stay tuned for the next book in the Blackwood Cellars series, *Red Velvet*, a friends-to lovers romantic comedy featuring Brody Blackwood, set at a fall wedding in Door County Wisconsin, coming September 14, 2021.

Turn the page for a sneak peek of *Red Velvet*!

CHAPTER 1

Few things pleased April Beckett more than taking a pan of sweets out of the oven. Even when she was at her lowest, the smell of baked goods always brightened her mood. She set the cupcake tins on two bamboo trivets, removed her oven mitts, and brought out her phone. After ensuring the cupcakes were angled correctly, she took a photo and posted it with the caption: *Red velvet beauties, waiting to be frosted. #bakersgonnabake #cupcakesofinstagram*

As she was setting the bowls and measuring cups in the sink, her phone pinged.

It had to be Brody.

Sure enough, Brody Blackwood, her good friend, movie buddy, and former crush, had commented on her post. *PLEASE say these are for Treatday Thursday.*

Of all her co-workers at Blackwood Cellars, no one appreciated her baking more than he did. She fired off a quick reply. *Of course! Bringing them in for Delilah's Bday.*

In response, he sent a series of smiley-face emojis.

His unabashed affection for her baking skills filled her with a warm glow. Even though she'd been seeing Chris for five months, she still harbored a tiny crush on Brody. How could she not? He'd been one of the first people to befriend her when she'd relocated from Santa Barbara to the Temecula Valley—an hour northeast of San Diego—to work for his family's company. And he was brilliant, funny, and totally hot for a self-proclaimed computer nerd.

She filled the sink with soapy water and shoved in the rest of her utensils. Once the dishes were done, she'd whip up the cream cheese frosting.

At the sound of a key turning in the lock, she froze.

Shit.

If Chris was making an impromptu booty call, she was ill prepared. Her faded sweats and messy hair were fine for a quiet evening to herself, but not for a night with her smoking-hot friend with benefits. Worse yet, her couch harbored dozens of tops, jeans, and dresses as she narrowed down the choices for their weeklong trip to Wisconsin. Since he kept his condo in immaculate condition, the disorder was bound to irritate him.

The door opened and Chris peered inside, holding a bike helmet under his arm. His forehead was damp with sweat, but it did nothing to diminish his good looks. Six foot two of lean muscle, thick black hair, and cheekbones that could cut glass. Factor in the skintight bike shirt and shorts he wore, and he was a sight to behold.

"Hey, April…" The words died on his lips as he took in the piles of clothing on the couch.

"Chris. I wasn't expecting you." Her hand flew to her head, where her topknot had unraveled to the point of no return. "How about I go freshen up? Why don't you have a seat on the…" Clearly, the couch wasn't an option. She pointed to the faded green armchair, where her spoiled Siberian cat had taken up residence. "Take the chair. Just give Princess Peach a shove."

Chris wrinkled his nose. "You know how I feel about cat hair on my clothes. And I won't be long." He sauntered over to the breakfast bar and frowned at the cupcakes. "Baking again? Butter and refined sugar are terrible for your waistline."

April cringed. Though she was on the curvy side, none of her previous boyfriends had ever criticized her figure. But Chris claimed he did it out of compassion. After enduring one too many lectures about her cholesterol levels, she'd vowed to seek out healthier baking choices. Yet here she was, breaking her word.

"They're not for me," she said. "I'm taking them to work."

"I thought you weren't doing Treatday Thursday anymore."

She undid her apron and hung it on a peg. "It's Delilah's birthday tomorrow. Red velvet cupcakes are her favorite."

"Why not bring in fresh veggies? Or a fruit tray?"

Because that's Healthy Hanna's job. If April was the devil on every dieter's shoulder, then Hanna from H.R. was the angel, with her array of heart-healthy snacks, like kale chips and radish hummus.

Chris turned his attention to the couch. "You donating a bunch of stuff to Goodwill? About time."

Did he think her clothes looked that bad? Granted, some of her outfits were out of style, but they weren't unwearable. "I was trying to pare down the options for my brother's wedding. We're going to be there for six days, and the weather might be iffy, since fall in Wisconsin isn't dependable."

"But you're not leaving for another week."

Did he just say "you're"? She gave a shaky laugh. "You mean *we're* not leaving for another week."

He leaned back against the breakfast bar and let out his breath. "Yeah. About that…?"

No. Please don't back out now.

"You promised." She hated how whiny she sounded, but he'd agreed six weeks ago. If anything, she'd been pleasantly surprised at how easily he capitulated. "After I went with you to the Oakland Triathlon, you said you'd do this for me."

"I never should have agreed to it. Attending a destination wedding? With your entire family? That implies we're getting serious."

"But—"

"You know how I feel about commitment. Right now, it's not an option."

That aspect of their relationship had never bothered her because she wasn't in love with him. Not the way she assumed love was supposed to be—a deep emotional connection that bound you to the other person, body and soul. But Chris was gorgeous, athletic, and driven. Much hotter than anyone she'd ever dated. Guys like him could have their pick of women. Yet, somehow, he'd chosen *her*.

She twisted her hands together. "I didn't ask for anything long-term. Just a date for Ollie's wedding. Six days. No strings. Think how much fun we'll have." When he didn't respond, she gave him a flirtatious smile. "We're staying in this adorable private cottage, right on Lake Michigan."

"April…"

"Plus, my family's really competitive, so you'll fit right in."

Whenever they asked about him, she rarely missed a chance to mention his athletic prowess. By bringing him to the wedding, she would finally be able to show them she'd landed someone worthy of their approval.

She held her breath, hoping he might reconsider. As the seconds ticked by, the loud thump of her heart echoed in her ears.

"I like hanging out," he said. "You're always up for a good time. But…"

She tried to keep her voice from breaking. "But I'm only worthy of a booty call?"

He groaned. "That's not what I meant. I'd be up for a normal vacation, like a weekend in the mountains. But weddings have this weird impact on women."

"What are you talking about?"

"I mean, one minute you're happy being single; the next, you're watching the bride walk down the aisle and wishing you were her."

"That's not going to happen," she said.

In all her twenty-four years, she'd never contemplated marriage—not to Chris or anyone else. She had yet to experience the powerful, all-consuming pull of attraction that led to a lifelong commitment. Right now, all she wanted was for Chris to make an effort. Some gesture that showed he cared.

"Sorry, babe," he said, "I can't do it."

Despite the warmth of the kitchen, ice-cold dread seeped into her veins. She grasped to find something—*anything*—to make him change his mind. "What about your plane ticket? Do you really want to waste all that money?"

Though he wasn't hurting financially, he'd complained about the cost and the long layover. But she hadn't been able to find any deals or direct flights from San Diego to Green Bay, Wisconsin.

He shrugged. "I got a changeable fare, so I can save the credit for another trip. No big deal."

Not to him, obviously.

He glanced at his Garmin sport watch. "I should go. I still have ten miles left on my training. How about you call me when you get back? We can hook up then."

She stared at him, too stunned to answer. Canceling now was a dick move. She swallowed past the lump in her throat, willing herself not to cry. He'd hurt her before, but never like this.

If she were strong enough, she would call him on his shitty behavior. But before Chris, her bed had been empty for months. Even the crumbs of his affection were better than slowly morphing into a lonely cat lady.

"Sure," she muttered.

He leaned closer and stroked her cheek. "That's my girl. I'll make it up to you in the bedroom." With a wink, he headed for the door. "Have fun at the wedding, but try not to overindulge. Go easy on the sweets."

What the hell?

What was Delilah always telling her? To sit up straight, look people in the eye, and speak her mind. April had let her family walk all over her for years. It was time she stood up for herself. Even if the prospect made her stomach churn.

She clenched her fists, digging her nails deep into her palms. "No."

Chris did a double take. "No, what?"

"No, I can eat whatever I want at the wedding. And no, you can't make it up to me in the bedroom. Because if you bail this late in the game, then we're done."

"Don't be like that. Can't we just enjoy what we have?"

No. After being available for Chris whenever he needed her, after cheering him on at *all* his races, she'd asked him for *one thing*. Granted, it was a big ask, but he'd given her his word. By breaking it so casually, he'd shown her exactly how little she meant to him.

She shook her head. "I'm done, Chris."

He gave a huff of disbelief. "You're dumping *me*? Are you serious?"

Her insides twisted into a knot. Maybe this was a terrible mistake. If she acted like she was joking, she could still salvage things.

But what was she trying to salvage? A few quickies a week, with a guy who disparaged her weight and fashion choices? The occasional weekend away, spent watching him compete? For all the times she'd opened her heart to him, he'd never reciprocated. And even if the sex was decent, it didn't make up for the criticism or the hours of self-doubt that plagued her every time he joked about her "muffin top."

"This trip means a lot to me," she said. "And you promised

you'd go. If you can't be there for me, then I don't want to be with you anymore."

He rolled his eyes. "You're making this into a bigger deal than it needs to be. But if that's what you want, so be it. It's your loss."

With that, he was gone, slamming the door behind him.

For a brief, blissful moment, the fire inside April burned bright. Screw Chris. She was through with all his calorie counting and all his *rules*. Like no sleeping over. After they were done, he always dressed and headed for the door. No matter how many times she asked him to stay, he claimed spending the night would derail his morning run.

For once in her life, she hadn't given in like a meek little mouse. She snatched a cupcake off the cooling rack and ate half of it in one bite. Even without the frosting, it was delicious.

See what you're missing, Chris?

Then reality sunk in. Her brother's wedding was in less than a week, and she didn't have a date.

Showing up without a date shouldn't matter. She'd been single when her two older sisters had gotten married. And for every Thanksgiving, Christmas, and family vacation for the past four years. Except, this time, she'd bragged about her plus-one. If she didn't bring Chris, her sisters would assume she'd made him up. Just like Sam Jameson, the guy she'd invented five years ago to get them off her case. A lie no one had ever forgotten.

She couldn't face another minute without backup. With trembling hands, she sent Brody a text.

If you're free tonight, I need you. Code Red.

~

Want to read more of April and Brody's story?
Red Velvet releases on September 14, 2021

ACKNOWLEDGMENTS

For years, I've wanted to call myself a published author, and it's an incredible feeling to have my dream come true. But I never would have kept at it without the support of my friends, my family, and the amazing writing community.

First of all, I need to thank the professionals who helped me craft this book in its final form: Bailey McGinn, for creating such an adorable cover; Serena Clarke at Free Bird Editing for her detailed copy-edits; and Sandra at One Love Editing for her careful proofreading.

Back in 2008, I took a class entitled "Writing Your Novel," where I was fortunate enough to meet a wonderful group of writers (aka the FITWIGs). To this day, we still meet to discuss our creative endeavors and share delicious food. Thanks so much to Lolly Rzezotarski, Jennifer Motl, Lisa Minetti, Rufina Garay, Shlomo Levin, and Virginia Small for all the support.

Crafting a novel requires a lot of feedback, and for that I was lucky to have input from many talented, generous writers, all of whom read *Blue Hawaiian* in some incarnation or other: Haley Kral, Gail Werner, Jennifer Rupp, Amy Reichert, Susan Keillor, Michelle McCraw, Sadira Stone, and Lorelei Scott. Among the other writers who have offered advice and friendship along the way are Michelle Mason, Karma Brown, Sarah Cannon, Melissa Marino, M.K. Wiseman, and Lori Oestreich, along with the members of the Wisconsin RWA.

Navigating my way into the world of self-publishing was made more doable by the support of the two most fabulous Lizzes I know: Liz Czukas and Liz Lincoln Steiner. I owe them a huge debt of thanks, especially Liz Lincoln, who gave me helpful feedback on an earlier draft of this novel.

Throughout this journey, my critique partner, Tricia Quinnies, has been invaluable—not only has she read everything I've written, but she's lifted me up when I've been at my lowest.

Among the friends who have offered encouragement, my coffee-buddies Jackie Dhein and Andrea Wallus have been solidly in my corner for years. Thanks, too, to my good friend Kari Frommell, who was among the first people to believe in me, back in 2008, when I told her I wanted to start writing.

From the Luna side of the family, I owe a debt of gratitude to my brother, John, and his wife, Julie. More than once, John has talked me off the ledge when I'm too stressed to keep going. I'm also thankful that my late parents, Dulcie and Mario Luna, raised me in a household where creativity was so highly valued.

My two children, Tasmine and James—who were kids when I started writing but are now *adults*—have been an incredible source of support. Through all my highs and lows, they've listened to me, encouraged me, and helped me believe in myself.

Last, but certainly not least, my husband, Mike, has been all in, ever since he bought me a laptop for my 40th birthday and said, "Now you can go write your book." The journey from aspiring writer to published author has taken longer than I thought, but I'm grateful to have a partner who has convinced me, each and every day, that happy endings are still possible.

ABOUT THE AUTHOR

Carla Luna writes contemporary romance with a dollop of humor and a pinch of spice. A former archaeologist, she still dreams of traveling to far-off places and channels that wanderlust into the settings of her stories.

When she's not writing, she works in a spice emporium where she gets paid to discuss food and share her favorite recipes. Her passions include Broadway musicals, baking, office supplies, and pop culture podcasts. Though she has roots in Los Angeles and Victoria, B.C., she currently resides in Wisconsin with her family and her spoiled Siberian cat.

For sneak peeks, giveaways, and recipes from the Blackwood Cellars books, sign up for Carla's newsletter
www.carlalunabooks.com

www.ingramcontent.com/pod-product-compliance
Lightning Source LLC
Chambersburg PA
CBHW011115100726
47898CB00011B/3099